"Maybe I want to be alone."

John didn't say anything else for a moment and averted his eyes from hers. He cleared his throat. "Do you want me to look for a place for you?"

"Not really," Shelby said.

He opened his mouth as though to say something but instead snapped it closed, nodded and backed out of the room. "Good night, Shelby."

"Good night, John." She stood and shut the door.

Turning, she sank against it, fighting against asking John to come back so she wouldn't be alone, so she wouldn't be so conflicted about the decision she'd made to chuck her pseudo-life in Seattle and stay in Magnolia Bend.

A knock at the door made her jump.

She opened it to find John looking determined.

"Did you—" she asked, closing her mouth as he stepped toward her. His arms came around her, hauling her up against the hardness of his chest, as his mouth descended upon hers.

Dear Reader,

This book began with a character. Shelby Mackey appeared in *The Road to Bayou Bridge* (Harlequin Superromance, September 2012) as Darby Dufrene's girlfriend. The premise of that book involves a secret marriage—one neither Darby nor the heroine, Renny, knows about. In the course of the book, Darby falls back in love with Renny and leaves Shelby holding a bag of dreams.

I really hated that for Shelby...mostly because I liked her.

So the more I thought about her, the more I knew she had a story. Shelby always falls for the wrong guy. And even worse—she always falls for married guys.

In this book I gave her a hero who was also married—to the ghost of his wife. And I gave John and Shelby a reason to move forward and find love. I gave them a surprise pregnancy and the question of *What if?*

This book concerns grief and second chances, but it also deals with the concept of family and finding where one truly belongs. I hope you enjoy the beginning of a new series set in Magnolia Bend, Louisiana, and the story of two lost souls finding love in difficult circumstances.

As always, I love hearing what you think. You can find me at www.liztalleybooks.com or on Facebook at www.facebook.com/liztalleybooks.

Cheers!

Liz Talley

LIZ TALLEY

—

The Sweetest September

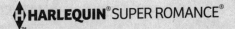

H HARLEQUIN® SUPER ROMANCE®

Recycling programs
for this product may
not exist in your area.

ISBN-13: 978-0-373-60862-1

THE SWEETEST SEPTEMBER

Copyright © 2014 by Amy R. Talley

Printed in U.S.A.

www.Harlequin.com

ABOUT THE AUTHOR

A 2009 Golden Heart Award finalist in Regency romance, Liz Talley has since found a home writing sassy Southern stories. Her book *Vegas Two-Step* debuted in June 2010 and was quickly followed by four more books in her Oak Stand, Texas series. In her current books, she's visiting one of her favorite cities—New Orleans. Liz lives in north Louisiana with her hero, two beautiful boys and a passel of animals. She enjoys laundry, paying bills and creating masterful dinners for her family. She also lies in her biography to make herself look like the perfect housewife. What she really likes is new shoes, lemon-drop martinis and fishing off the pier at her camp. You can visit her at www.liztalleybooks.com to learn more about the lies she tells herself, and about her upcoming books.

Books by Liz Talley

HARLEQUIN SUPERROMANCE

1639—VEGAS TWO-STEP
1675—THE WAY TO TEXAS
1680—A LITTLE TEXAS
1705—A TASTE OF TEXAS
1738—A TOUCH OF SCARLET
1776—WATERS RUN DEEP*
1788—UNDER THE AUTUMN SKY*
1800—THE ROAD TO BAYOU BRIDGE*
1818—THE SPIRIT OF CHRISTMAS
1854—HIS UPTOWN GIRL
1878—HIS BROWN-EYED GIRL
1902—HIS FOREVER GIRL

*The Boys of Bayou Bridge

Other titles by this author available in ebook format.

For my mother-in-law, Eretta, who has endured too much grief in her life. Finding happiness isn't easy and takes work, but love is always worth the effort. I love you.

Special thanks to Scotty Comegys and Greg Lott for teaching me about trusts, and Sam Irwin for teaching me about the sugarcane industry. All mistakes are mine.

CHAPTER ONE

SHELBY MACKEY HAD experienced a lot of bad sex in her lifetime, but she'd never made a man cry.

Sitting on the sink of a run-down bathroom in some Louisiana hole-in-the-wall grocery store/bait stand/bar, she focused on the man in front of her, who was breathing hard and blinking away honest-to-God tears. The yellow glow of the naked light-bulb over his left shoulder kept bobbing...or maybe it didn't. After all, she'd had two glasses of wine before moving on to gin and tonics. Shelby couldn't remember how many of those drinks the tall stranger had bought her, but they likely were responsible for the disgusting bathroom spinning.

He had dark hair—a sort of brownish-red that a poet might describe as a sunset sinking into the horizon. But he'd covered the rusty-brown with a well-worn cowboy hat. That damn cowboy hat had made her lose every inkling of good sense she had.

Or maybe the five—or six—drinks had done that. Whichever.

Results were the same—she teetered on a chipped sink, her panties nowhere in sight.

A faded country ballad still played in the background, and as she watched the man grapple with what they'd done against the bathroom sink, she noted he had a thin white scar along his chiseled jawline.

The sex hadn't been bad. But not good, either. Sort of desperate and fast. Shelby hadn't cared, because for a brief moment she'd felt desired. And being wanted had been way more powerful than even the deadly combination of cowboy hat and booze.

Green eyes looked down at her, swimming with a flurry of emotions—a sort of "oh, hell, look what we just did." She released the fists she'd knotted in his simple white button-down shirt and slid to the linoleum.

"Wow," she muttered, which was totally inaccurate. Not wow at all. She tugged her cashmere sweater over the bra he'd not even managed to unhook and gave him an embarrassed smile.

No. This wasn't awkward.

He didn't say anything. Just looked like she'd smacked him in the head with a baseball bat. Mechanically, he turned, dealing with the absurd pink condom she'd handed him minutes earlier. He tossed the wadded napkin in the waste bin and stayed with his back to her.

"Uh, you okay?" she asked, looking for her pesky watermelon-pink panties he'd tossed…somewhere.

Shaking his head, he said, "Oh, God."

"What? Are you okay?"

He shook his head. "I'm sorry. I shouldn't have done this."

Jeez. He apologized like he'd just tossed his cookies on her grandmother's wedding china. Or like he'd accidentally stepped on a kitten. Or tracked dog shit in the house. Like it was...something bad.

He spun and his eyes reflected anguish.

"You don't have to apologize," she said, trying on another smile, pretending like this wasn't what it was—a guy apologizing for having sex with her. "But if you can help me find my panties?"

If anything, he grew even paler at the suggestion. Wild-eyed, he glanced around. "We're in a bathroom."

"Ding. You're correct," she said with a decided slur. Gin did that to her. Okay, gin did that to everyone.

She didn't want to look back at him. Didn't want to see the despair and guilt in his eyes. He regretted this whole thing. Wished he hadn't gotten wasted and agreed to *help* her in the bathroom, which she'd made code word for *screwing me against the lavatory.* It was almost as if...her gaze flew to his left hand.

"Oh, crap." She grabbed the tanned hand with the noticeable white stripe on the ring finger. She hadn't noticed it in the dark bar, but could see very well in the blinding reality of the ladies' bathroom. "You're married?"

He glanced at the hand she held in hers and jerked it away, using it to tug up worn jeans that still gaped. The sound of his zipper was deafening. Shaking his head, he closed his eyes and exhaled. "Not anymore."

He opened those pretty eyes and their gazes met. A sheen of tears remained, but there was more—sadness over the words he'd just uttered. The regret made Shelby feel even worse. Head swimming, gut rolling, she stepped away and spied her panties hanging on the paper towel dispenser over his shoulder.

"I'm so sorry," he said again.

Shelby ignored her panties and instead turned away from him. The water came out of the faucet ice-cold. Why had she turned on the water? No clue. She needed something to do, something to prevent her from telling—oh, cripes, what was his name again? Josh? Joe? Did it even matter?

Shelby stuck her shaking hands under the water and splashed her face, not even caring that it would make her mascara run. She didn't want to look at him. Didn't want to see the utter abhorrence for her and for what they'd drunkenly done.

After the past few days, she felt close to losing it. Close to doing something like…screwing a stranger?

Too late, sister.

The sound of music roared into the bathroom before muted silence fell again.

Well, hell.

He'd left. Just flippin' walked out after an apology she didn't even want.

What an ass.

Shelby looked at herself in the speckled mirror and tried hard not to let her tears join the water coursing down her face. Not only had she impulsively gotten drunk and laid, but the guy she'd chosen for such an honor hadn't even bothered to stick around and buy her a drink for her trouble.

Not that she needed another drink.

The sound of crickets came from somewhere in the bathroom. Her phone. Crap. Where had she left her purse? Shelby swiped her face with a paper towel, grabbed the panties she'd bought last week thinking her now ex-boyfriend Darby might like them and searched for her purse.

She found it on the window ledge next to the only stall, the torn condom package sitting right beside it. At least she hadn't been too drunk to remember to protect herself. She'd bought a box in Baton Rouge, hoping she and Darby could finally take their relationship to the next level.

But then she'd found out Darby was married. Okay, so the man hadn't *realized* he was married to his high school flame when she'd started dating him. The whole thing was a big shocker for everyone involved. But by the time Shelby made it down to Louisiana to try to talk him into coming back to Seattle and the interview with her father's firm, her perfect prospect had fallen in love with his, uh, wife.

Yeah, another married man in her life. It was becoming a thing with her.

"Shit." Shelby sighed, picking up the bright red package, her heart aching at the thought of being back at square one. She felt like a blooming fool... even if none of it was her fault. Guess falling in love was like contracting measles. Bam. Just happened despite one's best efforts. Darby was off the menu.

No more visions of her in a wedding dress smiling at the dark-headed Southern boy with the alligator grin.

Stick a fork in her dream of respectability.

Done.

The phone went silent just as the self-loathing took over. This was what her life had come to—driving the memory of heartbreak away with random stranger sex in a backwater crap hole. She'd never sunk so low.

"Perfect, Shelby," she whispered, leaning onto the stall door. The bathroom still spun a bit but she remained upright. The worst of it was she couldn't drive in the state she was in, and she was utterly alone on her little venture out to tour Louisiana plantations. She'd either have to sit at the bar and drink water until the drunk wore off…which could be a good five or six hours, or swallow her pride and call Darby and ask him to come get her. Neither one appealed to her, but she guessed that was too damn bad.

She'd come to terms long ago that if she waited on Prince Charming to arrive on a white steed, she'd be worm food before he showed up.

As always, it was up to her to figure out a solution.

She dug her phone out of her purse, noted her missed call was from Delta Airlines and asked Siri about cab service. What good was having a couple of million bucks sitting in a bank if you couldn't pay an exorbitant cab fare once in a while? But no dice on a cab. Wasn't even a taxi service out this far.

So she dialed the number to Beau Soleil, Darby's

childhood home. The man owed her a ride back to Bayou Bridge. Time to go back to Seattle.

Goodbye, Louisiana.

So long, life she thought she'd have.

JOHN BEAUCHAMP CLOAKED himself inside the pickup truck that had seen better days, tossing his beat-up cowboy hat onto the bench seat and leaning his forehead against the steering wheel.

His chest felt like he'd been hit with a wrecking ball, tight and achy, the way it had been the entire day of his wife's funeral a year ago. He needed to cry. He needed to punch something until his knuckles bled…until the pain went away.

What in the name of Jesus had he been thinking in there?

He hadn't.

That was the problem.

He'd come to Boots Grocery to drink away the pain and ended up screwing some blonde chick in the bathroom. Like it meant nothing. Like he hadn't just betrayed the vows he'd made eleven years ago last month. Like that would lessen the hurt.

No. The pain never abated, and trying to extinguish it with some bar bunny had done nothing more than release crushing shame.

John felt in his pocket for his keys, pulled them out and reached toward the ignition, but then remembered—he was drunk as a sailor and couldn't drive.

Since his younger brother, Jake, was on a fishing trip, he'd have to call his older brother to pick him up.

No. He didn't want to see the pity in Matt's eyes, nor the unstated disappointment that would quickly follow. Getting drunk wasn't something they did in the Beauchamp family. Hell, naw. Praying was what they did in the Beauchamp family.

But that hadn't gotten him anywhere, either.

Goddamn it.

Nothing took away the damaged part of himself, nothing healed the open sore, erased the knowledge he hadn't been there when she died…hadn't even had a chance to try and save her. How could God let that happen to Rebecca, the sweetest, most wonderful person in all of Magnolia Bend? Hell, in all of St. James Parish. Why her and not someone else?

Why not him?

John tilted his head back and punched the dashboard. "Ow."

He shook his hand out and sank back onto the worn leather, the world tilting crazily. He needed to buy a new truck. This one reflected who he was—dinted, dinged and worn out. He had the money, but something stopped him every time. Because he didn't want to change, didn't want to move forward.

And now he'd not only drunk himself sick on the anniversary of that day, but he'd shamed himself with Shelby.

That had been the bar bunny's name.

Shelby.

She'd had nice straight teeth, a big laugh and sugar

in her smile. He'd thought maybe she could make the dull throb go away. Someone named Shelby ought to bring sunshine, but in the hard light of that bathroom, he'd seen the same emotion reflected back in her eyes—sadness.

"Shit," he said into the darkness, wiping the moisture from his eyes. He allowed his head to slide from the headrest, and listing sideways, he flopped onto the bench, knocking his old hat to the floorboard. The seat belt jabbed him in his back, but he ignored the discomfort and instead fastened his eyes on the stars twinkling out the window in the deep purple Louisiana sky.

All his life he believed in heaven. In God. When your daddy's a pastor, it's pretty much expected. But for the past year, John had stopped believing in anything except the morning sun and the pale moon. Except the rain that fell straight onto the cracked earth and the tender shoots stretching up from the ground. He'd believed in nothing but what he could see.

An empty house.

A made bed.

A lonely man.

And then he didn't care if the tears came. He only cared that he'd loved Rebecca and she was gone.

Gone like the whiskey he'd just used to numb himself...

Just plain gone.

CHAPTER TWO

Ten and a half weeks later

THE DUST BOILED up around her rental car making Shelby squint to see the tractor rolling along the rows of tall plants. Sugarcane. That's the crop John Beauchamp grew on the thirteen-hundred acres owned by the Stanton trust. Or at least that's what Annie Dufrene had told her when she'd called with the report...and unstated questions.

But Shelby hadn't given any answers.

For one thing, the private investigator was her ex-boyfriend's sister-in-law. For another, Shelby hadn't told a soul the reason she had to find John Beauchamp.

Yeah.

The gravel road wound through the green fields leading her to a white-columned farmhouse with a wide front porch. The hedges out front needed a good trim and the flower bed had long gone the way of despair. A patch of gravel indicated a parking area, so Shelby rolled to a halt there, sucking in deep breaths of air-conditioning and tried to still her pounding heart.

You can do this, Shelby. You have to do this. It's only right and fair.

With shaking hands, she pulled down the visor and looked at herself in the mirror. She looked good. The Louisiana humidity had been chased away by a cold front and so her bouncy blond hair looked like something out of a shampoo ad. She'd applied her makeup with a careful, light hand, and the taupe-and-orange-striped wrap dress emitted a polished vibe. She looked just right to tell a man she'd met only once that she was having his baby.

Yeah.

She still couldn't believe she was pregnant, but the visit to the obstetrician a month ago had confirmed what she'd tried to pretend away when the monthly bill hadn't arrived. She had no clue how it had happened. Even in the drunken haze, she remembered the condom being tossed into the trash can, the torn package she'd scooped up. Proof she'd been responsible.

The fact the stick had awarded her with two blue lines had caused her to literally drop to her knees.

Pregnant.

She'd immediately lost the lobster she'd choked down at dinner with her parents and afterward had lain half dressed in the bathroom of her parents' guesthouse wondering how in the hell something like this could have happened. Then she convinced herself it was a false positive. Had to be. But to be certain, she'd schedule an appointment with her doctor, where three weeks later the *wub-wub* of the fetal heartbeat had crushed her with reality and some other feeling she couldn't identify…something that had led her back to Louisiana to find the man she'd wrapped her legs around in a moment of desperation.

Before she'd heard the heartbeat, she'd planned to make the mistake go away. *Abortion* wasn't a pretty word no matter how one dressed it, but Shelby thought it best for everyone concerned. She'd made the appointment with her doctor in Seattle, researched the procedure on the internet and told herself it was the right thing to do. She'd even cleared her substitute teaching schedule in order to have the procedure on a Thursday and be able to return to school on Monday.

Not easy, but best.

Until she heard the heartbeat.

She hadn't known what the doctor was doing when she squirted cold lube on her stomach and moved that thing around. And then…there it was.

Whoosh, lub, whoosh, lub.

And that's all it took—Shelby fell in love with her baby.

Simple as that. Never would she imagine the pull to be so visceral. But at that moment, she knew there would be no abortion. She couldn't erase this mistake the way she erased assignments from the dryerase board at school.

Armed with a prescription for prenatal vitamins and various pamphlets, Shelby had strolled out of the doctor's office a different woman than when she'd strolled in, for now she was an expectant mother.

She felt different than being an accidentally knocked-up loser who didn't even know who the father of her baby was. Correction. She knew the father was a guy named Josh or John Beau-something who'd been in Boots Grocery, the unfortunate grocery/bar/bait stand, the second Friday in September.

Of course, it had crossed her mind to forget all about him…and the uncaring way her child had been conceived. Yes, *her* child. Not his. But that didn't sit well with her. In the past, she'd tried to slide around corners and hide from truth, and if she was going to have a baby and raise him or her to be a good, productive, honest citizen, she had to start out on the right foot.

And that meant finding the man who'd cried after having raunchy, impetuous sex with her…and telling him she was pregnant.

So when Thanksgiving break had rolled around, she'd bought a plane ticket back to the state she'd hoped never to see again. Then she'd called Annie Dufrene. Two days before Shelby was set to fly back into Baton Rouge, Annie sent her a fax on one John Beauchamp. Thirty-four years old. A widower. Sugarcane farmer. Resides at 308 Burnside Hwy 4, Breezy Hill Plantation. No children. Parents living. Two brothers and one older sister. Registered driver, organ donor and no arrest record.

Biggest relief ever—he hadn't lied when he said he was no longer married. At least that small thing had gone right.

So here she was in the middle of Louisiana on a nice fall day about to shock the boots off the poor man.

For a good five minutes Shelby fiddled around in the rental, double-checking her phone messages, updating her GPS and wadding up gum wrappers and tucking them in a tissue. Finally, with nothing more to piddle with, she opened the car door and climbed out into the cool Louisiana afternoon. The tractor still ambled along in a half-planted field. Behind it trailed several men, tucking what looked to be sticks into the furrows. In another field, a huge combine thing cut sugarcane, or at least that's what she assumed.

She knocked on the door twice, but no one seemed to be inside. Or anywhere around the outside of the house.

Maybe she should have called. But how awkward would that have been?

"Yes, hello. John? It's Shelby…Shelby. You remember me? Mid-September, Boots Grocery, watermelon-colored panties?…Yeah, well, guess what? I'm having your baby."

Didn't seem too kosher…not that Shelby was Jewish. Still, seemed like something a woman should tell a man face-to-face. But she'd been here for almost fifteen minutes and no one was around. Surely someone should have seen her driving up. How long should she wait?

Shelby glanced back at the field. Tractor still churning…or doing whatever tractors do.

Sighing, she sank onto the top step of the porch. There were rocking chairs framing a bank of windows, but sitting in one seemed presumptuous… like she was an old friend, familiar enough to sit on his porch. But she wasn't an old friend…or even a new one. Shelby was nothing to this man…and he likely wouldn't feel too "friendly" when she delivered her news.

She glanced at her watch. Twenty minutes had passed. Hadn't someone seen the car come up the drive?

"Hey," a voice came from her left.

Shelby turned and peered over the overgrown sweet olive bush to find a young sunburned guy in sagging jeans and a flat-billed cap staring at her with suspicion. She stood. "Oh, hey. I wondered if anyone was around."

"If you're sellin' something, we don't want it," he said, wiping his brow with a soggy blue bandanna.

"Well, how do you know you don't want it?" Shelby asked.

"If I ain't offered nothin' I don't have to choose whether I want it or not. Stands to reason it's easier to say I don't want to buy nothin'."

Roundabout logic, but it made sense.

Shelby walked down the five concrete steps. The guy with the bowlegged gait, stained T-shirt and bright blue eyes narrowed his gaze.

"I'm not selling anything, but I *am* looking for John Beauchamp," she said.

"Out there on the tractor." He pointed at the big

green tractor. It was so far away Shelby could see only the outline of a figure inside the cab.

"Oh," she said, licking her lips, trying to look calm.

"You here from the church, then?" he asked, shoving the bandanna in his back pocket.

"The church? Uh, no."

He lifted his brows. "Well, the boss—"

"But I do need to speak to Mr. Beauchamp. It's important," she interrupted.

The kid shook his head. "We in the middle of harvest and don't quit for nothin'. Not even a pretty lady."

Shelby didn't know what to say. Seemed evident the worker wasn't about to fetch John off the tractor. "But this can't wait."

"Guess I can take you out if you want. Boss will have to stop then." He gestured to a golf cart on steroids. "I'm Homer. Been working for the Stantons forever. Reckon I can decide you're all right and take you out to do whatever business you got with Boss Man."

Boss Man? Had she entered a time warp? "Thank you. I'm Shelby." She stuck out her hand, but Homer waved it away, lifting his hands and showing streaks of grease on his palms.

"I'll just say how you do." He bobbed his head.

Southerners were weird sometimes. And charming. But mostly weird. "You called Mr. Beauchamp Boss Man but you said this land belongs to the Stantons?"

"The boss married a Stanton and runs the place

for the family. Ain't nobody works this land the way Boss Man do. Even ol' Mr. Stanton, who died right there in that tractor of a heart attack, didn't love it like Boss, and there ain't nobody left to run this place, which is a shame since this land's been worked by Stantons for long as I can remember and way past that. Boss's wife died last year in an accident."

"Oh," Shelby said, not really wanting the history lesson, not really wanting to soften over John losing his wife. She wanted to get on with telling John about the baby and go back to a place that made sense to her.

Homer cracked another smile. "You ain't from here, are you? You talk funny."

"I'm from Washington State."

"Well, tell the president 'hey' for me when you see him."

Okay, she wasn't touching that one. "Will do."

"I'll get a towel outta the barn for you to sit on. Don't want to mess that fancy dress up," Homer said, loping off toward the barn.

Shelby waited, fiddling with the key chain and double-checking she'd locked the rental car since she'd left her purse on the floorboard. Of course no one was around to make off with it, but living in Seattle most of her life had ingrained certain precautions.

But then, sometimes taking precautions failed. She stood here living proof about to climb into a cart and bump out to a tractor operated by a man who was going to get the shock of his life. Yeah, sometimes in spite of a best effort, shit happened.

Like getting pregnant.

When Homer came back around, he carried a faded striped beach towel, which he placed on the seat of the cart. "Here ya go." He patted the towel.

Shelby eyed the new boots she'd bought before peeing on the pregnancy test stick and learning her life would go from single, focused substitute teacher to single, unfocused mother. Somehow the sleek knee-length boots she'd bought to make her feel better about the whole Darby fiasco seemed frivolous for her new role, but that didn't mean she wanted them spattered with Louisiana mud.

Minutes later they took off, rolling over ruts in bone-jarring fashion. Shelby clung to the handrail attached to the roof of the cart and focused on not sliding out since the seat belts looked to have been cut out.

She watched the green tractor in the distance grow larger. It still chugged along, workers scurrying behind. Finally, when the motorized cart Homer called a mule got within a hundred feet, the big tractor stopped. Seconds later the stranger from the bar climbed out, looking tired and puzzled.

Homer hopped out of the cart and jogged over to John Beauchamp whose edges looked sharper than she remembered. Sobriety did that. "Brought you a pretty lady who says she needs a word with you. I'll come back for her in a few. Gotta get this part over to Henry."

John glanced over to Shelby, his eyes narrowing, face bewildered. Shelby wondered what he thought. Probably had that same sinking feeling she'd had when her boobs had grown heavy and achy and the telltale crimson flow hadn't appeared. Pure dread.

"Thanks, Homer, but you better give me the part. I'll drive it over to the combine. Can you take over here for me?"

Homer saluted before scrabbling up the tractor into the cab. He called down, "Sure thing, Boss Man."

John frowned, shaking his head. "Stop calling me that."

Homer cackled. "Hey, it's what you are."

Shelby sat still as a puddle, watching John walk toward where she held a death grip on the handle. This wasn't going the way she'd planned, but then again, things were all over the map in regards to plans lately.

Readjusting an old ball cap on his head, John stopped beside the driver's seat, glancing back at the men standing behind the tractor, drinking water. They all stared, questions in their eyes, at the woman dressed for brunch sitting in a mucked-up cart in the middle of a cane field. "Go on, fellows. We need to finish this field today. Already late on this planting."

The men leaped into action as the tractor lurched forward with Homer at the helm.

Shelby took a moment to take stock of the man she hadn't seen since he'd slipped out of the bathroom that fateful night. John's boots were streaked with mud and his dusty jeans had a hole on the thigh. A kerchief hung from his back pocket, and the faded chambray shirt he wore stretched across broad shoulders. He looked like a farmer.

She'd never thought a farmer could look, well, sexy. But John Beauchamp had that going for him… not that she was interested.

Been there. Done him. Got pregnant.

He looked down at her with cautious green eyes… like she was a ticking bomb he had to disarm. "What are you doing here?"

Shelby tried to calm the bats flapping in her stomach, but there was nothing to quiet them. "Uh, it's complicated."

He slid in beside her, his thigh brushing hers. She scooted away. He noticed, but didn't say anything.

"Complicated," he repeated as though tasting the word. "You didn't go back to…Seattle, was it?"

"No, I went back."

"But you're here again." His words held the question.

She glanced at him and then back at the men still casting inquisitive looks their way as they followed the tractor down the furrows.

John got the message and stepped on the accelerator, this time heading toward the huge combine sitting silent in the opposite field.

Shelby yelped and grabbed the edge of the seat with her other hand, nearly sliding across the cracked pleather seat and pitching onto the ground rushing by the wheels. John reached over and clasped her arm, saving her from meeting the hard ground.

"You good?" he asked, releasing her arm and making no apology for the abrupt launch and turn.

"Yeah," she said, finding her balance, her stomach pitching more at the thought of revealing why she sat beside him than at the actual bumpy ride.

So how did one do this?

Probably should just say it. Rip the bandage off. Pull the knife out. He probably already suspected why she'd come. If it had been anything other than her being pregnant, she'd have found him before now.

As they turned onto the adjacent path, Shelby took a deep breath and said, "I'm pregnant."

He made no sound, but she felt his reaction. Glancing sideways, she saw him go rigid, knuckles white on the steering wheel.

"Pregnant?" he said, his voice low, perhaps even angry. "By me?"

"That's why I'm here."

"That's very unlikely."

"Oh, I am. Went to the doctor. Saw the heartbeat on the ultrasound. Pretty sure there's a baby in there."

He slowed down and eyed her in the brightness of the afternoon, looking as if he studied an insect that had landed on his windshield. Squash or let it blow away on its own? "I understand the concept, but it's not mine. We used a condom. I remember because it was bright pink and I'd never seen anything like that before."

"Yeah, I thought pink condoms were kind of fun, but that's not important. Or maybe it is, because something went wrong with it. Besides you ran out before—" She snapped her mouth closed, wishing she hadn't mentioned his running out. The fact he hightailed it like a coward was the least important part of the whole travesty. "The condom must have broken. Or did you notice any, um, leakage maybe?"

His head snapped around. "No."

For a moment he didn't say anything and she wondered if he was searching his memory for that night. "Look I don't remember much, but I'm pretty sure I would remember that. I was drunk but not stupid."

"I'm not lying."

John frowned. "I'm not saying you are, but I can't accept you got pregnant that night."

"Look, I'm not thrilled, okay? I'm only here because I thought you should know."

"Are you sure it's mine?"

She almost slapped him. Would have been melodramatic and very Scarlett O'Hara-like, fitting considering she sat in the middle of a field in the Deep South feeling rather beat down. "Thanks for the unspoken accusation that I'm a whore. And a stupid one at that."

John slammed the brakes, his arm catching hers before she could slide forward into the dashboard. "I'm not calling you anything. A woman I barely know shows up saying she's pregnant, I think I'm entitled to ask a few questions."

Shelby yanked her arm away and shifted even farther from him. "I came to tell you. That's it. I don't expect anything from you. I can take care of the baby on my own."

John sank against the cracked bench seat, looking as if someone had taken the starch out of him. "Just give me a sec, okay?"

Shelby didn't say anything more. She got it. She'd needed a lot of moments herself over the past few weeks.

For several minutes they sat; the only sounds were the tractor humming, the occasional shouts of the men working the fields and their mingled breaths, which was vastly different from the last time they'd been together. Very sober. Maybe too sober for the reality that had just crashed into both of their worlds.

"So what are your plans?" he asked. "Are you going to, uh, move forward with the pregnancy?" He sounded choked, as if the words stuck in his throat.

"Yeah. At first I thought about taking care of it—"

"Oh, God," he breathed, rubbing a hand over his face. "I can't imagine. I can't—"

"I know, but my first reaction was to erase the mistake we made then I could just move forward, but…" She trailed off, wondering how she could put into words what she'd experienced when she'd seen the heartbeat, heard the rhythm established by a life growing inside her. It was almost sacred.

John's eyes met hers, his gaze still convoluted, still shocked. "But what?"

"I heard the heartbeat," she whispered, swallowing the sudden emotion. Something warm crept up her spine. It wasn't an *aw* emotion. More like something that might eat her and swallow her whole. Not danger, but something life altering, something that made her palms sweaty.

John said nothing, merely turned his attention to the field full of glossy green leaves of sugarcane stirring in the slight wind. Captured stark against the horizon, he stood in sharp relief. John was a man shaken to his core.

"I'm sorry," she said, after several more seconds of nothing from him. The knot in her stomach grew tighter. She didn't know what to do, how to make it better for him. Or her.

"Me, too," he offered, his eyes fastened on the horizon.

"If you'll take me to the house now, I'll let you get back to work," she said.

John scratched his head beneath the Ragin' Cajun ball cap. "Not yet. Let me run this part out and then we'll go back to the house."

Shelby didn't want to spend any more time with him. She wanted to go to her hotel room in Baton Rouge, take a bath and curl up beneath the coverlet with the TV drowning out everything in her life. Escape sounded perfect, but obviously John wasn't going to let her slink away. The knot inside her tightened and twisted. "Fine."

After handing off a part to someone named Henry and bumping back along the original path, John headed to the farmhouse. It appeared around the bend, plain and lonely against the cerulean background. A turn of her head showed her John's stoic profile, jaw squared as he contained his emotions.

Okay. She'd done it. She'd told him about the child growing in her belly. Their child. Mission accomplished. Now all she had to do was go back home, tell her parents, move out of the guesthouse, get a permanent job, take a birthing class, register for preschool, start a college fund....

Oh, dear God.

Parenting wasn't for wussies…and she'd be alone.

Sweat broke out on her upper lip and her body started to tremble as the enormity of her situation, combined with the residual anxiety from telling John, crashed over her. Her teeth chattered as the knot inside her unwound, releasing some strange hormonal thing that smothered her.

John stopped the cart and climbed out.

But she couldn't move.

Silly as it was, all the emotion she'd balled inside over the past four weeks rolled over her, rendering her, well, overwhelmed.

"Shelby?"

Oddly enough, during the middle of what was possibly a panic attack she realized she liked the way he said her name. He had a drawled Southern accent quite different from Darby's soft Acadian dialect. Maybe a slight lilt.

Shelby waved her hands as if she could make the panic enveloping her go away. "I'm just a little—" Gulping deep breaths, she couldn't finish.

"Jesus," John said, taking huge steps around the mule to reach her side.

"No, don't touch me," Shelby said, brushing away the hand reaching for her, shrinking from him.

"It's okay. Breathe."

Shelby wanted to say something biting like what in the hell did he think she was doing, but she couldn't seem to care enough to be a smart-ass.

"Come into the house," he said, taking her by the forearm, his touch as gentle as his words. "We'll have some tea or something and take a few minutes to process all this."

"I just wanna leave," she said, teeth still chattering, her breathing ragged. She figured if she didn't get out of there, away from him, she might hyperventilate. "I told you. That's it. I'm done."

He stiffened again, but didn't release her arm. "I understand, but you need to gather yourself before you drive. Come inside. It will be okay."

"It won't be okay," she said, inhaling deeply, trying to find her calm, trying to find herself in the hysteria edging in. How dare he even imply such a thing? *It will be okay.* What a fat lie. She might be resolved to her fate, but having the baby of a stranger was not even remotely *okay.* "This is a screwup of enormous magnitude."

"You're right, but it will be okay."

"Stop freaking saying that."

He clamped his mouth shut and studied her for a moment. The same perusal he'd given her earlier. Scientific. "You don't need to drive. You're upset."

"Duh. You think?" Shelby drawled, the anger, the lack of control pissing her off. She'd had a plan. Tell him. Leave. But somehow her body…or her mind… or something…hadn't gotten the damn memo to play it cool.

He didn't respond. Just stared at her. And tugged on her arm in an insistent manner.

"Fine," she said finally, struggling to her feet. "I'll gather myself and have a cup of tea. We can even pretend we're normal people."

Again, nothing from him. He released her arm as she stood.

Shelby took a deep breath, relieved her task was nearly over. Now someone other than her doctor knew about the life knitting together within her womb. Of course, she'd shared that information with a man she didn't know beyond the investigative report sitting in her sock drawer…and the fact he sang off-key to old George Strait songs when he danced.

Wordlessly, side by side, they climbed the steps. When they reached the top step, where Shelby had perched a mere half hour ago, John stopped.

Shelby turned around, still fighting the edging panic.

"You're not alone, Shelby."

His words did what he meant them to do. Found their way inside her, creating a small bit of warmth in the midst of the madness of her life.

John stood there, handsome as sin, saying the right thing at just the right moment.

Damn him.

He was still the bastard who had treated her like a fungus, impregnated her with a child and implied she was some sort of whore.

But he knew exactly what to say.

And as he took her hand and pulled her toward the door, she realized he also knew exactly how to make her feel cared for.

And that was more dangerous than any other feeling she'd had since seeing him again.

CHAPTER THREE

JOHN LED SHELBY up the steps of the house that had been his home for a decade, every nook and cranny known and loved despite the flaws. Inside, he quaked as much as Shelby did. Outside, he maintained a semblance of control. Like always.

Shelby was pregnant with his baby. Or at least she said she was. The irony of the situation rubbed him, bitter and biting.

Rebecca's desire for the pitter-patter of little feet had been a driving force in their marriage for the past year of her life. With her death, the thought of children ceased to exist. And now, he'd gotten what he'd once desired so greatly…at the hands of a drunken hookup in a crappy bathroom off Hwy 5.

God had a sense of humor. Or maybe he didn't. Maybe God liked to sucker punch John for the hell of it.

He pulled the screen door open, holding it with his boot as he turned the century-old iron doorknob and pushed inside.

His yellow Lab sat, tongue lolling, ready to greet him.

"Down, Bart." John pushed the hairy beast with

the generous kisses off his thigh and walked inside the cool darkness of the living room, turning right and escorting Shelby toward the kitchen. Bart followed after them, tail threatening the doodads on the low antique tables Rebecca had scattered throughout the foyer and formal dining room. He should pack them away, but something held him back.

It always did.

"You have a dog," Shelby said like she'd never seen one.

"Yeah. This is Bart." John released her hand and pulled out a chair in the kitchen. He didn't know why he'd grabbed her hand to begin with. Maybe because for a moment she looked like a lost child and he hadn't wanted her to run away. "Here. Sit. I'll boil some water for tea."

Bart sat, too. Right at Shelby's feet. She patted the dog's head, causing Bart to nudge her hand for more.

John never made tea because he always went for a beer at the end of a long day. In the pantry he found some boxes of herbal tea that had expired a few months before. Tea didn't go bad, did it? Probably. But this would have to do.

He found the kettle and lit the flame on the stove, eyeing Shelby out of the corner of his eye. Her teeth had stopped chattering, and though she was pale, she looked less panicked.

The woman was almost too pretty, with flaxen hair likely achieved in a high-end salon. Wide blue eyes were framed by inky long eyelashes; high-rounded cheekbones and a mouth he remembered thinking belonged on a pinup girl. Plump and made for sex. Large breasts, nice legs and a waist that was still trim despite her pregnancy. A freaking Playboy Bunny of a woman.

God.

He filled the kettle at the sink and tried to figure out how to handle the situation. Shelby had seemed offended when he asked if she was certain the child she carried was his, but he had to ask, right? He knew nothing about her, and she'd seemed more than willing to pull that condom out of her purse that night.

Of course, it didn't mean she was morally loose.

Morally loose? Jesus. He sounded like his father.

Stay away from those kind of girls, Johnny. No girl who gives it away is worth your name, and if you knock her up you'll have to marry her.

So should he insist on a blood test? How did those work? Maybe the baby had to come first before they could test and that was months away. He didn't know how to handle this situation. Hell, who really knew how to handle this situation? He felt like he'd fallen into a well and was treading water with no foothold on the slick walls, no way to heft himself up.

He focused on what he could control. "Looks like all I have is Apple Orchard or Peachy Keen."

Shelby stopped petting Bart and the dog whined his displeasure. "Either, as long as it's caffeine-free. I'm not supposed to have caffeine."

John put the kettle on and stepped toward the back door, whistling for Bart to come. Reluctantly, the dog stood and waddled to the door. "Go tee-tee," he said out of habit.

When he turned, Shelby had a weird look on her face. "Go tee-tee?"

He shrugged. "Started when he was a puppy. Somehow changing the term to *piss* seemed wrong."

The kettle whistled, and John grabbed a cup, plunked in a tea bag and poured the water. Then he grabbed himself a beer. He'd allow himself only one, though he felt like he needed a six-pack to deal with the woman sitting at his kitchen table. But he needed to get back to the fields.

Pulling out the chair beside her, he slid the cup to her and cracked open his beer. "Feeling better?"

"Yes and no," she said, lifting the tea and inhaling. Just like Rebecca. The memory punched him. "Thank you for the tea."

"You're welcome. So…I'd like to talk a bit more."

"I assumed that's why you made me come inside and drink this." She didn't look happy about his wanting to know more. What had she said? *I told you. Now I'm done.*

"So what are your immediate plans regarding the pregnancy?"

"Immediate plans? Go back to Seattle, break the news to my parents and find a permanent teaching job." She fiddled with the teacup, bending a finger around the rim. Her nails were clipped short and painted a soft pink. Definitely a nice manicure.

"You're a teacher?"

"I teach high school math. My last teaching

assignment in Spain ended this past spring, and I
didn't come stateside in enough time to interview for
a permanent position. It's hard to pick one up mid-
year so I've been substituting in the Seattle school
district on a part-time basis. The baby's due in June,
so I should be able to maintain a permanent position next year."

"The baby's due in June?"

"The due date's June 24."

"My birthday's the eighteenth," he said, wondering why the hell that even mattered. But even so,
the image of a small bundle cradled in his arms appeared. A son with dark hair and fair skin, his little mouth doing that lip quivering thing as he cried
annoyance at being taken from his mother's arms.

"I know. I hired a private investigator to find you.
I was fuzzy on your name." Her bite of laughter was
bitter and when she looked up he saw shame in her
eyes.

"I remembered yours. Thought it was a pretty
name." He'd remembered her name, the way she
smelled—like something sweet and expensive—
and the small encouraging sounds she'd moaned as
he pulled up her skirt.

He hadn't wanted to remember, but on dark, lonely
nights when he lay awake staring at the crack in
the ceiling he needed to repair, he recalled Shelby
and the way she'd felt against him. He hated himself for it.

For a few minutes, they each contemplated the
enormity of the situation.

A baby. Good God.

"So," she said. "I'm feeling a little better. I'm embarrassed I sort of freaked out. Guess it was everything built up. I'm not usually so...wimpy." Her smile was embarrassed, almost pained. "I won't keep you from your work."

John cradled his beer in both hands. "Are you staying in town?"

"No, I'm going back home to Seattle tomorrow. Besides, staying in town a few days is what got me in trouble in the first place." She gave a humorless chuckle.

"This is crazy," he said.

"Yes, it is," she agreed with a nod, "but it's not the end of the world. I can deal."

"I'd like it if you could stay at least a day or two," he said, suddenly alarmed about the finality in her voice. Did she think she could drop this bomb and walk away...and he'd just go back to cutting cane like the news she'd brought was equal to "I sideswiped your mailbox" or "I accidentally broke your window." This wasn't something a person confessed to and then walked away. This was about a child... his child. "Just give me some time to wrap my mind around this and help you."

"I don't need your help," she said, pushing the teacup away. "I'm not trying to interfere in your life. Just thought telling you about the pregnancy was the decent thing to do."

"And that's it? I get to know and that's all?"

Shelby's eyebrows knotted. "I didn't think you..."

She paused and looked hard at him. "You don't have to do anything. I didn't come here asking for money or a way out of this. I'm not a girl in trouble. This isn't the '50s or '60s. I can take care of the baby myself. I'm financially secure and mentally stable… mostly."

He made a face.

"I'm kidding," she said, her complexion pinking, her eyes resuming a less-tragic glint. "I'm mentally stable."

"But it's my baby, too." John set his beer aside and leveled her with the same look his father had used on him when he thought to take the easy way out. John wasn't going away. If that's what she'd thought, she'd been wrong.

She gave an exaggerated, slow nod. "Okay, so technically speaking, it's your child, but you don't have to be involved."

"Too bad," he said. "You came here to tell me I'm the father of the child you're carrying. Did you really think I'd say 'thanks for the info' and go about my life as normal? What kind of man do you think I am?"

"I have no idea what kind of man you are," she said, scooting her chair back, looking as if she might run for the back door. "I didn't think you would—I never considered anything other than…" She knotted her brow, twisting her lips as if searching for the right way to say she didn't want him to care.

"Doing the right thing?" he finished. "I believe

that's the way you put it. So why even tell me if you don't want anything from me?"

"Because you have a right to know."

"But not a say-so?"

"Why would you? You ran," she said, looking up at him. "Remember? You left me in that bathroom, drunk, ashamed and…knocked up. Why on earth would I think you're the kind of man who would stand with me? And why would I want you to?"

John felt as if she'd just hit him in the face with a wet dish towel. The kind of man who would run? Yeah. She wasn't wrong. He'd been running for the past year…from his family, his friends and the grief that consumed him. The only thing he hadn't run from was the incessant work he did in the fields as some kind of penance to his wife's family. As if he could make up to Carla Stanton the loss of her daughter by keeping the Stanton legacy alive in some way. Rows of cane and this empty house were all he had left in his life. Even knowing how pathetic it was to close out the people who loved him hadn't stopped him from soaking himself in work and regret. "Okay. I'll give you that. I ran. I was a total dick. For that I apologize."

Shelby's sculpted eyebrows lifted. "Oh. Thank you for apologizing."

"I know this is a hard situation. I'm not asking you to do anything other than stay a day or two so we can figure some things out together. Obviously, you've been carrying this burden by yourself. Maybe you could use my help. Maybe fate threw us together and gave us, uh, a baby for a reason. So whether you wanted me involved or not, I am."

Shelby looked annoyed. "You're making this complicated. It's not. *I'm* pregnant. *I'm* having a baby. *I'm* making the decisions. You provided the sperm. Job over."

"No. It's not that simple and you know it. I'm not going away just because you want me to. You're not being fair."

"What? I'm being more than fair. I flew down to tell you. I didn't have to do that."

"But you did. It was the right thing to do, and you can't legally keep me out of the child's life. I'm the father. You said so yourself."

Her eyes narrowed. "Why are you doing this? I live thousands of miles away. I can't give you what you're asking for."

"Well, I'm not satisfied being a phantom figure who mails a check once a month. Is that what you thought I would do? Never want to see my child?"

Anger burgeoned in her eyes. "I shouldn't have come."

"But you did."

"So you keep reminding me," she said. "I only wanted to tell you about the baby. I didn't want anything else from you…not even a check."

"Too bad." John stood and scooped up her cup. He walked to the counter and set the half-filled cup in the depths of the scarred farm sink. His feelings were twisted into a giant ball of so many emotions he couldn't begin to identify them, but in the midst of the disappointment, regret and anger was something that surprised him.

Joy.

Seemed impossible, since he hadn't felt an inkling of happiness in well over a year. But despite feeling out-and-out terror, inside John thrilled at the warm thought of a child in his life. "We made a mistake a few months back. Not you. Not me. We. Which means going forward is something we'll do together."

Shelby eyed the empty spot where her tea had been. "Why did you pick up my tea? And why do you think you have the right to decide anything about my future?"

John eyed the cup in the sink before turning back to her. "Sorry."

She glared at him.

"You're carrying something inside of you who is as much a part of me as you. You would deny me the right to know my own son or daughter?"

Shelby paled but said nothing.

For a few minutes, they stared at each other, once strangers with a compulsion...an urge to feel something that dark September night, now tied together by the tiny life growing within Shelby.

"I need to use your restroom before I head back to Baton Rouge," Shelby said, her voice firm and teacherlike. She seemed set on ignoring his last question. As if she could make him go away.

John studied her, seeing too much or maybe not enough of the woman beneath the highlights and sophisticated clothes. The woman beneath the expensive leather boots and jewelry that probably cost more than his broken-down truck. This was a woman nothing like his wife. But this was a woman he wasn't going to run from this time. He conceded the battle, but the fight wasn't over. "Down the hall to your left."

She stood up too quickly and hit the table with her thigh. His beer fell, emptying its contents on the table he'd inherited from his grandmother May Claire. He scooped the bottle from the table, droplets of yeasty beer mixing with the scent he remembered from that night long ago—a sultry warmth that belonged to a woman he'd never thought to see again.

A scent that belonged to a woman who carried a part of his future.

John grabbed a dish towel and wiped up the spilled beer, wishing he could fix his world as easily.

SHELBY WALKED QUICKLY down the dim hallway, looking for the bathroom…looking for an escape.

God, why had she come?

Of course, she knew why. She'd put herself in the shoes of a man who'd had a one-night stand and convinced herself she would at the very least want to know she had a child out there somewhere. Seemed ethical. The right thing to do.

But now she wished she hadn't said anything.

I'm not satisfied being a phantom figure who mails a check once a month. So what did that mean?

All the doors on her left were closed. Shelby tried

the first one, but it was an office, desk cluttered with paper and somehow lonely in the afternoon shadows dancing against the pale wall. Shelby closed that door and found the small bathroom next to it.

Twisting the antique crystal handle, Shelby closed herself in the narrow gray half bath and bolted the door. Silly, but she felt better having a locked door between her and the man she'd paid her ex-boyfriend's sister-in-law three hundred dollars to find.

Irony was such a bitch.

The bathroom showed a woman's touch. Embroidered antique towels hung on a ring and a pewter picture frame sat on the vanity. Shelby picked up the picture of the happy couple on the sugar-white beach. John was nearly unrecognizable with tan skin and a huge grin. The wife he held in his arms was small, brown and pretty in a wholesome way. Happy times for a couple that no longer existed.

Shelby set the picture down next to a small carving of a pelican perched in the corner. From the top of the pelican sprouted cattail and tumbling Spanish moss. The braided rug looked handmade in tones of blue and moss-green. Tasteful and simple. Most likely decorated by the woman in the picture.

Shelby sighed and ran water into the sink, blinking at herself in the mirror. She'd eaten her lipstick off long ago, but still looked much the same as she had earlier. She didn't look like a half-panicked pregnant woman. She looked, well, prettier than normal if not a little pale after having to impart the news to the man clacking around in the kitchen, cleaning up her spill.

Cleaning up her spill.

Yeah. Story of Shelby's life.

Stay a couple of days. Let me help you figure things out.

John's offer was tempting to a degree. She had hated being back in Seattle. The summer had been long and rainy, spent waiting on Darby. Then fall had come, along with the news Darby was in love with his...well, wife. Things had unraveled and hadn't gotten better. Her relationship with her parents was as strained as ever, so in one way not being in Seattle was fine, but she hadn't wanted the complication of John in her life.

So why did you fly down here to Louisiana?

She had no delusions of some sort of relationship with John Beauchamp. God help her, but she'd had enough of emotionally unavailable men, and one look at the dossier prepared on him paired with the memory of his eyes that night, and Shelby knew he still loved his dead wife. And even if he were available, there would be no time for romance between pregnancy and her teaching career. Besides she hadn't come down here wanting to be rescued. She'd meant it when she said she didn't expect anything of him. She didn't have a permanent job, but she had a solid bank account, and if all else failed, there was her inheritance. Money had never been an issue for her family.

No, coming down to Louisiana had allowed her to

escape the reality of Seattle if only for a few days...
and delay the ensuing disappointment and scandal
she would heap on her accomplished family.

Again.

Once the black sheep, always the black sheep. She
seemed destined to stay in the role she'd assumed
long ago.

Sighing, Shelby hiked up her dress and tugged
down her tights. Might as well—how had John put
it? Oh, yeah. Tee-tee. Long drive back to Baton
Rouge. She wasn't staying here in Magnolia Bend
any longer than she had to. If John wanted to talk
about the future of their child, he'd have to—

Shelby's last thought disappeared as she caught
sight of the blood in the crotch of her brown ribbed
tights.

She jerked her panties down and sank onto the
porcelain toilet seat. Heavier smears of blood in her
panties. Frantically, she grabbed some toilet paper
and wiped.

More blood. Fresh.

Oh, God. She was bleeding.

Why had she climbed in that damn rattletrap
mule? Bumping over those huge ruts in the field
couldn't have been good for the baby. And all this
drama and stress hadn't helped, either. She'd put her
baby in jeopardy, and now she was having a miscarriage right there in a dead woman's guest bathroom.

Jesus.

And suddenly she, who'd hated the life growing
inside of her for nearly a month, who'd penciled in

an abortion on her calendar, who didn't even know the father of her baby beyond his birth date and occupation, knew beyond all else she wanted to keep the small miracle housed within her body.

She stood, tugged up her underwear and tights, squeezed her legs together as if that could stop the bleeding and called, "John!"

Shelby heard the pounding of his boots and slid the lock open, pushing back the door.

"What is it?" he asked, wiping his hands on a towel, looking alarmed.

"I'm bleeding," she said, trying to stay calm despite the fear clogging her throat. Rough unshed tears made her hoarse.

John took her arm and pulled her gently from the bathroom. "It's okay. I'm going to call Jamison French. He's a doctor and one of my closest friends. He's not far away."

Shelby nodded, for the first time glad John stood beside her, glad to have someone to lean on. She didn't want to need him, but her mind felt frozen and all she could think about was keeping the baby inside of her. "I'm scared."

John escorted her to the chair she'd left moments ago and grabbed the cordless phone sitting on the kitchen counter. "I know you are, but I'm going to take care of you."

Shelby sank into the chair and tried not to cry. She wanted to be strong, but at the moment doing so seemed impossible.

John barked some things into the phone, softening

his tone with an apology. Shelby didn't pay attention to who he talked to. She concentrated on telling her body to stop bleeding, to stop trying to eject the small life she'd glimpsed on the ultrasound.

"We're going to my truck, okay?" John said, grabbing a set of keys. "Jamison's at the hospital, but he's going to meet us at his office. We're going to go in the back door."

"Oh, God," Shelby breathed. "I didn't want this to happen. Why is this happening?"

"It's okay," he breathed, helping her rise, smoothing her hair back.

"You say that a lot."

"Maybe we'll both believe it."

Shelby closed her eyes. "I hope that's true."

John opened the back door, pushing Bart out of the way and flipping off the lights. "No matter what happens, Shelby, hold on to the thought everything will be okay. I've forgotten how to do that, but suddenly it feels pretty damn important."

And when Shelby glanced over at him, she believed him…but that didn't stop the fact she felt dampness in the crotch of her panties.

CHAPTER FOUR

DR. JAMISON FRENCH's office looked nothing like her doctor's office in Seattle. The walls were a bright blue and the hot-pink chairs looked like something in a funky designer's office rather than an obstetrician's. The navy chevron-patterned changing curtain and a funny picture of kittens playing on the ceiling above the exam table seemed to make pelvic exams fun…uh, almost.

Dr. French rolled his stool over to where Shelby lay on the exam table, paisley paper gown open to reveal her white belly. The tech rolled the ultrasound transponder around in the gook on her stomach while the doctor focused on the soft *lub-lub* of the heartbeat on the monitor.

Feeling like she might heave up the oatmeal cookie she'd scarfed down hours ago, Shelby watched the small screen and the mass of…something that caused the swooshing noises. The panic inside subsided as she listened to the telltale sound of her baby's heartbeat.

"I'm not seeing anything that concerns me here, Shelby," Dr. French said, his blue eyes intense behind

his artsy glasses. Pointing to the screen he continued. "Heartbeat's strong for an eleven-week fetus."

"So why am I bleeding? Was it riding in that stupid mule?"

Dr. French nodded at the technician, who removed
the roller-ball thing and handed Shelby a few tissues
to wipe off the lubricant.

"No, your baby is safe in your womb and hitting
bumps or getting jostled shouldn't cause any harm.
About twenty percent of women experience spotting
in the first trimester of pregnancy. Usually caused
by implantation of the fetus, but since you're past
that point of your pregnancy, I don't think that's the
issue."

"Oh." Dread knitted inside her. What was wrong
with her? Had she done something wrong? She'd had
some wine and, oh, hell, a couple of vodka martinis
before she knew she was pregnant.

"When was the last time you saw your doctor?"
Dr. French asked, noting something in the thin folder
before setting it on the counter by the sink. The technician left, shutting the door softly, and the pretty
nurse who'd taken her blood pressure slid inside the
examination room and with a warm smile, started
doing whatever it was nurses did behind the exam
table.

"Two weeks ago. Uh, when I had the pregnancy
confirmed."

"And did he or she do a vaginal exam?"

"Yes." Shelby sat up and wrapped her arms around
herself, rubbing her arms. She didn't want a vagi-

nal exam. She couldn't handle something that made her any more vulnerable than what she currently felt. Tears sat on the horizon waiting for an excuse to make a debut.

"Hmm."

"What's that mean?" Shelby tried to not sound panicked. Her life had been flipped topsy-turvy, and the ground beneath her feet felt as thin as the paper gown she shivered in. Dear Lord. How did single mothers do this and not lose their minds? She felt out of control…and there was no one to hand the reins over to.

On her own.

Dr. French lifted his head from the chart and gave her a sincere, comforting smile. "Relax, lots of changes are going on in your body—like the alteration of pH levels, which can allow yeast to flourish. Any disruption of the cervical cells, like having intercourse, can cause those inflamed cells to bleed."

"I haven't had sex. Um, since that night." Shelby looked at the closed door. John sat right outside in the small waiting area. Did Dr. French suspect John as the father?

Silly, Shelby. Sure, the good doctor had question marks in his eyes when John hurried her in the back door like it was some secret abortion clinic and he was the preacher's son, but that didn't mean he suspected his friend of being the father.

"We'll take a look and see if that's what's going on. A woman's body during pregnancy is a mysterious thing."

Shelby stared blankly at him.

"If you'll just lie back and scoot your bottom right down here," he said, flicking on the gigantic light-bulb at the foot of the table.

"Oh, God," Shelby breathed.

The nurse placed a comforting hand on her shoulder. "It's okay, Shelby. Try and relax."

At this Shelby laughed…almost hysterically.

Yeah, sure.

Five minutes later, Shelby stood inside the small curtained dressing room, hands trembling and stomach pitching. As she pulled on her wrap dress, she beat back the self-pity threatening to wash over her.

Never had she felt so alone.

And there had been plenty of times in her life she'd stood by herself—the time she'd gotten lost as a child while on vacation, the time she found out her first love had only used her for sex, when she moved to Europe not knowing a soul and most recently in a bathroom at Boots Grocery. But enduring a pelvic in an unfamiliar office with the stranger who knocked you up standing outside scraped the bottom of the *you're-so-alone* barrel.

Shelby curved her hand over her still-flat stomach, imagining she could feel the heartbeat beneath her hand.

Still with me.

Tugging on her boots, she whisked back the curtain and cracked the door so the doctor would know she was dressed. Sinking on the funky pink chair beside the wall of cabinets, Shelby pulled her purse into her lap and pretended she couldn't hear the conversation between Dr. French and John.

"How do you know this woman again?"

Long pause. "I told you. She's an old friend."

Shelby almost snorted. Yeah. Two and a half months of old friendship.

"Her patient information sheet says she's from Seattle."

"Yeah." Aggravation in John's voice.

"I'm not trying to pry."

Another long pause.

"Okay, maybe I am. You call and say it's an emergency of the female variety, bring in a pregnant woman I've never seen before and then expect me not to ask any questions? I'm an *old* friend, too."

More long silence.

A sigh.

"Fine."

John's voice again. "Is she okay?"

"Sorry. Patient confidentiality," Dr. French quipped. A door shut and then Dr. French stepped into her exam room, annoyance in his eyes fading as he smiled. As the door clicked shut, he picked up her chart and grabbed a pen from his scrub pocket. Clicking it, he grabbed a prescription pad. "The good news is that at present, you're not losing the pregnancy. I checked your blood work and you have a slight infection. Here's a script for a cream that can help."

Shelby opened her mouth to ask—

"No, it won't hurt the fetus."

"Baby," Shelby said. What grew inside her had

ceased being a fetus. It was her baby…and she supposed John's, too.

"The small amount of cramping you've had is likely the uterus stretching a bit, making a nice home for your baby, and perhaps contributing to the bleeding. Still, I'd like to put you on limited activity for the next week as a precaution. Feet up. Lots of rest. It's evident you're tired and stressed."

Shelby gave an embarrassed laugh, brushing her hair back, suddenly self-conscious about the no doubt tangled mess of curls…not to mention the mascara shadow under her eyes, which made her look like a heroin addict. She wasn't interested in any man, but Dr. French was awfully attractive. How the tiny town of Magnolia Bend had netted both John the smoking-hot farmer and Jamison the sexy ob-gyn was beyond her. "I suppose it's been a bit stressful these past few weeks."

"Your body's going through a lot of change, so maybe a little doctor-ordered rest will be good for you…and hopefully once the inflammation is gone the bleeding will stop." Sticking his hand out, he shook hers. "I'd like to see you in a week. I'll be glad to forward my notes and your chart to your regular doctor in Seattle when you return home."

"So I need to stay in town?"

Dropping his hand, he took a second to think about her question. "If at all possible, yes. Miscarriage can be a complicated process. I don't think the fetus, uh, baby, is in danger, but until we see if this cream works, it would be better for you not to travel. So put your feet up and focus on taking it easy for a week. If the bleeding becomes heavier or doesn't lessen in three or four days, call me."

Then he was gone, leaving her once again alone in the exam room. Shelby tucked the prescription in her purse, and found a tube of soft nude lipstick. If she were a bit more presentable, she'd feel stronger... like she could handle walking back out into the reality of her life.

She lingered a few moments, combing her hair, wiping away the traces of tears, and then left the room, running straight into John, who was lurking at the door.

His hands curved around her upper arms, steadying her, and Shelby tried not to think about how good it felt to have someone so solid beside her. "Whoa. You okay?" he asked.

Not even close.

She lifted her gaze and saw worry swimming in his eyes. "I guess. I don't seem to be having a miscarriage if that's what you're asking."

The worry lessened a bit, but then he seemed to remember where he stood. His head swiveled as if checking for spies...or maybe nosy nurses. His eyes landed on the door they came in. "Let's go out the way we came."

She pulled away from him. "I probably need to talk to the receptionist. I haven't given anyone my insurance card."

"Don't worry. I'll take care of it," he said, taking her elbow again and guiding her toward the door.

"Stop," Shelby said, wrenching her arm away, feeling skeevy about sneaking out and not paying. "I don't need you to—"

"I know, I know." He held up a hand, his mouth growing rigid. "You can handle everything on your own."

He sounded mad…and maybe a little hurt. She wasn't sure because she didn't know him well enough to make a judgment.

An exam room door opened and a woman wearing a tent waddled out. Okay, it wasn't a tent, just a maternity dress that masqueraded as one. But still…yikes. Would she get that enormous? The poor woman might as well have had RMS *Titanic* stenciled across her side.

"John?" the ship, ahem, woman asked, a little V of befuddlement forming between her eyes. She smoothed the linen shift against her bulging stomach and sailed toward them, questions bouncing in her eyes. "What the devil are you doing *here?*"

"Shannon," John said weakly, his smile pained. "Uh, I'm here to see Jamison. This is his office."

"I know that, silly," Shannon said, inclining her head toward Shelby, her eyebrows raised in that age-old expression that meant *Who's your friend?*

"Oh, you mean what am I doing here with Shelby?" He turned his regard to her.

"Hi." Shelby did a little wave. "I'm a friend of John's."

"Oh," Shannon said, her expression still puzzled.

"Shelby didn't feel well and since Jamison's a close friend, I asked if I could drop in."

"Oh," Shannon said again, her cheeks dimpling as she gave Shelby a smile. "Lucky you. Dr. French is the best doctor around. Women even drive up from New Orleans to see him."

"Great," Shelby said, wishing she'd allowed John to tug her out the back door without resistance. This whole thing was awkward with a capital *A*.

"Well, we need to go. Tell Rob I said hello," John said, motioning Shelby toward the back door like a cruise director.

Okay, so she extended the ship imagery. Sue her.

"So are you new in town?" Shannon persisted, following them with the determination of a...

She was out of ship metaphors.

John paused, turning toward the inquisitive Shannon, but Shelby beat him to it. "Just passing through."

"For the week," John clarified.

"What?" Shelby snapped, realizing Dr. French must have told John he'd prescribed bed rest.

"You're staying with my sister, Abigail, at her bed-and-breakfast, right?" John said, his eyes beckoning her to go along with his statement.

"Actually, I was going to stay in Baton Rouge," Shelby said, giving John a look she reserved for naughty students. How dare he manipulate her?

Magnolia Bend was a charming little town, but she didn't want to spend her weeklong bed rest with John's sister. Something told her it would be too... too suffocating.

Shannon looked from him to her, now resembling a...buoy bobbing in the current? Or maybe a cork? Or a—Shelby was officially about to lose it. She wasn't sure what losing it might look like. She felt equal parts anger and hysteria.

"Laurel Woods is a lovely place to stay. I had my wedding reception there," Shannon said.

"Really?" Shelby said, a giggle rising to the surface. She bit her lip and tried to hold on to the anger.

"Oh, sure. It's one of the top bed-and-breakfasts in the area. Of course, we don't get many tourists because we're so close to New Orleans, but this time of year with Thanksgiving and the Candy Cane Festival around the corner, we see a few new faces."

"Huh, that's...interesting," Shelby said, glancing longingly toward the back door. She needed to get out of there. Screw the insurance.

"In fact my brother's playing at the street dance Saturday night after the tree lighting. Maybe I'll see you both there?" Shannon's question might as well have been a fishing line tossed into unknown waters.

Shelby couldn't seem to stop the nautical metaphors. Anytime she couldn't deal with situations she became plain silly...which meant if she didn't vamoose, she'd say something inappropriate.

"Maybe so," John said, tapping Shelby twice on the arm. "We better go."

"Tell your father I enjoyed his sermon last Sunday…and tell your mama hello, too," Shannon called out as John turned toward the door and nearly dragged Shelby with him.

Sermon?

Wait. John was an actual preacher's son? The whole back door thing suddenly made sense.

"Jesus," he said as he pushed out the door.

"Imagine that. A preacher's son calling on his savior. Now the whole back door approach makes sense. You go into liquor stores the same way?"

"That's not what this was about."

Shelby lifted her eyebrows. "Whatever you say, sailor."

"Fine. I wanted to get you in to Jamison's without everyone asking questions, and I knew you'd get treatment faster. It was an emergency, right?"

"Right."

"Doesn't matter. Shannon will tell the whole town about me being with a woman at the local ob-gyn's office."

"That ship just sailed, huh?" And that was it. Her sanity snapped and the giggling started. John stared at her like she was deranged.

She was. At least temporarily.

"Sorry," Shelby said, turning away, holding her belly, trying to find the remote control to her feelings. She teetered on the edge, the rollicking emotions pulling at her, making her wish for safe harbor from the storm.

Safe harbor.

The laughter boiled up again at the continued nautical nonsense, but she managed to stifle it. Turning around, she found John heading for his truck. He looked pissed, resigned, shell-shocked and pretty good in his jeans. She wished she hadn't noticed that last thing, but there it was.

The man who had impregnated her in the bathroom was pretty hot, sad and grumpy.

Hey, a girl had to look for silver linings somewhere.

JOHN OPENED THE door for the woman who he suspected was either crazy as hell or suffering the start of a breakdown. Could be both, but either way she'd rolled into his world and pulled the rug out from beneath him. He'd hit the proverbial dirt so hard his proverbial ass had bruises. On an actual literal level, his head throbbed and the churning in his gut was something no antacid could cure. World rocked was an understatement.

He could get perspective later, though. At present he needed to convince her to stay in town.

Which could be a huge problem on a lot of levels, but still…he couldn't help the inclination he felt to press Pause. He needed some time to think, some time to figure out possibly the rest of his life.

Shelby climbed inside the truck, allowing him to assist her, looking contrite after laughing like a cuckoo bird in the doctor's parking lot.

He shouldn't have been surprised. That night months ago, her vivacious laugh had first attracted him to her. Okay, if he were being honest, her body had been the first thing, but when she'd laughed, telling him lame jokes, he'd felt almost normal again. And then she'd flirted, pressing her polished nails against his chest, gazing into his eyes, telling him how good he made her feel…how much she needed someone like him to make her forget about the world.

That goddamn bright smile of hers and those baby-blues. By the time he was on his fifth beer, Shelby had been the answer to his prayers and he wanted to sink inside her, allow her to take the damn pain away and replace it with something as light as her laughter for just a little while.

God, send me something to take this damn pain away.

In John's mind, God had answered, delivering Shelby with her perfect teeth and lush body.

Yeah.

God liked to play jokes…or maybe it was more his punishment for Rebecca's death. *Thanks, God. Good one.*

John fired the engine, sliding a glance over to the woman who now sat solemnly, clutching her purse like it held the antidote to a horrible disease. Her knuckles were white.

"My sister has a bed-and-breakfast. You'll be close by so I can check on you."

"I have a hotel in Baton Rouge…all my things are there. Staying at your sister's place isn't necessary."

"This isn't just about you."

She didn't say anything, so he gave her time, rolling onto Main Street, heading back toward home. The postman gave him a curious glance…along with the woman who worked the dry-cleaning counter. John waved because it was expected, but he knew they wondered why he wasn't out in the fields…and why a blonde sat next to him.

"True," Shelby said finally, settling her gaze on him. "I get that you're trying to do the right thing… that you feel bad about what happened that night—"

"You need help."

"I don't. That back there was a weird reaction to stress. I can't help myself sometimes," she said, looking sheepish, "but I'll be fine on my own."

"So beyond the half breakdown you nearly had, are you okay? I mean is the baby okay?"

"Yeah, Dr. French thinks it's an infection."

"I heard through the door. He said no traveling."

"He *recommended* no flying."

"Stay in Magnolia Bend." He tried to keep his tone neutral. Half of him wanted her to fly out of his life, but the other half clung to the thought this woman carried his son or daughter in her womb. He didn't want to feel anything for her. At all. But he couldn't let her go.

"I'm not sure that's a good idea," she said. "I don't belong here and it doesn't seem fair to you to invite questions. I bet your town is full of Shannons who will be disappointed in their golden boy."

John's mind flipped to an image of his parents. They'd be very disappointed, along with his brothers and sister. Well, maybe not Jake. Then his mind flipped to his former mother-in-law, Carla Stanton, and the churning in his gut intensified. When Carla found out he'd fathered a child with a random woman, she'd be devastated. The idea he could lose everything popped into his mind. But if he let Shelby leave, he could lose something even more unimaginable—his child. "Having time to decide how we'll handle this trumps what everyone else thinks. I shouldn't care what anyone thinks."

Not even Carla.

"But you do. You just sneaked me in the back door of the doctor's office. You had a life…"

"Key word is *had*," he said, his heart tripping over the truth Shelby had unearthed. He was ashamed of what he'd done that drunken night. He'd been untrue to Rebecca, sullying the day she'd left this earth with selfish desires. He'd sown this discord in his life and now he'd have to deal with the reaping. "Look, I don't know how to feel. I wish I could say I didn't give a damn about what people thought about me and the way I live my life, but—"

"You do?"

"I haven't attended a single social event in town since Rebecca died. I've been in mourning and people accepted that. So to show up in town with a beautiful woman at my side, having people stare makes me feel…" He left off because he didn't know.

Vulnerable? Guilty? And, yeah, maybe embarrassed he'd been so stupid. Getting a girl pregnant was a bonehead move and so unlike the salt-of-the-earth reputation he'd established in the town that had been home to the Beauchamps since the Civil War. Maybe if he hadn't been such a part of the community it wouldn't matter. Shelby was right. They weren't living in the '50s...though sometimes the small Louisiana town felt very much that way.

They passed the general store run by the Burnsides who were cousins on his mama's side and the old men sitting outside playing checkers and lying about the fish they caught raised hands in greeting. He then tooted his horn at his uncle, Howard Burnside, who stood outside the courthouse wearing his sheriff's uniform. "My whole family lives here."

"Strange."

"That's the way it is in these small towns. I know almost everyone who lives here...and they know me."

"So having me sit here pregnant from the one time you decided to take off your mourning clothes is a bit like crawling out from under a rock only to get pissed on?"

He had no reason to smile, but, damn, she'd nailed it. "I'd say that's an accurate depiction."

"So why do you want me to stay?"

"I can't let you traipse off to Baton Rouge and hole up in a hotel room without someone to look after you."

"Why? I'm a grown woman. I have a cell phone."

She had a point, but something inside him balked at her leaving. He didn't know exactly what he wanted in regards to the child, but if Shelby left Magnolia Bend, he might never know. Her leaving felt wrong. "Look, I know you can take care of yourself, but do me this solid—stay here. If something goes wrong, you'll have someone to help you. I'll get your things from the hotel. My sister won't pester you or ask questions. I swear."

"You'll be working so what does it matter if I'm here or in Baton Rouge?"

"I can visit you each evening. We can get to know each other better."

"Better than sex on a bathroom sink?" she snorted.

"Yeah, not my best moment."

"I'll say." After a moment, Shelby continued, "I don't need you to apologize for what happened or feel guilty. I don't blame you anymore than I blame myself. We both screwed up and fiddler's bill is steep."

"Yeah, but I wish the dance had been a little better," he said, recalling the cheap linoleum, the naked lightbulb and the way he'd made her feel when the realization of what he'd done washed over him. Not well done of him. Cheap, shoddy and now that he knew Shelby a little better, not deserved. "But it's too late for regret. Best both of us can do is to move forward, doing what is best for our baby."

"Our baby," she repeated, her voice sounding lost.

Right as he pulled onto the highway, Shelby touched his arm. Her hands were small, still polished and soft looking. Nothing like Rebecca's hands, worn from washing them too often at the preschool where she'd taught. Shelby's touch sparked something in him, something he'd rather ignore and keep hidden.

Hunger for something more than what he'd lived for the past year and nearly three months.

"For the baby's sake, I'll stay until I get the all clear from Dr. Jamison, but I can promise you nothing beyond that."

John looked over as she pulled her hand back into her lap and focused on the broken yellow lines of the road zipping beneath the old truck. "Okay, we can start there."

CHAPTER FIVE

THE LAUREL WOODS Bed-and-Breakfast had a polished shine that John's small plantation lacked. The house boasted plush Oriental carpets, shining mahogany and framed John James Audubon original paintings centered above marble mantels. The soaring ceilings and glittering chandeliers nearly overwhelmed, but the sincerity in Abigail Orgeron's eyes set Shelby at ease…something she needed in spades at the moment.

Abigail, for one, didn't ask a single question, as promised, merely ordered a smartly dressed young man to ready the Rose Salon and take up the shopping bag Shelby carried before waving Shelby into the dining room where a carafe of tea sat along with some pecan-studded muffins and perfect tea cakes.

"John, why don't you fetch some milk for the tea and call Birdie inside? The sun's about to set and I don't want her breaking her fool neck in that oak tree," Abigail said to her brother, dismissing him as she sank onto a velvet flocked chair of crimson. "Sit down and I'll pour you a cup of tea."

Shelby didn't want to be there and didn't want tea, but she sat down anyway. John glanced at her, concerned, but slipped through the swinging door no doubt leading to the kitchen. "You have a lovely place."

"Thank you," Abigail said, lifting the steaming pot and pouring the fragrant tea into a delicate cup. Handing it to Shelby, she smiled. "Hibiscus herbal tea. I can't tolerate caffeine this close to bedtime. Stay awake all night."

"Thanks," Shelby said, taking the cup and balancing it on her knee, glad she hadn't had to ask for decaffeinated.

"Sugar?"

"One spoonful, please."

Swirling the spoon and clanking it on the lip of the cup, Shelby glanced up to find John's sister staring at her with a curious expression on her face.

John's sister looked older than him. She had an elegant silver forelock that swept her inky shoulder-length hair. Her eyes were a clear green, cheekbones high, chin long, mouth generous. Her navy slacks and trim apple-green cardigan portrayed no nonsense and easy sophistication. Soft tan leather ballet flats backed up the impression. Here was a woman who chaired committees, ran a house like a field general and…waited for others to explain themselves.

Silence sat fat between them. Abigail sipped her tea, never wavering in her stare, waiting for someone, presumably Shelby, to clarify the situation.

Shelby shifted in her chair as John reentered carrying a carton of milk and dragging a young girl with tangled hair and a pair of binoculars around her neck.

"Mom, I can't believe you're making me come inside. I had just gotten my 'nocs trained on that woodpecker. How am I supposed to draw him in his habitat? This is preposterous," the tiny girl declared with a stomp of her sneaker.

"Birdie, you've been out there for the past hour and still have some reading to complete," Abigail said, her eye going immediately to the dirt left by the sneaker stomp. "You're tracking in the house."

The girl wore glasses that made her blue eyes look impossibly large. The skinny jeans made her more waiflike and the oversize Flash Gordon shirt didn't help. She looked exactly like her name. "It's Thanksgiving break, Mom. I'm not reading that stupid AR book over my holiday."

Abigail's eyes widened but she said nothing, turning instead back to Shelby. "Shelby, this is my daughter, Eva Brigitte. We call her Birdie."

"Hi," Shelby said.

The girl glowered but muttered, "Hey."

"Now, get cleaned up for dinner. Shelby is one of our guests tonight and doesn't want to hear our squabbling over homework." Abigail's voice brooked no argument.

Birdie flashed her mother a withering look and ran toward the stairs, leaving more zigzag dirt on the polished floor. She may or may not have muttered "whatever" on her escape.

John stared after his niece looking as perplexed

as Shelby felt. "Since when has she been fond of sketching woodpeckers?"

"Oh, it's those Audubon prints scattered all over the inn. She's so strong willed and—" Abigail waved her hand. "Let's not do this right now. Birdie is Birdie."

John's lips tipped up, softening him. "She's something else."

His sister nodded. "That's one way to put it. So, Shelby, how long will you be with us?"

"I'm not sure. Through Saturday?"

Abigail gave her the "you don't know?" look and then glanced toward John, the unspoken question in her eyes.

"At least through Saturday. Actually, I'm bringing Shelby to Thanksgiving dinner."

Abigail's eyebrows rose nearly to her hairline. "Really?"

Shelby swallowed, wondering if she should correct him or merely accept the fact she was stuck with John in Magnolia Bend for a week.

"It'll be nice to have a guest at our table. Friends are always welcome," Abigail said, sliding another glance to John. The unstated questions literally pulsed in the quietness.

Shelby knew Abigail wanted to grill John, but likely relied on Southern graciousness in order to bite her tongue. Shelby wasn't from the South so she said, "Just so you know, we're just friends. Met a few months back."

"Oh," Abigail said, her gaze meeting Shelby's. "I didn't know John had started dating again."

"We're *not* dating," John said, settling his hands on his lean hips. "Like Shelby said we're just friends."

"Yes," Shelby agreed. "Just friends."

"But he's brought you home to meet his family," Abigail persisted, unconvinced.

"I had some business to take care of down here," Shelby said, setting the half-empty cup back on the antique tea cart with a clatter. "Getting to spend time with John is a bonus of sorts. Unfortunately, my health prevents me from flying back to Seattle and spending the holiday with my own family. John volunteered to help me get settled here for a few days, thinking I'd enjoy the small town atmosphere better than the busyness of Baton Rouge."

"I knew she'd like Laurel Woods...just wasn't sure you'd have room," John said.

"I have room until Friday. This weekend the Candy Cane Festival starts, and I'm booked solid for a week. You're welcome to stay until then. What about your health? Is there anything special I need to know?" Abigail looked worried, as if at any moment she might whip out Lysol and start spraying.

"No, nothing contagious," Shelby said, almost laughing. Almost. 'Cause there wasn't anything really funny about being an unwed, unemployed single mother who'd conceived a baby in the bathroom of a roadside honky-tonk that also sold bait and beer during daylight hours. "I appreciate you putting me up on such short notice, but I think I'll head to my room for a shower and an early night."

"Can I at least make you a sandwich?" Abigail volunteered. She didn't look as worried anymore. "Ham? Turkey?"

"If you have peanut butter and jelly, that would be perfect," Shelby said, rising and scooping up her purse. "Thank you for the tea."

"Sure," Abigail said, setting her cup on the cart and standing. "Let me know if there's anything else you need."

"I'll walk her up," John said to Abigail.

Seconds later, they climbed the grand staircase to the second floor. The rooms were all marked by placards, most named after flowers. Shelby withdrew the old-fashioned skeleton key and inserted it in the keyhole, the whirring machinations releasing the lock. Vintage outside, modern inside.

John pushed open the door and Shelby sucked in her breath.

"Oh, wow," she breathed out.

"Yeah, pretty grand," John said.

The room had raspberry walls stretching up to a ceiling with insets and heavy crown molding. The huge bed sat on a platform, the green silk canopy gathered in the center, cascading down the sides of the ornately carved bed. Large linen European shams banked the profusion of needlepoint pillows and the plump duvet beckoned weary travelers to lay their burdens down and burrow within the depths. The elegant antique furniture complemented the room and the adjoining door gave a view of an enormous claw-foot tub.

Shelby eyed her bag sitting at the end of the bed. "Well, thank you."

John stared at her, his face impassive.

"You can go. I'll be fine. Your sister seems capable of handling most anything."

At this he snorted. "My parents should have named her Colonel so people would know what to expect when they find themselves facedown in the mud with tank marks on their back."

"It would be hard for a girl to go through life with the name Colonel. She'd never find a personalized key chain or snow globe," Shelby cracked, wanting him to go away, wanting him to stay so she wouldn't feel so alone.

His flash-bang smile surprised her. "That's the girl I remember from Boots."

"Yeah, I have a good sense of humor when I'm not hormonal, on the verge of tears or cracking up… though I bet you wish you had never answered that knock-knock joke at the bar."

"It *was* funny."

"Yeah," she said, walking toward the bed and sinking onto the plush comforter. "So…"

"I'm writing down my number." He picked up the notepad by the phone. "If you need anything…"

"I won't." She hadn't wanted anything from him in the first place. Her plan had been so simple—tell him about the child and fly back to Seattle. Okay, she hadn't *wanted* to fly back to Seattle and face the

music with her family…over turkey no less. She'd
imagined the scenario several times over the long
flight to Louisiana. "Pass the green bean casserole.
Oh, and by the way, I'm pregnant."

How fun was that?

Spotlight on her as she enacted the next install-
ment of "Shelby the Eternal Screwup"—a yearly
special airing near the holidays when family mem-
bers were apt to ask things like "How are you?" And
since Shelby prided herself on being honest and rel-
ishing the jolt on the faces of her brother, sister and
assorted cousins, the answer was always shocking.

"How are you, Shelby?"

*"Good, David. I lost my virginity to Dad's junior
partner, who swore he loved me and would marry
me when his wife died. How are you?"*

Yeah. That's pretty much how it went. Come to
think of it, saying, "I'm pregnant by a man I met
at a back-road honky-tonk" sounded tame by com-
parison. Maybe dropping that doozy over the white-
chocolate-cranberry cheesecake wouldn't be so bad.

"Look, Shelby, I know we're veritable strangers."

"Veritable?"

"Virtual?"

"We know each other carnally. That's pretty much
it."

He lifted both his eyebrows. "And that's all it took."

"Touché," she said.

"My point is that I'm here for you. You aren't
alone."

Shelby ran her hand over the fine needlework of

the velvet lumbar pillow. "It's been a tough afternoon, and you've been pretty damn decent."

He spread his hands. "What else could I do?"

"You could have done a lot of things that weren't as nice as what you did. I dropped a tornado on you and you didn't hide in a cellar."

"I don't have a cellar. This is Louisiana."

Shelby smiled and took time to study him in the golden light of the room. Despite the grimness shadowing his eyes, John Beauchamp was a fine specimen of a man. No pretty boy, he had a ruggedness that called to mind Clint Eastwood in his younger days. Brows that easily gathered into perplexity, a hard jaw that spoke of stubbornness and a sensual mouth that, though often drawn into a line, could curve into a wicked smile.

She remembered his scent, remembered the way his muscled chest felt beneath her fingertips, the way he'd kissed her...like a man starved.

Now that she knew he'd lost his wife over a year ago, she understood the desperation in his kiss, recognized the same need throbbing inside her. After Darby dumped her, her ego had been fragile and she'd been ripe for the plucking...or ripe for the— well, she wasn't going there. Suffice it to say, she'd been just as desperate as John to feel the touch of another person.

"Time to process all of this would be nice," he said. "So, I'll let you rest and say good night."

She nodded because she still struggled to believe her whole life had been turned on its ear. In six and a half months she'd become a mother…if she didn't lose the pregnancy. Process? Not a bad idea.

"Good night, John," she said.

For a moment he looked uncertain, like he wondered if he should extend his hand or offer a hug or something.

Luckily, a knock at the door interrupted the awkwardness, and Abigail hurtled inside, balancing a tray, which she sat on the desk.

"I hope it's enough," John's sister said, arranging the silverware on the napkin. A single yellow chrysanthemum brightened the tray holding a sandwich, fruit and a slice of pecan pie.

"It's perfect. Thank you," Shelby said, rising.

"Don't get up," John said, lifting the tray and crossing the room, setting it on the bedside table.

"I could have done that," Abigail said, eyeing her brother with an odd expression.

"I'll see you tomorrow," John said, glancing down to where Shelby sat, one foot hooked beneath her.

"You're in the middle of harvest." Abigail looked as if she'd been tossed in a lake. "You can't come here tomorrow."

"I'm not too busy for a friend," he said.

"Who are you?" Abigail asked.

"A man not that busy."

"Hmm," John's sister muttered before turning to Shelby. "Let me know if you need anything. Extra toiletries are in the bathroom. You wouldn't believe how many people forget basics."

"Thank you," Shelby called as Abigail headed toward the door.

John waited until his sister disappeared. "What about clothes…a, uh, nightgown?"

Shelby pointed to the plastic bag. "That's why I asked if you'd stop at the store. I nabbed a few things including an oversize shirt to sleep in along with a toothbrush. I can manage."

"If you'll give me your hotel info, I'll send someone to Baton Rouge to gather your things."

"Don't bother. Things are scattered all over the room, and I really don't want a stranger packing my personal items. I can climb out of bed long enough to do that."

"I'll drive you, then," he said.

"No. Just send my rental car over. Besides you looked pretty busy in your fields. Abigail seemed to indicate—"

"I'll be here at noon," he interrupted, tone firm. "Besides I need to stop in Baton Rouge for a part Homer needs."

John Beauchamp was a driven man. Easy for her to recognize since she'd been around driven people all her life. Her entire family was listed under the definition in the Merriam-Webster's dictionary.

"If you insist," she said.

"I do. Good night, Shelby."

"'Night." The door closed with a soft snick and Shelby fell back on the bed.

Jesus.

At that moment, she wanted someone, anyone,

to hold her. To tell her all would be okay. A mother to lean on would have been nice, but Shelby's mother had never been the type to welcome weakness. Maybe someone like Picou Dufrene, Darby's mother, would run a careworn hand over Shelby's brow and help her figure things out, but that thought was insane. Darby didn't belong to her anymore, if he ever had, so she couldn't lay claim to anyone in that warm, quirky family. Like always, Shelby was on her own.

Going back to Seattle to her family wouldn't change it.

Her parents weren't horrid—they'd never locked her in a closet or even missed any of her important ballet recitals or graduations—but Shelby had always felt they loved her because they were supposed to, ticking off a list on a job description. As for her siblings, Shelby's brother seemed to equate her with something a seagull vomited, and her older sister hadn't wanted Shelby in her wedding. Sela had even joked in front of the bridal party she didn't deserve a bridesmaid with less than a master's degree.

Yeah, Sela was a bitch who had required her husband to pack his testicles away the day they wed. What had Shelby expected?

Shelby dashed the moisture from the corner of her eyes, staring at the fabric gathered at the crown of the bed.

Alone.

She placed a hand over her stomach.

Please stay in there, little pea. It's me and you. We can do this together.

Even if John Beauchamp was the fly in the ointment.

CHAPTER SIX

JOHN JOGGED DOWN the steps of The Laurel Woods Bed-and-Breakfast wishing he could start running and never stop. Like Forrest Gump.

Or maybe he'd head over to Ray-Ray's and drink until he didn't give a hot damn about anything anymore.

Of course the last time he'd gotten drunk he'd gotten Shelby pregnant so maybe Forrest Gump had something with that whole cross-country jaunt.

But running wouldn't work…eventually a man had to stop, and reality would catch up. John climbed into his truck and punched the steering wheel, making the horn beep.

He didn't want his sister to come out and start asking questions so he started the truck, flipped on the headlights and got the hell out of there.

Jesus H. Christ, what had he gotten himself into?

The truck bounced down the drive, jarring him the same way Shelby had jarred him that afternoon, showing up with that little nugget—*I'm pregnant*.

Rubbing a hand over his face, he said the words that had been bouncing around inside him since

Shelby had uttered those words. "I'm sorry, Becca. I'm so, so sorry."

Of course his wife wasn't there to answer…but if she'd been there beside him, she'd have turned to him and said, "Don't even say it, John Miller Beauchamp. You dug this hole. Now you gotta fill it."

His Rebecca had been nothing if not tough. She wouldn't have smiled as she said it, but the forgiveness would have been there in her eyes. He'd never deserved her. Rebecca Lynn Stanton had been his greatest champion…and that's why disappointing even her memory made him feel like turning the truck into the big tree sitting at the end of the drive.

The cell phone sitting in the cup holder buzzed. He lifted it, expecting it to be Abigail, but it was his younger brother, Jake. News traveled fast in the Beauchamp family.

"Yeah," he said into the phone.

"Who's Shelby?"

"Shelby is none of your business."

"So you're out in the dating world again. Here I was thinking you were holding fast to the role of grieving widower."

"It's not a role."

"Yeah," Jake said, his voice softening from smartass to the hushed tone he'd used after the accident… after the funeral. John would rather have Jake stick with smart-ass. "You show up with a good-looking woman at our sister's bed-and-breakfast, asking favors, lip buttoned, and you think you can escape the inquisition?"

"Just leave it alone."

"Was it eHarmony or something? Lot of guys do computer dating. Even thought about it myself."

Bullshit. Jake Beauchamp didn't need a computer. Women fell in his lap. "No. It's not like that."

"Christian Mingle? The old man would approve."

"I'm not using a dating website."

"So how did you meet her? The Rev and Fancy will know by tomorrow morning. Rochelle Braud already told me she saw a strange woman in your truck, and Shannon Smith said you were at Jamison's office with a blonde. Jig is up, my brother."

John released a frustrated breath. This was the huge downside of living in Magnolia Bend. Nosy folk didn't have enough to occupy them. "She's just a girl I met."

"Why was she at Jamison's? Birth control?"

John smothered a bitter bark of laughter. Too damn late for that. "How about you back the hell off, Jake? Unless you want the same meddling in your life?"

Silence reigned on the line before his younger brother sighed. "Good point. I'm not prying. Just being there for you, bro."

John already knew this. His family had always been there for him...almost nauseatingly so, and Jake was a good sounding board even if he ran as wild as the kudzu growing along the Mississippi River. "I appreciate that, but at present I don't need help."

Liar.

"If you change your mind, I'll be at Ray-Ray's later. A cold beer always makes things clearer…but maybe you're getting a little something-something later? Am I right? Huh? Huh?" Jake cackled like an old woman.

"Goodbye, Jake," John drawled.

His brother sobered. "I'm just raggin' you. Besides if you're getting some, good for you. You've been wearing black for a long time, brother."

"I'm not wearing black."

"Figuratively speaking, of course. Later, bro."

John clicked off the phone and focused on the road in front of him. Part of him wanted to tell Jake about Shelby and the baby. The other part of him wanted to do what he'd been doing for the past year—withdraw and hide in the cave he'd made comfortable for himself.

Disappearing was easy to do when the light in your world was extinguished.

But he didn't want to think about Rebecca, grieving or even the cane still standing in the fields. He had to decide what to do about Shelby.

He wanted to hate her for riding into his world looking like a sex kitten, making him remember he was a man…not a robot. He wanted to hate her for making him want her. But most of all he wanted to hate her for dropping the bombshell she'd dropped hours ago. His child, the one Rebecca had wanted so badly was housed inside a woman he barely knew. The thought squeezed all the air out of his lungs.

Shortly after Shelby uttered those words, John had

felt resentment so intense it had stunned him in its ferocity. But when he'd entered the bathroom and saw the sheer desolation on Shelby's face, that kernel of hate dissipated. He hadn't a clue why. If she'd lost the child, everything would be easier. No one would have to know John's shame. Everything could go on as normal. But one look at the terror in her eyes— at the desire to keep their child in her body—and he'd changed. Hate turned to an odd desire for that child…for the hope he or she represented.

Maybe *hate* was too strong a word.

He'd never hated Shelby.

Only himself for being so weak.

John turned into the drive he'd turned into every day of the past decade, bumping up to the silent house illuminated by moon glow. Like a ghost, Breezy Hill sat, a relic of happiness. As he stopped and shifted the gear to Park, the old ginger tabby crept out of the small barn located out back.

Damn cat.

Rebecca had loved Freddy even when John threatened to use him as gator bait for sharpening his claws on the seat of the new lawn mower.

"You touch that cat and you better sleep with one eye open, John Miller," she'd said, brown eyes glittering as she propped her hands on slim hips. Rebecca's brown hair had always been cut chin-length in something she called a bob. Her mouth was wide and a few freckles scattered across her nose. She'd been cute, but not pretty. But beauty had never mattered to John. He'd loved everything about his wife—the long fingernails she used to scratch his back, the messy office full of travel books on places she'd never go and the way she cried over every present he gave her…even the blender. Beauty hadn't been a factor.

But Shelby was beautiful.

The first time he'd seen Shelby, he'd liked her because she was so different from Rebecca. Almost as if it was okay to hold her in his arms while they danced because she wasn't even close to being the woman he'd loved.

Still, like Rebecca, Shelby had made him smile. She was funny, and when she laughed, her blue eyes sparkled. He'd heard that term before—*sparkling eyes*—but had never seen it until he'd met Shelby. Even now, in the face of this difficult situation, she cracked jokes.

It occurred to him perhaps that was her coping mechanism. Maybe Shelby laughed so she didn't cry.

The cat wound around his ankles, its meows plaintive in the stillness. John walked to the porch steps and sank onto them, stroking the cat despite his profession of disliking the old thing. He'd fed it every morning, and some nights he sat outside and petted it, as if taking care of Freddy would make up for the fact he'd killed his wife.

Okay, so technically he hadn't killed his wife— Rebecca had died from an accidental gunshot wound. He hadn't been home when it happened, hadn't been the one to leave the round in the chamber. But he'd been the one to accuse her of wanting to leave him.

He'd been the one to make her feel guilty, guilty enough to want to please him by stopping by the gunsmith and picking up his repaired shotgun.

He shook his head. No time to think about guilt. No time to dwell on what might have been. He had to decide what to do about Shelby and the baby.

Telling his folks would be hard. The Reverend Beauchamp was a principled man, and also a good man. He'd never turn away one of his flock during times of trouble, including his own son.

But John wasn't ready to bring any of his family, other than Abigail, into this mess...yet.

First he had to get to know the mother of his child...and convince her he belonged in the child's life—as more than a check and weekly phone call. Maybe introducing his family to her wasn't the best way to do that. The Beauchamps were like a straitjacket—the more you fought against them, the tighter the binds got. But there was no way of getting around his family, especially if he took Shelby to dinner on Thursday.

"I'll think about this later, Freddy," John said to the cat.

Freddy meowed and rubbed against him insistently.

"Yeah, I'll do that, too," John said, and looked at the moon.

SHELBY WAS BORED to tears. Okay, not real tears, but that didn't matter. Lying in bed was only wonderful when one had a seven o'clock meeting and had to get up. When given permission to wallow via doctor's orders, it pretty much sucked.

For one thing, John's sister had obviously tried to create Old South ambience, and, alas, there was no television hidden in the ornately carved wardrobe.

To which Shelby said a modern version of "I do declare" that would have shocked Aunt Pittypat outta her hoop skirt.

And though cold air piped though vents somewhere in the room, there wasn't a ceiling fan. And Shelby always slept under a ceiling fan, except for that one time in Girl Scouts when she'd gone camping. Emphasis on the *one* time.

Fiddle dee damn.

So Shelby stopped counting the folds in the canopy, rose out of bed and ambled around, finding a copy of *The Sound and the Fury* in the drawer of the secretary. Of course, she'd rather bite her toenails than read Faulkner. She'd never cared for "the classics"—dusty books recommended by English teachers made her break out in hives. Those, along with snotty historical biographies, were what her sister, Sela, read. When Shelby had professed to loving Christian Grey and being tied up, her sister had literally lifted her nose and given her *that* look.

Made Shelby want to take a paddle to her sister... and not in a kinky way.

So she stared out the window. The Laurel Woods Bed-and-Breakfast was aptly named. Just outside the window, trees knitted together, holding mysterious woodsy secrets. Shelby had stared out, determined to enjoy the rustic peace. So far she'd spied a couple of bright red birds, one frisky squirrel and an ugly buzzard roosting in a huge tree.

Boring.

But then Birdie showed up.

The child wore skinny jeans and a hoodie. Huge binoculars dangled from around her neck. Her brown hair had been scraped back into a messy ponytail, as if she could care less, and on her back swayed a large backpack. Walking intently toward the big tree in which the buzzard sat, she immediately swung up on a lower branch and started climbing. The buzzard took flight, which Birdie didn't seem to notice. After scampering up half the tree, Birdie plopped down on a thick joint just as casual as she pleased.

Good gracious. If the child fell, she'd break her neck.

Surely, Abigail didn't allow her daughter to sit in trees without…did they make tree seat belts?

Birdie was partly visible through the half-bare branches. Shelby watched with bated breath as the child pulled off the backpack, sat a sketch pad on her lap and lifted her binoculars, training them on something to Shelby's right. Adjusting the knob thing on top, the girl grew still and focused.

Shelby sighed and wondered if she should say something to Abigail about the child being so high in the tree. Then again, Abigail seemed to know about her daughter's daredevil antics.

Turning away, Shelby looked around the room for something to do. Her phone had only 5 percent battery life remaining, and she'd left the charger in the rental car, which was parked at John's house. No playing on her phone. She glanced at Birdie one last time. The kid still perched, binoculars focused on the distance behind the house. Shelby pressed her face against the window and tried to see what the girl watched, but she couldn't see beyond the edge of the woods.

Something in the girl's demeanor nagged at Shelby so she glanced back at Birdie, waiting for the girl to pick up her sketch pad and start working, but she never did. Instead the girl's mouth fell open in that age-old expression of "I can't believe what I'm seeing."

Shelby wrinkled her nose.

What the devil was Birdie watching that would render her so engrossed?

Any other time and Shelby wouldn't care. But she was bored out of her gourd. Not to mention, some inner teacher Spidey sense told her this was not about birds.

So she pulled the oversize T-shirt serving as her nightgown over her head and scooped up the dress she'd worn yesterday. Thankfully, the dress was a rayon blend and didn't wrinkle, but the stained tights were hopeless. She netted three points tossing her balled-up tights into the metal trash bin. The new cotton undies were a bit blousy, but the hot-pink socks featuring a popular boy band logo, which she'd grabbed at the Dollar Store, would work fine for stealth. She left her knee-high boots beside her purse and sneaked out the door.

No one was in the hall. Abigail had said she wasn't full until next week so no surprise there. A soft runner ran the length of the shiny floor. Shelby padded to the end of the hall where an antique rocker and a bookshelf nestled near a wavy-paned window. She peered out, cursing the authentic glass. Despite this, she could still make out the large privacy fence and the houses backing up to it. There appeared to be a small subdivision with cookie-cutter houses and requisite postage-stamp backyards directly behind Laurel Woods.

So Birdie wasn't bird-watching. She was people watching.

The little spy.

Shelby chuckled and craned her neck to see if she could make out who the child watched with such fascination. Out of the corner of her eye she saw someone plunge into a lap pool. Someone naked. Not just naked...but tight male ass naked.

Whoa. Birdie wasn't just spying—she was a peeping, uh, Birdie. So what to do about that?

This was a child and a naked dude. A responsible adult would find Abigail and squeal. But maybe not yet. Maybe she needed to know more. Something about the girl's pluck and natural curiosity carved a tender place in Shelby's heart. Had to be hard having a mother like Abigail. Again, teacher Spidey sense blipped and she decided to track down Birdie later to suggest she not spy on naked dudes in their lap pool no matter how nice the view was.

"Shelby?"

She jerked around to find Abigail standing at the head of the stairs holding a tray. John's sister wore her hair pulled back into a knot, a deep blue sweater and the same flats from the evening before. She looked like a librarian catching someone making out in the stacks.

"Oh, hey," Shelby said, turning with hopefully a nonguilty smile. "Just checking out the, uh, view."

Abigail snorted. "No view out that window. I fought like the devil trying to preserve this historical area, but I didn't win. They built that subdivision last fall. I tried to fence them out and mask the sounds of a busy neighborhood with the water feature out back."

Shelby moved toward her room, abandoning her own spying on the very interesting Birdie. "Well, my view's lovely and I didn't hear anything."

"I'm lucky most of the rooms face the woods on either side of the house. I haven't had trouble, but I would have preferred the solitude." Abigail set the tray on the bedside table. "Nice socks."

Shelby lifted her foot and wiggled the One Direction socks. "I feel cool, but maybe I'll leave them for Birdie."

"Don't bother. She thinks boy bands are stupid… and boys are disgusting."

Yeah. Right. "Well, she's only…eight or nine?"

"Try twelve," Abigail said with a smile. "A little small for her age."

Twelve? Shelby thought she had stretched it by suggesting eight. Of course, Shelby didn't know a lot about elementary-aged kids. Neither of her siblings had procreated, professing no urge to overpopulate the earth—something about the ozone layer and stretch marks. And by the time students hit high school and Shelby's desks, most had gone through puberty.

"I brought you some oatmeal, a soft boiled egg and dry toast. John said you were sick or something and I didn't know if you wanted anything rich. I have some Bananas Foster French toast if you'd rather that?"

Oh, yum. Shelby's stomach growled…but then she thought about the diet guidelines in her healthy pregnancy books. Maybe something low fat and easy on her stomach would be a good idea. "This is fine. Thank you."

"John called and said he would pick you up at noon." Abigail's remark was more a question than a statement, said the way a mother would say it…with that little unspoken "And?" at the end.

"Great," Shelby said.

Abigail stood there for a moment, looking indecisive. Shelby knew she wanted to ask about her and John, but was too polite to do so. And Shelby wasn't going to help. That was John's cross to bear.

"Okay, if you need anything else," Abigail said, still not moving.

"Nope," Shelby said with a smile, sinking onto the bed, wishing now she'd just left her T-shirt on. She'd forgotten about breakfast, which was crazy since suddenly she could eat a small horse.

Abigail walked toward the door, casting wistful glances back at her.

"Thanks, Abigail."

John's sister turned. "Oh, good gravy, just tell me. Are you seeing John?" So much for his sister not asking questions.

Shelby played dumb blonde. "Of course I'm seeing him. He's picking me up at noon."

Irritation flashed in Abigail's eyes, reminding Shelby of her brother. "Oh, stop it. You know what I mean. Y'all say you're just friends, but John has never had any female friends. He's a farmer."

"Farmers don't have female friends?"

"You're good at avoiding questions, but I'm the only girl in my family, so I'm good at getting around the bullshit," Abigail said with a feral smile. "So are you dating? Because he's never mentioned you. None of us even knew he—"

"Maybe he didn't want his family to know his business. I don't like my family sticking their noses into mine. I'm the baby of the family so I'm good at avoiding everything. I win," Shelby said, trying for lightness, lifting the toast and taking a bite. It was good—a homemade multigrain. Good for Shelby and good for baby.

"We're not like most families," Abigail sniffed.

"We're very close and we've been very worried about John."

"He doesn't strike me as a man who needs his sister to manage his life or screen his dates."

"That's not what I'm doing," Abigail said, propping her hands on her hips, looking even more like a librarian. This time Shelby had talked too loudly… or lost a book. Deadly librarian sin. "I suppose the only way he could have met you was online."

"Boy, you're determined, aren't you?" Shelby said, "Besides what's wrong with online dating?"

"Online dating isn't real," Abigail said.

Shelby made a face. "I know plenty of people who've met online and have good relationships. One of my friends married a guy she met online. Besides, John's a big boy. He can do what—"

"One would think," Abigail interrupted, abandoning the open door, moving back toward Shelby. "On the outside, he's tough. Always has been. But inside he's tender."

Just because a man had been hurt by losing someone he loved didn't mean he was tender. And even though her own sister was a bitch extraordinaire and unlikely to care about Shelby's happiness any more than she'd care about the local grocery bag boy, Shelby understood the need of an older sibling to look out for her younger brother. Abigail meant well, but Shelby bet she wouldn't like the same sort of prying in her own life. "Hurt like you?"

Abigail's eyes widened. "We're not talking about

me. We're talking about John and the shit he's gone through the past year."

"I already know he lost his wife." She'd only asked Annie for location and basics. His wife had been listed as deceased, nothing more.

"It's the how she died that's the problem."

Shelby's face must have indicated she had no clue what Abigail spoke of.

"You don't know how she died?"

"I didn't want to pry."

Abigail sank onto the desk chair. "His wife's name was Rebecca. She died last year…in September."

The hair rose on Shelby's nape. John had wanted to forget. That's why he'd been at Boots.

"She had gone into Gonzales to her mother's and popped by the gunsmith's to pick up John's shotgun. She was carrying it inside their house when it accidently went off. The smith had left a round in the chamber during the test fire. John was the person who found her."

"Oh, God," Shelby breathed, dropping the toast onto the plate.

"It was a freak accident. John couldn't have saved her even if he'd been there when it happened."

Shelby shook her head.

"He found her that evening on the back stairs of Breezy Hill. Would have been traumatic to find anyone who'd died from a gunshot wound, but she wasn't just anyone to him, was she?"

The toast felt like a brick in her stomach. Shelby turned away from Abigail. "That's horrible."

"Yes. Horrible, but now you see why I'm concerned. Maybe I shouldn't stick my nose in—"

"No, you shouldn't. Look, I understand the inclination. John's obviously been through a great deal, but, trust me when I tell you he's not being irresponsible. We haven't jumped into anything." Except reckless, unprotected sex that resulted in pregnancy.

"Even so, this whole thing, him bringing you to Thanksgiving is—" Abigail paused as if weighing her words "—quite frankly, odd. John's the steadiest member of our family. He doesn't do things like this. I'm sorry if my honesty offends you."

Shelby stared at the woman trying to figure out her brother's life. What could Shelby say after learning about the way Rebecca Beauchamp had died? The whole idea of how hurt John was made her ache…and sent flashes of reservation through her body.

Tread carefully, Shelby.

"I'm sorry," Shelby said, for lack of anything else.

"Me, too," Abigail said, a glimmer of appreciation flickering through the sadness in her eyes.

For a moment they both faced each other, Shelby lost for words to capture the feelings swirling inside, Abigail studying her.

"I'm not offended by your honesty, and I appreciate you telling me about John's wife. I needed to know," Shelby said finally.

"Just be careful with him, okay?" Abigail turned and exited, softly closing the door.

Shelby flopped back onto the unmade bed, feeling both irritated and incredibly sad.

What had happened to John's wife was some heavy stuff. He'd found his wife dead on the back porch steps…absolutely unthinkable.

And Abigail thought she could protect her brother, which was touching, but there was no need to protect him from Shelby. To her, John was merely another man she couldn't, wouldn't, shouldn't be interested in, because he was in love with the memory of his wife.

Yep, Shelby really knew how to pick 'em.

Handsome? Check.

Enigmatic? Check.

Committed to another woman? Check.

And this one was dead. How did a girl compete with that?

She didn't want to feel anything toward the man who'd cried after having sex with her. But she knew, of course, that deep down inside under all the warning and caution signs she'd nailed over her heart, something drew her to the man…something more than the baby cradled in her womb.

Just be careful with him. Abigail's words were good ones to live by. Maybe if she'd had John's sister around, she wouldn't have believed Kurt, the lawyer at her father's firm who had professed to love her and taken her virginity, and then went back to his wife. Or maybe she would have done a better background check on Darby Dufrene.

Sighing, she rose, determined to ignore whatever

drew her to John, and managed to choke down the rest of her toast. Then she allowed the hot water in the bath to soothe her tense muscles, relieved to note only a small streak of blood on the washcloth. After using the cream prescribed by the doctor…oh, the humility of being a woman…Shelby tried her best to pin her hair back with the three bobby pins she scrounged from the side pocket of her purse. Thankfully the Transportation Security Administration had missed them during the preflight screening. Lacking her makeup kit meant she had to employ emergency tactics with her one tube of pretty plumtastic lipstick, using it to highlight her cheekbones so she didn't look like something John's golden retriever barfed up.

Finally, after fastening her David Yurman loops and sliding on her boots, she walked out, prepared to wait downstairs for John. But she ran into him coming up the steps.

He smelled like he'd been in the fields, but it wasn't unpleasant. Just an odd scent of sugarcane. And man.

"Hey," he said, expression guarded, making her wonder just how much he'd processed from yesterday's news. He didn't look any more at peace.

"Hi," Shelby said, waiting for him to turn and start back down the stairs. He didn't budge.

"How are you?" he asked, meaning clearly, was she still bleeding?

"I'm good. Better than yesterday," she said.

He examined her, reading between the lines. "Did you get rest? Been off your feet?"

"Yes, drill sergeant," she said with a salute.

"I'm worried about you traveling today. Jamison said bed rest. My truck isn't a bed."

"It has a bed," she said, trying for lightness, not wanting to spend a long hour in the car with an overly anxious John.

"Not the same thing," he said. Wish not granted because obviously John wasn't the lightest of folks… and now she better understood why.

"I'll be fine."

"Maybe you should stay here."

She crooked an eyebrow. "You going to fold my panties?"

"I can," he said, a teeny smile flitting across his lips before disappearing.

"I insist on going with you. I'll rest all afternoon. Pinky swear." She didn't wait for him to respond, merely headed downstairs. Lying around Laurel Woods Bed-and-Breakfast with no TV or gossip magazines felt like punishment, which made riding into Baton Rouge to fetch her things sound as good as winning tickets to the Emmys and sitting next to Hugh Jackman. Being totally desperate for interaction was an understatement.

And that the handsome farmer was every bit as gorgeous as the Aussie actor was an added bonus she didn't want to acknowledge because she didn't want to remember the way he'd touched her…the way he'd kissed her. The memory of his taste and touch paired with the pain in his past made her weak, made her want to fix him.

Being a sucker for broken guys isn't cool, kiddo. Never works. Guard yourself, Shelby. You can't fix broken like this, so take the friends-only route. Safer, better traveled and won't leave you in a ditch.

Abigail stood at the bottom of the stairs, wearing an old-fashioned white apron and a smear of flour on her cheek. She looked like a commercial for Duncan Hines.

"Are you sure you're okay to travel?" she said, looking worried. "Of course, I don't know what's wrong with you, but I'm concerned nevertheless."

"Such a worrywart," Shelby said, trying again to lighten the mood. Jeez, these Beauchamps were a dark bunch. Shelby had grown up with the Addams family and they still weren't as gloomy and anxious as these two.

"Understatement of the year," John said, swinging open the front door.

"I'm the older sister. That's my job," Abigail said with obvious reference to the words she'd spoken to Shelby earlier. "Why don't you stay for dinner tonight, John? I'm making pork roast and homemade French bread."

"Got to get back to the fields," John said, and a tiny dart of disappointment snagged inside Shelby. Why? What should it matter to her that John wasn't coming back to eat pork roast? It shouldn't.

She felt vulnerable because she was on her own and still slightly scared she might lose the pregnancy that had brought her to Louisiana in the first place. That was it. Had to be. She wasn't attracted to him. Didn't want to mean anything to him.

Okay, she *was* attracted to him. The man made a chambray shirt and worn jeans look movie star sexy…so no use lying to herself about that one.

Guard yourself, chickadee.

Right.

"Drive safely," Abigail called as they crossed the wide porch with the freshly painted rocking chairs and ferns dropping dried fronds. A pair of pumpkins flanked a fancy arrangement of cornstalks, hay bales and bright mums. In the bright light of day, the Laurel Woods Bed-and-Breakfast reminded Shelby of places she'd never known…opposite of the sleek steel world she'd inhabited.

John's old farm truck idled in the drive. It had obviously been running the entire time John had been inside. What was up with that? Was that a thing? Just leave an unattended truck running?

Then John jogged around and opened the passenger door for her.

You're not in Kansas anymore…not that she'd ever been to Kansas in the first place.

Of course, it wasn't like there were no well-mannered men in Seattle, but something about the easy way things were done down here—a sort of "this is the fabric of who we are"—struck her as a good, gracious way to live one's life.

Didn't mean she wanted to live here. Because above all else, Shelby Mackey knew she didn't belong in Magnolia Bend.

CHAPTER SEVEN

JOHN SLID BEHIND the wheel, and with a quick wave at his worrisome sister standing on the porch in her apron, they bounced down the rocky drive. John winced as they hit a pothole and darted an apologetic look at Shelby.

"Hitting a pothole is not going to cause a miscarriage. I asked your doctor friend."

"I know," he said, though she could tell he hadn't known any better than she had. Blind leading the blind.

A few minutes' worth of highway sped by. Cows dotted pastures and the brilliant sun stretched over the flat alluvial plain as they wound around the road chasing the Mississippi's edge.

John cleared his throat. "Tell me about yourself, Shelby."

"Huh?"

"About your life in Seattle, parents, siblings, the students you teach."

"Oh, so we're going to backtrack, huh?" she asked.

John shrugged, drawing attention to his broad shoulders. She'd always been partial to strong, manly shoulders. Really, who wasn't? "Well, I don't know much about you. Might be a good idea to correct that since we're sharing, uh, such an intimate sort of…thing."

There was that.

Shelby inhaled, wishing she didn't have to reveal the impersonal world in which she'd been raised. John obviously had a caring family. Shelby obviously had a family of cyborgs. "I grew up in Seattle."

"You like it there?"

Did she like it there? Hmm. "Well, it's lush and green from all the rain. My parents have a boat and my favorite times are on the Sound—something about the briny air. When I was young, I wanted to spend all my time at the piers eating fish baskets, sucking down ice creams and running through packs of gulls making them scatter. Other than my stint at Oregon State and the years I spent in Spain, it's all I know."

John looked out at the flat land dotted with trees and the occasional bayou as if he weighed his world against the world she'd presented. "What about your folks?"

"My father's a successful attorney, partner in a large firm. My mother's family owns a company for which my mother is CEO and always at the office. I have an older sister by six years who works in L.A. as an executive for Warner Bros., and my brother's a plastic surgeon. He lives in San Diego."

John glanced over, eyebrows raised.

"Yeah, and I'm just a teacher."

"Just a teacher is a pretty important thing," he said

in the quiet space left after such a self-deprecating statement. "My late wife, Rebecca, was a teacher, too."

Of course she was. Probably ironed all his T-shirts, gave blood at every drive and babysat for free, too. One of those too-good-to-touch girls Shelby had never been. "What did she teach?"

"Preschool, but she worked with kids who had disabilities."

Exactly. Saint Rebecca. "That's a tough job."

"She loved it, though," he said, sliding his gaze back over to her. "I bet you do, too."

"Never wanted to be anything else. When all my other friends played dress-up or tea party, I'd have all my stuffed animals lined up and I'd be in front of my mini chalkboard teaching. I amused my parents greatly until I actually set education as my major."

John made a "huh" sound in the back of his throat. "So why Oregon State?"

"'Cause they're the Beavers," she deadpanned.

"And you don't like the Ducks?"

"I would have looked hideous in highlighter-yellow. And I refuse to quack at football games."

That made him laugh, and he looked good when he laughed. The corded muscles of his neck stretched, and his delicious mouth begged to be nibbled. Hardness melted into something most touchable.

"Actually the campus was gorgeous," she said. "And it took me away from home." Far away from scandal and the colossal mistake she'd made when she was eighteen. Her parents hadn't even cared she hadn't made it into Stanford or the other "more academic" schools her brother and sister had attended.

"You said you're teaching in Seattle now?"

"Presently I'm substituting. My plans weren't concrete when I came back from Spain, so I didn't interview for any permanent positions." Because she thought she'd be planning a wedding. Like a moron, she'd thought she'd be Mrs. Darby Dufrene, wife to the junior attorney in her father's firm. Stupid, stupid Shelby. "I've been staying in my parents' guesthouse until I figure out a permanent job. Then I'll get a place near wherever I end up teaching."

"So your parents are supportive about the baby?"

"I haven't told them yet. Only you." Shelby glanced down at her hands.

"Why not?"

"Because," she said, knowing it sounded lame.

"Because?"

"What's with the interrogation? I didn't want to tell them yet, okay?" Because they would flip out not at the social stigma of being an unwed mother, but because Shelby had been so stupid as to get knocked up by some random dude she didn't know...and who could be dumber than dirt. "Let's just say I don't have the most supportive family so I've put it off. Besides, I felt like you should know first."

"Why?"

"Is that all you can ask? Why?"

He glanced over at her and said nothing else.

She exhaled. "I don't know why I haven't told them. I'd planned on doing it over Thanksgiving.

You know eat turkey, tolerate your siblings and drop the bomb that you're pregnant by a stranger. Could've been fun telling my mother she'll be a Nonna in June, but instead I'm stuck in the home of Skeeter Burnside. By the way, who is Skeeter Burnside?"

"Oh, you saw the sign," John said, a flicker of amusement in his face. "He's my uncle Skeeter. He holds the state record in the long jump and participated in the 1976 games. Has a bronze medal."

"Wow," she said, not sure how much enthusiasm she should use in responding to that comment.

They drove a few more miles in silence before he cleared his throat. "What I meant was why did you tell me first?"

Shelby fidgeted with the seat belt. Fact was she had no clue why she hadn't told her parents. Though they worked long hours, she lived on the family estate and could have caught them at breakfast before they left for the gym and dropped the news. But she hadn't.

Not to mention, she'd still not told them about the split with Darby. In fact, her mother had assumed her departure for Louisiana was another attempt to talk Darby into interviewing for Mackey and Associates. To date, she hadn't felt strong enough to admit how badly she'd screwed up again. "I don't know. When I lay there in that doctor's office listening to the heartbeat, I felt so powerless and so full of…I don't even know. Hope? A new beginning? Fresh start?"

He said nothing.

"So that night I lay in bed and a realization hit me—if I want to raise this child to be strong and ethical, I have to start with being that way myself. I have to do the right thing. Telling you about the baby seemed the first step in that process. Coming clean with my parents and pulling up my big girl panties is the next step."

John turned off the highway, cutting through to the interstate, but remained silent, which chafed her. Here she was being totally honest, laying it all out, and he couldn't bother himself to say a simple "thank you"?

Maybe he wasn't thankful. After all, since she'd turned up at his doorstep with the news, she'd been nothing but a problem to him.

When John reached cruising speed on I-10, he glanced over at her again. "Stay here."

"Beg your pardon?"

"In Louisiana. Stay here with me. For a while longer. For the pregnancy."

Grappling with that bomb of a request, Shelby snapped her gaping mouth closed and stared out at the trees whizzing by.

Stay here?

In Podunk, Louisiana, with a man she didn't know beyond his preference in underwear—which was boxers, by the way.

Staying with John made no sense.

"That makes no sense," she said.

"It makes some. You have little support at home. No apartment. No job."

"Thanks for pointing out what a loser I am," she drawled.

"I'm not," he said, his mouth firm, his demeanor serious as a funeral director. "But you need support, and I'm offering you some."

"Why would you want me in Magnolia Bend bringing the shame? Lemme ask, do I get a scarlet *A* to wear and everything? Will I have to always use the back door?"

"So I screwed that up," he said, a flush rising to his cheeks as he veered the truck into the lane indicating Baton Rouge. "I apologized."

"You did," she admitted.

"I was up half the night thinking about what to do."

"And this was what you came up with?"

She watched uncertainty flit across his face. "Yeah."

"What will you say when people ask you about me? There's going to be talk."

"Sure, I accept people will talk, but I don't want you going back to Seattle. I want you to stay."

"With you? Or get an apartment? Does the town have apartments?"

"You can stay with me at Breezy Hill," he said, though he didn't sound so certain anymore. "I'm here for you and the baby."

Something struck inside her—a buried need for someone to want her. Inside the smart-ass with the big boobs and the bright smile was the girl who wanted to be loved. She knew herself, but it didn't matter. This particular yearning had been the cause of many a downfall in her life. Still, John wanting her in his life enough to weather the community's censure made her heart ache. He risked his reputation for a chance to…what? Share in the life of their baby? "I can't. You're still mourning your wife and…and…I can't just move in."

"Why not? I have four bedrooms and it's just me and Bart. None of Rebecca's family lives here anymore. Her mother moved to a patio home in Gonzales before Rebecca's death."

"What's she going to say about her former son-in-law who runs her family business shacking up with some floozy."

"You're calling yourself a floozy?"

"You know what I mean. This is a crazy idea."

"Breezy Hill is *my* home and Rebecca's mother promised me after Rebecca died I would stay there. Carla holds the trust, but I run the company with the understanding it will become mine upon her death. Don't worry about Carla—I'll make sure she understands you and I are essentially roommates." Again, uncertainty shaded his voice.

"You're going to tell her we're roommates?"

"Yes, but even if we were more to each other, she has to have foreseen the possibility I would find someone new someday. Besides, the business relationship works—the improvements I make to the land increase the value. There's no reason to change anything."

Shelby made a noise in the back of her throat. "I

wouldn't bet on that. You're thinking like a businessman, but for Carla it might be more personal. So what about the baby? Making a baby isn't something 'roommates' do."

"That was a onetime mistake. I can make her see that."

His words slapped her and she turned away, trying to remember she had no right to be hurt. What they'd done in that bathroom *was* a onetime thing. But in the outside world people wouldn't see it his way. When the baby bump popped up, there would be suspicion, and Shelby doubted John's former mother-in-law would accept a onetime screw as a valid explanation. But then again, what did she know about John's relationship with Rebecca's mother?

John exited at College Drive and after a few minutes pulled into a Chinese restaurant parking lot.

"Are you hungry?" he asked.

Does a nun pray? "Yeah, but I'd rather finish this conversation first."

He shifted into Park, killed the engine and turned to her. His green eyes roved her face and tugged at her heart despite her insistence the man meant nothing to her. "I get this is out of left field."

"Or right field. Or out of the blue. Or…" She shook her head.

"When I thought about you leaving, I could hardly breathe."

Shelby couldn't stop her heart from aching at those words.

"I want to be there for every part of your pregnancy. Neither of us planned this, but you don't have to go through this alone. I can't go to Seattle, but you can stay here. We can have this baby together." His words were like soft silk, enfolding her, brushing against the clenched resolve.

"But we're strangers."

"We know enough about each other to make a rational judgment call," he said.

"You can't possibly use *rational* in a sentence describing me."

"Fine. You're funny, pretty and haven't told my sister Birdie's been spying on their neighbors. So I'll add loyal to children to the list."

"How did you—"

"You glanced out at where my niece sat in the tree as we were leaving…and you smiled a secret smile. I caught Birdie yesterday with her sketch pad prop."

Shelby couldn't stop the grin. "Poor Abigail. Her daughter's Harriet the Spy."

"More like poor Birdie," he said, pulling the keys from the ignition. "Abigail will find out and be appropriately appalled. Birdie may never climb another tree."

Shelby turned to him so they held each other's full attention. "I don't want to make something not so great worse."

"Maybe it won't be worse."

"I can't imagine not going back to Seattle. These whole few months have been surreal. I keep waiting to wake up."

"I understand. Take a few more days to decide.

We won't mention the pregnancy to anyone until you figure out what you want."

"Why do you want me to stay so badly?"

John's eyes sparked with something she couldn't name. He lifted his hand and laid it on her stomach, the heat searing her, making her start, before warmth curled in both her girl parts and somewhere around her heart. "Because you carry hope for a life worth living."

Shelby swallowed, sudden emotion sticking in her throat. Christ Almighty. How could a woman argue with something like that?

She pressed her hand on his, and he turned it over so they held hands. The moment shimmered with tenderness, something neither had between them. Here they sat, virtual strangers, united by an unborn child…an unborn child who gave them each a new beginning.

Releasing his hand, Shelby redirected her gaze, afraid she might tear up. Her emotions had been roller-coastering for the past weeks. She'd cried over a tampon commercial for cripe's sake. "Okay. I'll consider staying for a while. I wholly acknowledge you're part of this baby and, therefore, have certain rights."

"Thank you," he said, using the hand he'd pressed into hers to remove the keys from the ignition.

"Now let's go grab some dumplings. I'm starving," Shelby said, scooping up her purse, tired of the tangle of her life.

"It's rare I leave the fields during harvest so let's do this right," John said, his face more relaxed.

Yet his words seemed to speak of larger things in their life. Still for that moment, Shelby focused on not overthinking every word John said. He wanted her now, but she'd been in this same position several times before, her heart overruling her head. She needed to proceed carefully because now the stakes weren't just about her.

They were about the tiny life inside her.

CHAPTER EIGHT

THE NEXT TWO days followed a pattern. John rose before the sun, ate oatmeal, drank black coffee and worked till the sun went down. After overseeing the loading of the cane, he showered, shaved and headed to his sister's place, where Shelby waited.

He couldn't flatter himself thinking Shelby looked forward to seeing him—she was bored and probably would have welcomed a zombie for company.

Of course, he pretty much fit that description after a day in the fields and a long night of tossing and turning. He'd brought her several magazines about fashion and whatever the Kardashians were up to. Glancing at those covers—at the antics of whoever those people were—made him feel not so bad about the mess he and Shelby had created. He'd also brought her some chewing gum, one clutch of flowers he'd grabbed not knowing if it would say something other than "Feel better soon" and a deck of cards so she could play solitaire. He'd tried to talk her into reading *The Sound and the Fury,* but she'd looked at him like he'd sprouted a horn in the center of his head.

Rebecca had always loved the classics, and the

Faulkner book along with a Truman Capote collection had been a gift to Abigail when she'd opened the bed-and-breakfast. Southern authors for a Southern home.

Shelby, however, wasn't impressed, and when John took a hard look at the books on Rebecca's shelves in her office, he had to agree with Shelby. Dry words, old times in a glossy new cover.

Each evening he and Shelby faced the cooling darkness of his sister's porch—her sipping tea, him a longneck. They'd talked about the weather, the Seattle Seahawks' record and how they'd both loved visiting Cozumel. Inane conversation designed to help each of them gauge how it might work if they were to cohabitate while awaiting the birth of their child.

But today would be the true test for him—Thanksgiving Day at his parents' house.

Ye gods.

Pulling into the drive of Laurel Woods, John checked his reflection in the rearview mirror. He'd trimmed his own hair because he hadn't had time to go by Tammy's in town. It looked okay, though he'd nicked a spot behind his ear. His green eyes looked tired, but they always did at harvest. Not bad but not his best. Been a long time since he was at his best.

Climbing out, he studied the females assembled on the porch. Shelby sat in a rocker, wearing the wrap dress and boots she'd worn Monday. Her hair looked shiny and she wore equally shiny lipstick. Looked like a city girl—a good-looking city girl. His sister wore a long skirt and a dark shirt, which was pretty much standard for her. At one time Abigail had been a bit more frivolous and not so grown-up. Her lousy cheating ex-husband, Calhoun Orgeron, had fixed her good. No more Abi…just serious Abigail. Birdie wore a black hoodie, skintight jeans and a sullen look. Dollar to doughnuts, she'd gotten busted spying on that California nutcase who had moved into The Haven behind Laurel Woods.

"Happy Thanksgiving," he called, climbing the stairs.

"What's happy about it?" Birdie asked, her tone caustic enough to blister paint.

"That's enough, missy." Abigail jabbed a finger at her daughter. "Straighten up. Pawpaw and Fancy don't want to stare at your sad face all day long."

Birdie's narrowed eyes softened. Even if she was miffed, Birdie loved his parents and would never bring any grief to them. "Whatever."

Shelby watched their interaction, her blue eyes amused at what unfolded. Shifting her gaze to his, she mouthed "busted."

And just like that, the doubt, the feeling he'd been too rash in asking her to stay, lifted. "Now that's settled, you gals ready to roll?" he asked.

"We can take the wagon," Abigail said, with a wave at the staid Volvo station wagon listed in the dictionary as an antonym for *sexy*. "More room and much safer than your old truck. Let me grab the sweet potatoes and the caramel pie first."

"Why don't I drive Shelby? She may not want to stay for football and the annual Christmas cookie bake."

Shelby opened her mouth, likely to disagree, but Abigail beat her to it. "Good idea. I told Mom I'd help her decorate the tree, too, and you know how long that takes. Story behind every flippin' ornament." Abigail disappeared into the house. Birdie kicked the railing of the porch and glanced over at Shelby. She wanted to say something, but wasn't the kind of kid who piped up on her own.

"Birdie, everything cool?" he asked.

"Sure. Punished until the cows come home, and Mom is making me go apologize to Mr. Lively for spying on him. I mean, what did he expect? He swims naked."

"Mr. Lively? Is he the—"

"Yeah. New art department head at the high school. He's totally hot and I have to note worth the effort…if you know what I mean," Birdie said, almost too matter-of-factly.

John tried not to react to the obvious implication about Mr. Lively. Birdie didn't even manage a blush, just stuck her little chin out like she dared him to say something.

"Okay, I'll spread the word," John said, and it made Shelby laugh. Her laugh was nice. Not a tinkling sound like Rebecca's. More low and velvety.

Shelby smiled at Birdie. "Maybe your mother needs to go with you to apologize. Maybe she needs some Mr. Lively."

Abigail came out holding two dishes. "Birdie, get the door. Jeez, I would appreciate your helping me sometime. Do you ever think about how much I have to do? Do you ever wonder if I might need some help?"

Birdie took the pie from her mother. "Mom, will you come with me when I apologize to Mr. Lively? Please." The girl looked over at Shelby and John with a spark in her eye.

"Of course, I'm going with you. Do you think I would allow you to go to that weirdo's house alone?"

Birdie mouthed "wow" before saying, "It's not nice to call people who are different names, or so you told me when I went to preschool."

"Oh, well, I should have said 'odd' and not 'weird.' Better?" Abigail clipped down the porch steps, balancing the casserole, and turned to wait on them with a crooked eyebrow.

John waited for Shelby to pass. "You look nice, Shelby."

"Thanks, John."

"Speaking of weird," Birdie muttered under her breath, following her mother to the navy Volvo that could dissuade a sex addict from approaching Abigail.

Silently he followed Shelby to the truck he'd left idling in the drive. In the formfitting dress, her backside swayed, and he couldn't help admire the view. Her pregnancy hadn't seemed to change her smoking body one iota. He'd have to keep his eye on Jake today...if his brother showed up.

Halfway on the ride into town, Shelby looked over at him. "I'm nervous."

"Don't be. They're going to stare a little and wonder a lot, but my family, annoying as they can be, is welcoming. Plus, you already know Abigail and Birdie. My brother Matt and his wife, Mary Jane, will be there, along with their two boys—Wyatt and William. Hopefully, my younger brother, Jake, will show up. And then there's Aunt Lucy and Uncle Carney, Gram and Mr. Jenkins. That's probably it."

"Sounds horrifying," Shelby said.

"Relax," he said, turning out of the drive. "So what happened with Birdie?"

"Your sister was dusting the rocker at the end of the hall. Something about the Christmas tree. And she saw what I saw that first morning. Um, Mr. Lively in the buff…and Birdie watching him."

He tried not to smile. "Interesting. And what about you? Feeling better?"

"Yes, and I appreciate your distracting me from being so nervous that I might hurl."

John rolled through the Magnolia Bend city limits sign, coming face-to-face with the fact today wasn't a regular workday. No one sprawled on the porch of his uncle's store, no cars cluttering lots, even the square where the crumbling courthouse stood had only Mrs. Dryden walking her ancient Italian greyhound. The wind blew at a nice clip, the sun played hide-and-seek with the clouds, and John Beauchamp, the son of the pastor of the First Presbyterian Church of Magnolia Bend was bringing the girl he knocked up at an infamous roadside bar home to holiday dinner.

"You want to bail on the turkey and dressing?" John asked.

"No. I just wish I had a better answer every time someone, aka your sister, corners me on our relationship. You know everyone is going to sit there eating pie, trying to figure out what's going on between us."

"And what would they think?"

"That I'm some bloodsucking parasite trying to get my claws into you."

He glanced sharply over. "You think that's what they'll think?"

Her shoulders sank. "I don't know what they'll think. Only that they will."

"Okay, so maybe that's the worst thing," he said, pulling onto Second Street where his parents' 1800 French Revival sat in the middle of the street surrounded by graceful oaks, looking postcard pretty and very much at home on the street strewn with old homes. "Or maybe they'll be happy to see me with someone who makes me happier."

"I make you happier?" Shelby asked, her head snapping around so quickly her hair lifted off her shoulders.

He pulled in the drive next to his uncle Carney's '57 restored Chevy truck, surprised at his words, but, yeah, though the past few days had been hard, he'd felt more himself. "Oddly enough, you've made me forget how bad this year has been."

And it was true. For over an entire year, he'd

existed in robotic fashion, smiling only when someone cracked a joke, and even then only because it
was expected. Otherwise, each day was the same—
empty house, hard day and lonely evening with a cat
he'd never wanted in the first place. But after he'd
conquered the horror over how badly he'd screwed
up three months ago, an unexpected protective
feeling and burgeoning fondness for Shelby had
bloomed. The woman was such an enigma, bringing unexpected laughter in the middle of despair…
and she had every reason to be as unsettled as anyone over the fact she was pregnant.

"Only a bit, huh?" she said, eyeing his parents'
home. "This looks like something out of *Cat on a
Hot Tin Roof.* In fact I feel like a cat on a hot tin
roof. Ouch."

"It's been in our family since my great-great-
grandfather Earl bought it back from his mistress.
I like the irony a preacher lives here." John killed
the engine, climbed out and hurried around to open
Shelby's door, but she'd already climbed out.

Closing the door she turned to him, her blue eyes
full of…something. But the moment felt intimate, as
if admitting she made him happy had moved them
to a new stage…a stage he was afraid of entering.
"Thanks for saying that." She smiled.

Her lips were glossy. Usually he didn't like kissing
women who wore sticky gloss, but at that moment
he wondered what she tasted like. He couldn't remember. Sweet? Spicy? Minty? "For saying what?"

"That your life isn't worse because of all this."

"I didn't say that. I said you made me a bit happier. Key word is *bit*," he joked.

Yes, he'd actually made a joke. Strange. No, not a joke. Flirting. Shockingly, it felt fantastic.

Her eyes twinkled as she laughed. "Now I remember why I wanted to dance with you, Josh Beauchamp."

"Who?"

"That's what I told the private investigator I thought your name was. Josh or Joe."

Holy crap, they both flirted with each other. "I remembered your name."

She gave him a smoldering look. "I'm memorable. Sue me." And then she sauntered off with a little laugh. And he stood there, very, very much aware of Miss Shelby Mackey, the woman he'd invited to live with him.

Damn.

He felt… He couldn't name the feeling…but he'd felt it before. A long time ago when he'd first met Rebecca Lynn with her subtle smile and surprising wit. It had been at the Dairy Palace. She'd attended school in Baton Rouge up until her junior year of high school so he'd never met her before that day. Once he did, he couldn't keep his eyes off her. This was how it felt at the beginning.

John didn't want to move in that direction. He wasn't ready to flirt. But even as part of him dug in his heels, the other part stepped toward this woman carrying his child. Something within him stirred, and it wasn't just about being a father in less than seven months. It was interest.

In Shelby.

Not a good idea, bud. Things are about as clear as bayou mud.

He grabbed the ice chest he'd strapped down in the back of the truck, lifting it over the scratched edge. He was back to bringing the drinks again à la bachelor. Jake would probably be responsible for the rolls which he'd no doubt bring from Betsy's Bake Shoppe.

As he headed toward the front door following Miss Fancy Pants, he saw someone he'd not expected on the porch, sitting stock-still regarding him with a stunned look on her face.

Rebecca's mother.

And Carla Stanton wasn't happy about what she'd witnessed.

CARLA WAGUESPACK STANTON had seen much in her sixty-nine years. She'd endured her papa driving off into a bayou dead drunk. She'd sat through the funerals of both her parents, her brother who'd perished in Cambodia, her husband and her most precious gift of all—her beautiful daughter. But nothing had ever hurt her more than to see John Beauchamp flirting with the pretty blonde he'd brought to Thanksgiving dinner.

The pain struck hard and fast, and for a moment, she couldn't manage a breath.

This was it. The day had arrived when John stepped

back into a world without Rebecca. He'd made the leap she'd been unable to make. She should be happy for him. But she wasn't.

Seeing him with that other woman made her daughter's death all the more horrific.

If only…

So many *if onlys* in regards to what had happened that September day. But none could change the outcome—her baby had died alone, terrified. Carla would never forgive herself for that…and she'd never forgive John, either.

So to watch him laugh with the blonde felt like he'd walked up and slapped her in the face.

When he saw her ensconced in the rocker, the laughter in his face slipped away. His expression went from surprise to shame to dread.

"Carla," he said as he climbed the steps to his parents' house, the blonde beside him looking suddenly wary.

Smart girl.

"Hello, John. I suppose your parents didn't tell you I was invited."

"No, but I never asked. How are you?"

"Well as can be expected. My hip has been bothering me and Dr. Peevy's been talking about replacement." Her eyes shifted to the blonde. "You have a friend."

He nodded and the girl swallowed, clasping her hands behind her back, forming a smile. "I do. This is Shelby Mackey. She's a friend of mine from Seattle."

"Oh?" Carla said, not bothering to rise. She shouldn't

have to be polite to the girl with the diamond earrings and the big tits. Shelby was the intruder here,
not Carla, who'd been coming to Thanksgiving dinner
at the Beauchamps ever since her daughter had married into the family. "I never knew you had friends in
Seattle."

The girl extended her hand. "How do you do?"

Carla took the hand only because her mama had
raised her with manners. Her grasp was warm and
firm, which made her even less likable. "Not very
well if truth be told."

"Oh," Shelby said, casting a glance toward John.
"I'm sorry to hear that."

"Carla was Rebecca's mother," John said.

"No, I *am* her mother. That never changed," Carla
said, eyeballing John with a firm look. Rebecca's
death hadn't changed who Carla was. She'd always
be her baby's mama.

The blonde dropped her hand, noticeably paling
as she cast a startled glance at John. Receiving no
help, she mumbled, "I'm sorry for your loss."

"Yes, well, perhaps so, though if I'm reading
things correctly from my viewpoint, you benefit
from the cause of that pain."

The blonde's eyes widened and she shook her
head.

"Carla," John said, warning in his voice.

"No, it's true, isn't it? You two are dating?"

"No, we're not dating," John said, his green eyes
crackling with more emotion than she'd seen in a
while. Change wafted in on the Louisiana breeze.

She felt this in her bones as much as she felt the arthritis, and she didn't like the thought of the world moving on, forgetting what had happened, abandoning her daughter.

Logically she knew life went on, but logic was a piss-poor companion to a brokenhearted woman.

Shelby blinked. The girl had pretty eyes, the kind you saw in Miss America contestants, intentionally guileless, placid on purpose. But then her eyes changed. Shelby wasn't as dumb as she looked. "He's right, we're not dating. I'll be living with him."

John's head jerked toward Shelby.

Carla rose, her hip screaming in protest. "Living with him?" Ice hung off her words even as anger fired deep in her belly. John was out of his mind if he thought he could invite someone to live at Breezy Hill.

"In a technical sense. I'm considering relocating to Louisiana, and John has kindly offered me a place to stay," Shelby said, her smile pasted on in a most determined manner.

"You're going to stay at Breezy Hill?" Carla said, shifting her gaze to John as the anger boiled over into fury. They could say whatever they want about being friends. Carla could tell it was more. She wasn't stupid.

"I'm happy to help out," John said, his gaze intent.

"You're happy to help out?" Carla repeated.

"Carla, Shelby's a friend who needs a place to stay. Don't turn this into something it's not," John said.

Carla shook her head. "No. Not going to happen.

That house belonged to my husband's family and you're not going to use it for…whatever you think you're going to use it for. It belongs to the trust."

And I control the trust. She didn't say the words, but John knew the score. Had he even thought about how this would look? His wife not even cold in the ground and he'd replaced her?

"I think you misunderstand the situation, Carla," John said.

"No, I don't think I do."

"This doesn't have to do with Rebecca."

"Don't say her name," Carla hissed, her control slipping away. Today was Thanksgiving, a day to reflect on blessings. What was she to reflect upon? How empty her life was now? How utterly alone she was?

"Carla," John intoned, reaching a hand toward her. "Don't do this."

"Don't do what? Feel the way I feel? She was my daughter."

"And she was my wife," he said, his voice lowering, the hurt still there. Carla hated herself for it, but hearing the pain in John's voice momentarily satisfied her. She wanted him to still feel that pain, to still feel guilt over Rebecca's death, because it meant her daughter existed in some small way. Her fingerprints stayed behind.

"I'm leaving. I'm not eating dinner with—" Carla shifted her gaze back to the blonde who stood looking as if she wished to be anywhere other than where she stood in her fancy boots "—your *friend*."

Carla didn't wait for either Shelby or John to say anything more, merely pushed past the two of them, noting the expensive scent of Shelby's perfume, and entered the Beauchamp house. Francesca "Fancy" Beauchamp came around the corner just as Carla bent to scoop her purse off the old church pew sitting in the foyer.

"What's wrong, Carla?" Fancy asked, waving a wooden spoon in her direction. "Oh, I forgot I had this spoon. You're not going, are you? We're about to eat. Waiting on John."

"I'm not staying, Fancy. Today is too upsetting for me."

"Too upsetting?" Fancy repeated. "Oh, honey, you don't need to be alone today. Stay with us. We're family."

Carla looked at Fancy in her ruffled apron with her perfect hair and warm smile and wanted to slap her silly. Family? No, she wasn't family. She was a sad charity case for the Beauchamp family.

Let's invite poor Carla. She has no one.

"I'm just not feeling up to snuff today, Fancy. No need for me to ruin everyone's dinner."

"Oh, Carla, don't leave. Abigail made the caramel pie you like."

Like caramel pie would keep her at the table with the woman trying to take her daughter's place, and, for Christ's sake, *living* at the Stanton family farm. The thought of Shelby standing in the kitchen where Carla had raised Rebecca made Carla hopping mad. She might do something inappropriate like throw a roll at the woman…or wrap her arthritic fingers around her pretty throat. Or maybe kick her fathead son-in-law in the balls for even thinking about letting another woman live at Breezy Hill.

What was he thinking?

She thought about Shelby with her blond hair, blue eyes and big knockers and knew what he was thinking.

"Sorry, but I'm leaving." Carla shouldered her purse as John and Shelby entered the front door. Fancy turned toward John, took in Shelby and Carla could see the dawning in her friend's eyes.

That's right. John has moved on, and I can't stand to sit here and watch.

"Carla's leaving," Fancy said to John.

"I know," he said, his expression void of emotion. "I wish she wouldn't."

Carla walked past them, trying to keep her eyes on the door and not on the woman standing there looking so put-together, so voluptuous…so damned alive. "Well, we all wish for things we can't have, don't we?"

"Carla," Fancy called, obviously distressed by her antics. She hated to disappoint her friend, but she just couldn't do it. Every nerve in her body throbbed with anger, and the slightest scrape would send her plummeting toward can't-take-it-back.

"Happy Thanksgiving," she called back, nearly tripping over the ice chest John had left on the steps…and her tears.

Oh, my sweet Rebecca, I'm so sorry you're not

here. But I'm not going to make it easy for him. I'm not letting him replace you with that stranger. I'll do whatever it takes.

CHAPTER NINE

SHELBY STOOD IN the foyer of John's childhood home, trying not to hyperventilate.

What a shitfest.

For a good ten seconds, she, John and his mother stood looking at one another while the rest of the house moved around them. A kid darted across the hallway yelling about a rubber bracelet, pots and pans clanked in the kitchen somewhere beyond John's left shoulder. All seemed perfectly normal, but it was far, far, far from normal. Like maybe in the next stratosphere of not normal.

"Well, that was, uh, awkward," John's mother said with a rueful shrug, her eyes darting from Shelby to John and then back to Shelby again. "I'm sorry."

She'd settled sharp eyes on Shelby. "It's okay," Shelby said because the woman seemed to be waiting on her to grant her pardon.

"Mom, this is my friend Shelby Mackey. Shelby, this is my mom, Francesca Beauchamp. Everyone calls her Fancy."

The older woman, who barely came to John's shoulder, wiped her hand on her apron and extended it. She wore a pink rubber cancer awareness bracelet and a sincere smile. Wispy hair the color of rhubarb stuck out at arranged angles and her eyes were as green as John's. "Happy to meet you, Shelby. Welcome to our home."

"Thanks for having me," Shelby said, taking the slightly damp hand extended.

"There he is," a booming voice sounded behind her.

"Happy Thanksgiving, Dad," John said, accepting the hug and slap on the back given by the man exactly the same height as him. "Dad, this is Shelby Mackey. She's a friend who will be staying with me for a while."

The man had sterling hair, a broad tan face and deep brown eyes that crinkled slightly. "Oh? You're staying in Magnolia Bend for a while, are you? At John's place?"

Well, hadn't she just said as much to Rebecca's mother?

She hadn't meant to make that commitment. No good reason to stay in Louisiana other than it was far away from her family and their disappointment. She was a stranger here, and bearing the stares of the people in Magnolia Bend would be uncomfortable at a time she'd feel awkward enough.

But John and those few minutes beside his truck earlier had pushed her in his direction. Whether she wished it or not, she felt something for him. She had no clue what that was—maybe some misplaced need to have the father of her child in her life or maybe leftover attraction from that night. Or maybe she wanted someone to take care of her, which was so screwed up. But somehow the words had flown out of her mouth.

"For now," she said. "I'm thinking of relocating from Seattle." She extended her hand yet again. "Starting over."

Starting over wasn't a bad concept.

But doing it in Magnolia Bend? She liked it fine—except for the mosquitoes—and so far the people had charmed her. The town could be a good place to raise her baby. Plus, John would be nearby so he could take a role in the child's life. But she wasn't sure about anything at this point. Only that by summer, God willing, she'd be a mother.

"I'm Reverend Beauchamp, but you can call me Dan. Do you have a place to worship?"

"Really, Dad?" John groaned.

"Hey, it's my thing," the older man grinned, slapping his son on the back again. "Come on in the den. The Cowgirls are getting their butts handed to them. Shelby can visit with your mama in the kitchen."

John cast a questioning look in her direction and Shelby smiled. Part of her didn't want him to go. Okay, all of her didn't want him to go, leaving her alone with his mother and God only knew who else. "Go ahead. I'll be fine. I think."

"Of course you will," Fancy said, picking up a wooden spoon from a nearby table. "I need help with the gravy. You cook, Shelby?"

"Um, I can boil water," she said, making a face. She'd always intended on taking cooking classes, but never had. Her family housekeeper, Mosa, was a fantastic cook and had allowed the lonely Shelby to assist on occasion, but Shelby's skills were limited. "And stir things."

"Perfect." Fancy grinned, motioning her toward the area where seconds earlier pots had clanked.

They swooshed into the large kitchen. Abigail buttered rolls, Birdie squatted on the floor beside an ancient Irish setter and a woman with long blond hair frowned at a layer cake. A huge island created from a worktable sat in the center of the bright blue kitchen. A cat perched on the windowsill watching as if it were maestro of the commotion unfolding.

"Everyone, this is Shelby," Fancy announced.

"We know. She's been staying with us," Birdie said, not bothering to look up. The dog wagged its tail in greeting...or in appreciation of Birdie's petting.

"Welcome, Shelby," Abigail drawled, going back to buttering the huge popover rolls.

The other woman lifted her gaze to Shelby. "Hi, I'm Mary Jane, Matt's wife. We're glad you're here. It's good for John."

Shelby didn't know what to say. "Oh, well, I thank you all for letting me tag along."

Fancy waved a hand. "Enough chitchat, we gotta finish up this dinner. I'm hungry as a bear in spring. Shelby, dear, you come over here and help me with this gravy. Birdie, run out and see if Uncle Matt is done with the turkey."

Birdie gave an elaborate sigh, but rose and headed

toward the back door. The dog followed, tongue lolling, eyes adoring. The cat coldly assessed those gathered, licked its paw and turned, dismissing everyone. Shelby had never had a single pet her entire life and the thought of having them as a part of a family seemed weird...and somewhat unsanitary.

For the next thirty minutes, Shelby, clad in a spare apron, learned how to make gravy from drippings while chatting companionably with the others about the Macy's Thanksgiving Day parade and the fact the forecast predicted rain for the upcoming Candy Cane Festival. Shelby didn't contribute much, just savored being part of a process she'd never experienced before—holiday dinner preparation.

In her family, they gathered in the evening around lit candles to eat the dinner Mosa created with Cornish hen, oyster dressing, a few gourmet side dishes and a sparkling champagne and/or Washington Riesling. It was all so very elegant and civil.

Not so this meal with its macaroni salad, candied yams and green bean casserole made with soup. One-word description—*Southern.*

John popped his head inside the kitchen. "Shelby, can you break away?"

She had been filling cups with ice and stared at the job half-done.

"Birdie, take over for Shelby," Abigail said, oven mitts on both hands.

Requisite huff sounded, Birdie took the stack of cups from Shelby.

"Wash your hands first." Abigail nodded at the farm sink.

Shelby surrendered her task and followed John out the back door where several men stood staring at a huge pot. A golden turkey hung from a nearby hook, permeating the air with deliciousness. Her stomach growled in response even though she didn't eat meat.

"You've already met my father. This is my brother Matt," John said, indicating the man who stood an inch taller and several inches wider than him. He looked like a football player or a prison guard. Rough, no-nonsense, more similar to John than not. The other man seemed nothing like John or Matt.

"And this is the baby of the family—Jake."

Jake was shorter, but very put-together. Auburn strands caught in the sunlight and his blue eyes swept down her body with appreciation and thoroughness. Chiseled pretty face, crinkled blue eyes and white smile. He reminded Shelby of a crocodile, seemingly placid, but ready to gobble at the slightest provocation. His body language screamed "I'm here to serve you but don't think you'll catch me."

"Hi," Shelby said, donning a smile. "I appreciate your family having me for lunch."

Jake arched an eyebrow, his eyes amused. "Thanks for sacrificing yourself. We'll try to make it painless."

John frowned.

Jake grinned bigger. "What? She just said we can have her for lunch, and you know how I love blondes."

"See what I deal with?" John said.

Car doors slammed around front.

"Ding dong, the witch is here," Jake cracked.

"Stop calling your aunt a witch," Reverend Beauchamp said, scooping up a huge aluminum pan, heading toward the bird.

"If the broom fits…"

John jerked his head toward a path winding toward a small garden. "Walk with me?"

Matt and Jake exchanged knowing looks.

Shelby fell into step with John, and as soon as they were out of earshot, he said, "I'm sorry about what happened with Carla. Mom didn't say anything about inviting her."

"You can't help Mrs. Stanton feeling the way she does."

"No, but I could have talked to her beforehand. Or we could have skipped coming."

Shelby caressed the blossom of a yellow rose arching over the path. "I wouldn't want you to miss this. Your family's nice."

"They're a little too much at times."

"I like them," she said, lifting her gaze to his.

"You said you'd stay."

She nodded. "The devil made me do it. I felt a little defensive and judged by Carla."

"She's always been so reasonable," he murmured, shifting his gaze to the trees swaying behind the house. A small creek ran the length of the backyard, an oddity in the middle of a town.

"Grief changes people…as you are well aware."

"She wants to stay damaged," he murmured. "I don't."

His words brushed against the reservation she felt at blurting out she'd stay. John wanted to heal...and maybe she could be part of that. He had a good reason for wanting to move into the sunshine of life.

"Maybe so," she said, "but I understand the way she feels. Breezy Hill was her home and now it's not. Her daughter was your wife and now she's not. Bitterness grows like a weed over something like that."

He nodded. "And now there'll be a baby. Not going to be easy for her."

"I'm pretty sure she'll hate my guts."

"She wouldn't go that far."

Shelby didn't say anything. How could she? She didn't know Carla, didn't know anything about her grief...or even her daughter. But something told her Carla would definitely go that far and maybe further. Hadn't she said something about the trust? Could Carla force John out of the house? Take away the farm?

Maybe her staying wasn't such a good idea. John shouldn't have to choose between her and what he loved.

"Thank you, Shelby."

"For?"

"Staying. I can't make any promise other than I will be there for you."

"I never asked for anything, John," she said, meeting his gaze straight on. She might be down, but she wasn't out. Shelby didn't need him. She'd

learned over the years how to take care of herself—
physically and emotionally. No one had to pick up
pieces for her.

"No, you didn't, and I admire you for your in-
dependence as much as I admire you for taking a
chance and staying in Magnolia Bend. We'll have to
feel our way around this thing, but I want to do it."

"Define *it*."

His forehead crinkled. "Having a baby."

"That's already happening," she said.

"Living with me?"

"You sound confused. And we are talking about
a platonic relationship, aren't we?"

He nodded. "I don't know if I'm ready for anything beyond friendship."

"You were ready for something more a night almost three months ago."

"That was different," he said.

"Define *that*." Shelby crossed her arms.

He gave her a hard smile. "Busting my balls today,
aren't you?"

"No," Shelby said. "I'm setting my parameters.
Start with the night we began."

"I drowned myself in Jack Daniel's so I didn't remember. I wanted numbness, but then you walked
into Boots and I felt something more than I thought
I could feel. I wanted to feel you against me, have
someone touch me with something other than com-
passion."

His honest words made her stomach flip and her
heart ache. She couldn't fool herself—John Beau-

champ still loved his wife. He was as inaccessible as every other man she'd ever been with. This wasn't anything other than two people making their way through something they'd never thought could happen—parenthood. Love wasn't part of the equation.

"Okay," she said.

"Okay?" he repeated, moving them farther away from the house. "What does that mean?"

"I'll move into Breezy Hill and give us a chance to know each other, to become a team for our child."

Relief combined with something she couldn't pin down reflected in his eyes.

"I have an appointment with Dr. French tomorrow morning. Afterward I'll arrange to move some things from Seattle."

"Do I need to take you to the doctor?"

"No, you need to work," she said with a smile. "I looked up sugarcane farming, and you've been generous in taking so much time away. I'm a big girl, used to taking care of myself. No need to put yourself out."

"Actually it's been nice to have someone to share my evenings after a long day in the field."

Shelby smiled at his admission. Oddly enough, she knew what he meant. Living in Spain, she'd dreaded going home. In her classroom, energy hummed, students joked and she had purpose. In her small flat, she'd rambled around lonely as a coot on a winter's lake. Perhaps that's why she'd attached herself so firmly to the handsome, warm Darby Dufrene. He'd made her feel not so alone, and he seemed just the sort of man her parents would approve of. Maybe her feelings for Darby hadn't been love. Maybe she didn't know what love was. What she did know, however, is things with Darby hadn't worked out, and she'd looked for comfort elsewhere and ended up pregnant.

She had to deal...and now she had someone to help her.

"Thanks for being my friend and giving me a place to stay until I figure things out."

John's gaze lightened. "Not sure I'm being a good friend if I have a selfish motive in wanting you to stay."

"I know. I understand your motive," Shelby said, placing a hand on her belly.

John took her hand. "Still, thanks for staying."

"Let's see if you say that in a few months when I'm bloated, gassy and cranky."

His eyes widened.

Shelby withdrew her hand in case she got too used to his touch and wanted more. "Well, that's what it says in my pregnancy book."

For a moment, he looked horrified then shrugged. "Red beans do that to me and I survive."

"Oh, Lord, I'll make sure we don't eat those," Shelby said.

"I'll stay away," he said, moving back toward the big house where kith and kin awaited the carving of the turkey. "Would you mind letting me borrow the pregnancy book? Or giving me the name of a good one? I'd like to know what I'm up against."

"I have several. You can take your pick."

"So we're doing this?"

"We're doing this."

John broke into a smile, and Shelby was reminded of the man in the photo sitting in the guest bathroom at Breezy Hill. "Together."

"Together," she agreed.

USUALLY THE FRIDAY after Thanksgiving, John took a break from harvesting and went duck hunting with his father and brothers, but since he had missed so much time with his crew, he stayed at Breezy Hill, rising with the sun to make up for lost time.

Of course it was move-in day for Shelby, too. Not that that was any reason to miss hunting with his dad. Or at least that's what he told himself.

He'd stayed up late the night before, cleaning out the guest bedroom Rebecca had decorated with her old college bedding. They had rarely used the room, saying it would make the perfect nursery when the time came. But that time never came, of course, so it had gone largely ignored. He'd found soft sheets and washed the towels so they'd smell fresh. He'd scrounged around and found some flowery-scented soap in the back of his bathroom cabinet and some nice-smelling wood chips. He couldn't remember what it was called, but the scent reminded him of a summer day. He'd poured it in a bowl and set it on the nightstand, but then he thought it looked stupid and dumped it out.

Basically, he felt nervous as a kid on prom night, and for a guy who'd already scored with his date, that felt silly. But he wanted her to like his house, wanted her to stay and not go back to Seattle, taking the child with her. Even though it had been less than a week since he'd learned his baby grew in her belly, he didn't think he could bear that loss.

Perhaps many would think it strange to feel so strongly about the baby in so short a time, but it didn't change the fact something moved inside him every time he thought about a child in his life.

Shelby said she would wait until his day was over before she came, so he'd left the fields early to shower, shave and grill a few steaks. He'd picked up some potatoes and a bagged salad. If she wanted dessert, he had Blue Bell ice cream in the freezer.

At seven o'clock, a car pulled into the drive. He peeked out between blinds that—he ran a finger over them—needed dusting. A silver Lexus?

Seconds later, Shelby climbed out of the luxury sedan. She wore jeans, a long-sleeved Henley shirt and running shoes. Her hair was secured in a ponytail which swung as she took in his house. He didn't want her to know he stood there spying on her like some creep, so he stepped away from the window, but he didn't miss the expression on her face—doubt reflected in the orange glow of his porch light.

He moved back, nearly tripping over Bart, who sprawled at his feet.

"Damn it, Bart," he muttered, righting himself and heading for the door just as she knocked.

Bart barked, lunging toward the door. John caught him, shoving the big brute back as he pulled open the door. Through the screen, he saw her tentative smile.

"Hey," she said, pushing back an escaping chunk of hair, "I'm here…to live with you and stir up tons of rumors and cause your former mother-in-law to make a voodoo doll of us both."

"Well, in that case, come on in," he joked, stepping back and kneeing Bart. The dumb dog panted a welcome, his brown eyes happy to have another human to give him a crumb of attention. "Where'd you get the car?"

"It's a lease. I returned the rental."

"Been busy, huh?"

"I can get things done. Something smells good. Did you fix dinner?" She craned her head around his shoulder, toward the kitchen.

"Real men don't cook. They grill," he said, suddenly uncomfortable. Or maybe it was merely nerves.

Shelby dumped her purse on the hall table. "Hello, Bart," she said, petting the dog sitting at her feet. He looked as if he'd found a new reason for living.

For a moment, standing with his hand flat against the closed door, John disassociated, his mind scrabbling, fixating on the fact this couldn't be his life. His mind zoomed away, dissecting the scene before him: a beautiful woman, a dopey dog, dinner on the table and John teetering on the cusp of a future he'd never, ever thought could happen. Then he zoomed back into himself, snapping into the thought that his life was what it was. He couldn't stay on the perimeter anymore. Time to move forward.

"Come in the kitchen and wash up."

She trailed behind him and he sensed she took in his home in a new way…as someone who would live here rather than making a onetime stop. "I stayed stuffed from dinner yesterday so I haven't had much to eat. Suddenly I'm starving."

"Yeah, about my family yesterday—"

"Don't you dare apologize. They were wonderful. I felt like I was in a movie."

"National Lampoon?"

Shelby laughed. He decided he loved her throaty laugh. Made him hungry for more of her.

But he wasn't supposed to feel that way.

"Well, they *were* funny."

"And you ended up next to Aunt Lucy." He faked a shudder. "She can't hear dynamite and thinks discussing her health issues counts as conversation."

"But it was educational. I now know how difficult it is to mix up the swishy medicine for the thrush she got from the strong antibiotic her doctor gave her for the infected boil on her butt…and how turnip greens, whatever they are, affect your aunt the next day. She ate quite a few servings of that dish your neighbor brought, so I feel pretty bad for her Home Health nurse today."

John snorted, pulling out the plates he and Rebecca had picked out at Dillards twelve years ago.

The irony he'd be sharing his first meal as a—God he could barely think it—single man hit him between the eyes. But he ignored it, swallowing the pain of moving on, determined to put one foot in front of the other.

After refocusing himself, he loaded the plates and took them to the breakfast table where on Monday he'd first shared tea with Shelby. Setting the plate in front of her, he sank into the chair he'd always sat in. Then thought better of it and switched to the one next to Shelby. New perspective needed.

"This looks good," Shelby said, eyeing the steak, "but I think you should know I don't eat meat. Uh, some fish and shellfish on occasion, but—"

"You don't eat meat?"

Shelby's cheeks bloomed pink. "I'm sorry. I should have told you."

"No," he said, shaking his head, trying to comprehend why someone would refuse meat. He wasn't sure he knew anyone who didn't love a good cheeseburger or a perfectly grilled filet. "I noticed you didn't eat turkey yesterday, but it never crossed my mind."

"John, it doesn't offend me. I don't expect you to know everything about me…yet. This is all new."

No shit.

"You want me to take it off your plate?"

She shook her head. "How about I slide it onto yours? I bet you worked hard today and can handle some extra protein." She smiled and the pink faded.

For the next few minutes, they ate, silently chewing. John's mind flipped through how hard it was to start dating again, and Shelby's mind flipped through God only knew.

Wait. He wasn't dating. This was dinner essentially between two roommates. Roommates who'd had sex. But drunken sex didn't really count, did it? So why did it feel like a date?

Because Shelby was single and had spectacular breasts. Oh, he'd not forgotten their perfect plumpness topped with dusky pink nipples he'd seen only through the black lace bra. His mouth watered, so he picked up his beer, chastising himself for remembering how much he'd liked her rack.

Or maybe it felt like a date because whether he liked it or not, he *was* single…but without spectacular breasts, thank God. Having breasts might have made dating more challenging. Not that he was ready for dating.

Or maybe it felt like a date because he was nervous? For some reason, so much was at stake. He wanted to handle Shelby, the baby and becoming a father in the right way. But what was the right way? Up until now the only thing he'd managed to do was keep Shelby from flying back to Seattle. He hadn't thought much beyond that, and now she was here in his kitchen, living here, showering down the hall. He swallowed at the thought of Shelby naked, water sluicing down her curves. He'd never seen her naked, but he could imagine.

Don't, Beauchamp. Leave it alone.

"The Candy Cane Festival starts tomorrow.

Would you like to go? We could hear some music and, uh, eat?"

"Are you asking me out?"

Heat rose to his face. "No. I thought you might want to see more of the town. My parents sort of expect me to go. My cousin Richard's the mayor and the Beauchamp family always sponsors the lighting of the town tree."

"Sure. I've never been to a Christmas tree lighting."

He didn't respond, just finished off his steak, pulling the filet she'd delivered onto his plate into position. "We're not dating."

"I know. It's just some people might see us as more than what we are if we go out together."

"I don't care anymore." And he didn't. People had been bugging him to move on—go to football games, poker night, singles bingo at the church. Last year he hadn't gone to the festival. Hell, he hadn't acknowledged beyond a few presents for his niece and nephews that the holidays had even come. No tree, no colorful lights, no silly blow-up snowman in the yard. But this year he felt like acknowledging the season he'd always loved. He'd deal with Carla later. "Fact is, we'll always have something between us…and in almost seven months that something will be fairly evident."

Shelby poked at the salad. "They'll know that in two months unless I'm one of those women who doesn't look pregnant, just fat. We'll have to break the news to our families at some point. Or we could let everyone keep speculating."

Something sank in his stomach at the thought of sharing just how badly he'd screwed up on the anniversary of Rebecca's death. He knew out in the real world people had children out of wedlock all the time, but his family had always lived by the good book, expecting John and his siblings to follow the same. His father and mother weren't judgmental, but he suspected deep down they'd be disappointed in his lack of control, even as they understood what had propelled him to act so rashly. "Speaking of parents, how did yours react to you staying here in Magnolia Bend?"

Shelby glanced up, her eyes shuttering. "I sent my mother's assistant a memo instructing her to send my things. She hasn't called so I'm assuming she has little to say about it."

Wow. He must have made a face because she followed that with "My family's different than yours. We're not big on communication."

His family overcommunicated. If one stood up too fast, he might break the nose of a family member who had it in his business. "Would you like more salad? Dessert? I have ice cream."

Her laugh was dry as sand. "Families are tough, aren't they?"

He deadpanned, "Tough? Naw."

"Don't worry, I'll tell my parents about the baby… maybe when Junior is six or seven years old. I can attach the picture with the memo."

He said nothing because since Rebecca had died, he hadn't been good at handling his own family much less someone else's. Even so, he felt bad for the pretty woman shuffling salad around her plate, sorry that she had no one to depend on. His parents might be disappointed in him, but they would stand beside him, giving him whatever support he needed. He started to tell her this, but could see she didn't want sympathy.

Shelby sat silently for the rest of dinner, lost in thought. He allowed her to keep to herself, busying himself with picking up the plates and feeding Bart, who'd patiently waited on the kitchen rug, occasionally thumping his tail when someone cast an eye upon him.

"I'll grab your luggage," he said finally, after waiting several seconds for her to snap out of the reverie she'd fallen into.

She blinked. "Are you sure you want me to stay? Once I unpack my toiletry bag, it's done."

He studied her, taking in her bright blue eyes shining with doubt. "I want you here."

Something in her face relaxed, and he swore she looked relieved. "Then go grab my bag."

CHAPTER TEN

SHELBY SANK ONTO the bed with the faded pink quilt and eyelet-edged pillows.

"So this is it," she whispered, glancing around at the simple bedroom with its white furniture, muted blue braided rug and the sturdy rocker nestled in the corner. The large windows flanked a window seat and seemed to be the highlight of the room.

John came in rolling her suitcase and carrying a small Louis Vuitton bag. "Is this okay?"

"Fine, thank you," Shelby said, sounding more like she spoke to a bellman than the man she'd be living with for the next...she didn't even know how long she would stay. And when it came down to it, she still didn't know why she'd agreed to stay. The closest she came to any good reason was the look in John's eyes when he'd asked her. Something about the desire for something more had pulled at her, making her think staying in Louisiana was the right decision.

John waited for her to say something more. Finally, he cleared his throat. "Uh, you never told me what Jamison said today. I mean, if you don't mind my asking?"

"Of course not. Dr. French said everything looks good. No more spotting, the heartbeat is strong. I'm suffering from a little morning sickness, but he said that's a good sign. In a week I'll be officially into my second trimester and less likely to miscarry."

"I have a lot to learn."

"We both do," she said, taking the smaller bag and setting it on the window seat. "The room's nice."

"This was Rebecca's room growing up. We turned it into a guest bedroom. Mine's down the hall, uh, if you need anything," he said, shifting in his boots, darting a glance at her before clearing his throat. "You have your own bathroom right through there."

She turned toward where he gestured, noting the door leading into a dim room. "Perfect."

So uncomfortable. So much left unsaid. So much unknown.

"And there's a TV in the den with satellite TV, room in the fridge for things you like. Make yourself at home."

"I need to pay you something for letting me stay here. Put something toward utilities."

"No, you're a guest."

"Am I? Maybe in your mind, but in mine, I need to feel like I'm pulling my weight."

He studied her for a moment. "Fine. You can split utilities with me, but I'm not accepting rent. That feels silly."

"I can look for a place in town."

"Even sillier. You'd be alone."

"Maybe I want to be alone."

He didn't say anything else and instead averted his eyes from hers. For a few seconds he didn't speak. "Do you want me to look for a place for you?"

"Not really," she said, sinking back down on the bed, not understanding why she prodded him, why she'd suggested moving out when she'd just gotten there, when she knew he wanted her there. Of course, she didn't know why she did anything anymore.

John stood silent in the spare room, the room where his wife had no doubt played Barbie dolls or the Dating Game, looking as lost as she felt. After a moment, he straightened and with an enigmatic glance said, "Got to get to bed. Morning comes early."

"I didn't mean to sound ungrateful. You've stepped outside your comfort zone to give me a place to stay, to help me when I feel sort of...lost."

He opened his mouth to say something, but instead snapped it closed, nodded and backed toward the door. "Good night, Shelby."

"Good night, John," she said.

Bart appeared outside the door and followed his master down the hallway, leaving Shelby to her own mixed-up thoughts.

Shelby shut the door, and turning, she sank against it, fighting against asking John to come back so she wouldn't be alone, so she wouldn't be so conflicted about the decision she'd made to chuck her pseudo life in Seattle and stay in Magnolia Bend.

The knock at the door made her jump.

She opened it and stepped back to find John looking determined.

"Did you—" she asked, closing her mouth as he stepped toward her. His arms came around her, hauling her up against the hardness of his chest, as his mouth descended upon hers.

The kiss was everything John was—hard and punishing, then soft and hungry, but way too short.

He released her, stepping back, looking a bit shocked at his actions. "We're not dating."

Shelby swallowed. "Okay."

He pulled the door closed, the clip of his boots mimicking her racing heart.

"But I don't think we're just roommates," she said, lifting a hand to her lips.

CARLA LEAFED THROUGH the old photo albums. They sat next to her chair for easy access. She loved running a hand over the old photos of her and Hal's dating days. She'd been a little thing with a trim waist, bobby pin curls and pencil skirts. Then she graduated to bell bottoms and fringed vests while Hal showed off his mutton chops. And then the '80s with the shoulder pads and big earrings. And Rebecca.

Rebecca had been a gift from God.

She and Hal had struggled so long to have a child, losing one pregnancy after another, even burying a son who'd nearly made it full term.

They'd given up, resigned to a life with nothing to dote on but the teacup poodles Carla loved so much.

Then one day, she'd felt a flutter in her stomach.

Carla had been forty years old and assumed it was something she ate not agreeing with her, and so she ignored the successive gurgles in her stomach, frowning at her favorite jeans when they didn't button. Finally, fearing the worst of news, she'd gone to the doctor. A tumor had to be growing. Or maybe she suffered some other horrible malady. She prepared herself for bad news, but after the doctor completed the exam and called for an ultrasound of her stomach, she'd lost it. Crying and shaking at the lot she'd drawn in life, she'd lain there while the technician glided the transducer over her swollen stomach. How would she tell Hal she was likely dying?

When the doctor came in and asked her if she wanted to know the baby's sex, she nearly fell off the table.

"Baby?" she shouted. "What in the hell are you talking about?"

The doctor had looked confused. "You know you're pregnant, don't you? Jesus, Carla, you're five months along."

After crying for thirty minutes, Carla had laughed all the way home, windows down, wind catching hair she had to color with Miss Clairol every four weeks.

Rebecca had been a beautiful, wonderful gift.

Carla turned through the pages of hundreds of baby shots—first time eating carrots, first time in the pool, first recital—until she came to Rebecca and John's senior prom picture.

So young and already so in love.

Rebecca grinning up at John as she stuck him with the boutonniere pin. The next page showed them at college, backpacks slung as they stood in front of Rebecca's dorm at LSU. A few more pages and it was their wedding. John in his tux, Rebecca with Carla adjusting the veil, cake being crammed in mouths, limo pulling away.

Carla slammed the book closed, the sadness inside her replaced with something ugly. She knew this, but didn't stop herself from setting her course against this new relationship John pursued.

He can't do this, my sweet Rebecca. He can't write you off like you never existed, can't replace you with that woman. She's not going to live in the place you loved so much, claiming your life. It's not fair. Not fair.

Carla set the photo album carefully aside, causing Dim Sum, her apricot poodle, to lift his head and blink hazy eyes at Carla.

"Go back to sleep, Dim," Carla cooed before reaching for the address book she kept on the table between her chair and the huge beat-up recliner Hal had always kicked his feet up in. Though she had complained about it for years, she hadn't been able to dump the recliner. The man had loved the plush leather chair with its vibrating massage feature. To some degree, it felt as if he were still with her.

Running her finger down the column in her address book, she found the name she sought: Remy T. Broussard, attorney-at-law. Lifting the phone, she dialed the number of the man who had handled the Stanton trust. She'd never intended to wrench the farm and house from John. After all, he'd loved Rebecca and his grief had been palpable. And though she'd spent some time blaming him for Rebecca's death—him and that damn hunting and all those damn guns—she knew he'd suffered the loss of her daughter. Leaving him at Breezy Hill had been easier than facing the truth—that everything had changed when Rebecca died.

But she hadn't examined the results of the promise she'd made to John in the darkness of his grief. She hadn't foreseen the eradication of the Stantons from the land that had been theirs for nearly two centuries. John had stayed, working the land, existing as a shell of a man, throwing every waking hour into growing and harvesting the cane. For a while, it had been enough, but she owed him nothing more. Happiness couldn't be gifted to him so he could live out the dream he'd built with her daughter with another woman.

So John would have to choose—Breezy Hill or blondie.

That was Carla's ultimatum, unfair or deranged as it may seem.

After leaving a message for Remy to call her back, Carla hung up, settled into her chair and turned on her story, happy with the thought she still had power over something in her life. She didn't wish John ill, but she wasn't watching him get everything he wanted.

JOHN SPENT THE morning trying to forget the dumb-ass thing he'd done.

He *kissed* Shelby.

Last night something inside him snapped and he found himself reaching for her, hauling her against his body and kissing the daylights out of her…for no apparent reason other than he'd lost his mind.

He'd been going back to tell her about the shower—the cold and hot water lines connected backward—so she wouldn't get the shock of her life when she slipped into the shower. His mind had jumped to the fantasy of a voluptuous Shelby naked beneath the spray, water flowing down her sleek back, over her fine full ass.

When she'd opened the door, she'd had the look on her face—half little girl lost, half desirable woman. Before he knew it, she was in his arms. He'd surprised her, but she hadn't resisted. Instead she'd melted into him as if she'd been waiting for him to toss his resolve away.

She'd tasted like sadness and hope, bubble gum and something spicy and wonderful. Warm and tempting, Shelby's curves had softened against him, and desire flared inside him. All his good intentions of being a friend dissolved like a fart in the wind. All he'd wanted was to sink inside her, inhale her sultry scent and forget about how damn hard it was to live in the world in which he existed.

When he stepped away, her blue eyes had reflected raw desire. He'd been so tempted to step back inside and kiss her again, but good sense overrode the horniness rearing inside him.

Like a moron he'd stuttered, "We're not dating," and shuffled away.

But he'd lied.

Well, not lied. Because he and Shelby weren't dating...but they were something.

Homer rocked alongside John's tractor in the mule, his expression grim and his presence jarring John from contemplating what he had or didn't have with the pretty blonde he'd not seen since the night before. "Soldier harvester's down again. Gonna have to go over to Smiley's and see if I can't find a few parts that might hold her this season."

Damn it. He wanted to get the northwest field harvested to the ground and he'd need the soldier harvester. "Go see what you can find. I'll shift Red and the boys over to the south field. He's finished planting the new field with the LCP 85 sugarcane. Southeast field is cut to stubble and off to the mill."

Homer nodded and rolled away, leaving John to climb into the combine and tackle the field full of cane grown from first stubble. If he worked long enough today, they could get another two loads to the sugar mill. Thing was, he didn't want to work, which shocked the hell out of him. Work had been the only thing to keep him going this past year. He'd eaten, breathed and slept sugarcane, diversifying his crops, working a small plot of a test variety he'd played around with, even putting in some soybeans in the fields he'd burned off and plowed. Farming had been his life.

But tonight he would take Shelby to the Candy Cane Festival in Magnolia Bend.

People would stare. But that would be better than enduring their sympathetic glances. Having Shelby beside him would feel different. Occasionally she'd brush her arm against his, and the scent of her sultry perfume would tickle his senses. Those pretty lips would curve into a smile, tempting him.

He shouldn't be eager to be with Shelby tonight. Too soon to step off that ledge. After all, she'd shown up not even a full week ago with news that would have most men running.

But John hadn't run; he'd walked toward her.

For one year and three months, he'd been living in a near-catatonic state—numb and content to stay that way. Shelby's news about the pregnancy had been like putting a screwdriver into a light socket. He had snapped awake, disoriented to find himself back in the world he'd shut the door on. He didn't understand why...only that he'd come back from a hard place. Maybe all bereaved had the same experience—living in a fog until one day something or someone smacked them and they gasped for breath, claiming life over death.

Tonight he'd go to the Candy Cane Festival and take a deep grateful breath, even if he was scared as hell about how Shelby would fit into his life.

As the tractor rolled down the rows cutting the glossy cane to second stubble, John's mind drifted back to the last time he'd attended the Candy Cane Festival. Rebecca had missed her period and had immediately jumped to the conclusion she was pregnant. They'd been trying for so long and she'd been taking shots that made her crazy emotional. She swung from gleeful to depressed in the span of an hour. He'd been miserable trying to please her…trying to have sex with her after she checked basal temperatures or whatever she did. She'd even paged him from the field, causing the guys to crack jokes and break into renditions of "Afternoon Delight." And there had been nothing romantic about it—pants down, work up an erection and then think about the Asian porn he'd borrowed from his roommate in college. He'd hated trying to get pregnant with Rebecca because it made her not her normal self.

But that night at the tree lighting, his wife had glowed with happiness, hinting to his family how different things would be the next Christmas, making everyone's eyes dance with excitement over the thought of John and Rebecca finally becoming parents.

The next festival had been different all right just not in the way Rebecca had hinted.

The following Monday she'd started her period, and they'd spent the next few months with the same routine masquerading as a sex life, and by September Rebecca was dead.

So it would be bittersweet returning to the festival tree lighting with a pregnant Shelby—a virtual stranger to his family.

He closed his mind to the irony and rolled on, cane mowed down like men under assault, falling this way and that in neat little rows. If only life would fall into place as simply as the cane.

He'd learned nothing in life was simple, and having Shelby around, making decisions about the baby and dealing with the fact he wasn't a ghost of a man—that he had feelings and desires again—would not be easy.

The time he'd thought would never come had arrived. He was moving on without Rebecca.

But whether he could hold on to any expectation of something with the hot blonde living in his guest room remained to be seen.

CHAPTER ELEVEN

SHELBY CHANGED HER outfit three times, marveling at how her pants could be loose when she was nearly three months pregnant. She needed to be more cognizant of eating better, resting and practicing yoga or visualization or something that made her stomach relax from the knots twisting inside.

John kissing her hadn't relaxed the knots. Instead he'd tightened them with a new expectation whether she wanted to acknowledge it or not. His breaking through the barrier they'd established, the unwritten rules to their relationship they'd agreed upon standing in the garden only the day before, had allowed all the need, want and desire she'd shoved to the back of her mind to come forth. She'd never intended on John being anything but her baby's daddy.

But now she wasn't so sure about things.

As evidenced by her care in dressing. She pulled on jeans that slimmed and heels that lifted her ass. Selected a shirt that hinted at a little cleavage, and she'd taken special care with her makeup, highlighting her cheekbones, applying two coats of mascara and tracing her brow bones with shimmer. She'd walked into a cloud of Bond No. 9 Bleecker Street after her long hot shower and again fully dressed after she'd decided she'd have to deal with the silk blouse and somewhat loose jeans until she received her things from Seattle.

In other words, she treated tonight like it was special.

After slipping on her heels, she'd walked downstairs, passed the closed door where she could hear the shower still running, sat at the table and waited. It was a good ten minutes before the shower shut off, and then John bumped around up there, no doubt going through the same routine she'd just gone through. Without a bra and lipstick, of course.

Shelby listened to several voice mails from the substitute teacher bank and read a handful of emails from friends in Spain before John arrived with a smoothly shaved jaw and still-damp hair. The smell of Irish Spring tickled her nose as she registered the ridiculous-looking red-green-and-white-striped knitted sweater.

"Nice sweater."

He set a pile of magazines on the counter and looked down at his sweater. "Yeah, my sister knitted us all one to wear for the lighting every year. Kinda expected."

Shelby smiled because though he looked a little silly, he wore the somewhat misshapen sweater because he loved his sister. Pretty sweet guy. "It brings out your eyes."

"How can you tell? The only light is from the vent hood."

"I'm being positive."

"So I've noticed," he said, riffling through some papers on the built-in desk beside the door. Bart whined from his bed. "Can't come this time, Bart."

The dog's head sank to the floor.

Finally, John's eyes met hers, his gaze dropping, skimming the collar of her ice-blue silk blouse with the tiny triangle pattern, the gold belt with snazzy jeweled buckle and the ridiculously high heels she knew would make her feet hurt but wore anyway. After he finished taking her in, his gaze returned to hers. "You look like a rich girl."

"I am a rich girl, but that's not all there is to me."

"No, it's not, but you look like you're trying to make a statement."

Shelby unbuttoned the third button. "Only for you."

Awareness flared in the depths of his eyes. "You are something else, Shelby Mackey."

She didn't say anything because she was afraid he might say exactly what that was. *Something* was rather broad. Besides he'd used the same descriptor on Birdie days before.

"I shouldn't have kissed you," he said.

Her stomach took a nosedive. He regretted it. Of course he did. So why was he studying her lips like they were chocolate and he had PMS? "Maybe not. But you did."

Her words bounced and stuck. He moved back, tearing his gaze from her. "I should have listened to common sense. Nothing about going there again is a good idea. Sex is not what we need."

The hell you say.

"Presumptuous, aren't you?" She kept her tone light.

"Guess I've presumed a lot lately, but I wasn't talking about you. My words were at myself. Last time I listened to the voice below my belt and not the one in my head, we fell into a little trouble."

"You have a voice below your belt? Does your doctor know about this?" she teased.

He gave her an exasperated look.

"I know what you mean, John, but I wish you wouldn't regret the kiss. You have to stop beating up on yourself for feeling something."

"Maybe so," he said.

"You know what?" Shelby interrupted. "How about we let go of the guilt for now?"

He nodded slowly. "Maybe so."

"You like the word *maybe,* huh?" she said, picking up her purse, trying to move him from where he stood, figuratively and literally. More and more she realized John had spent a year on hold—no emotions, no laughter, no teasing, no wanting. That night in September, whether he knew it or not, he had moved back into the land of the living. But knowing and doing were two different things. Shelby knew firsthand. Her first love had turned out to be a creep, and her second had been in love with another woman. Like a dog with a bone, she'd held on, hoping she could force something meant to be.

But John clung to something that could never be.

Sometimes it was hard to let go and be moved. Staying put was instinctual, but fighting against the push and pull of change, unwilling to believe you have no control, was what everyone did. Eventually, destiny and fate would have their way.

Best thing to do was stop worrying about the destination and enjoy the journey. Or that's what she told herself daily.

John got her message about leaving and picked up his keys and followed her out the back door.

"I'll drive," she said, indicating the car she'd leased sitting in his drive.

"Something wrong with my truck?"

"No, but I need to get gas." Shelby dug her keys out of her bag and dangled them. "Or you could drive?"

"A car?"

"Oh, real men don't drive cars?"

"I can drive the hell out of a car, but I don't want the men in town thinking I've gone soft."

"Jeez, the machismo is thick around here," she said, glad he'd relaxed into someone easier to spend the evening with. Maybe he'd stop looking at her like a ticking bomb.

"We take our manhood seriously," he said, grabbing the keys.

Ten minutes later, after a detour for gas at The Shortstop, they pulled into the bank parking lot.

"We're a little late so no good spots left. I spent too much time in the fields," he said, taking her elbow when she nearly tripped stepping onto the curb. He looked down at her heels, his mouth indicating disapproval, but then something flickered in his eyes, a sort of acceptance of her frivolity or maybe even an appreciation of her attempt to please him. Yeah, Christian Louboutin knew what a man liked.

"You spent too much time primping," she teased.

His green eyes reflected mock outrage. "I ran out of hot water because someone was in the shower for three days."

"I had to shave my legs."

A flare of sexual awareness struck in the glow of Christmas lights strung around the Cut-N-Curl even though there was nothing really sexy about shaving legs. Well, unless it was in a porno—somehow those random hygiene procedures became opportunity for a three-way in the shower. But still, desire exploded right there in the middle of downtown Magnolia Bend.

John's eyes moved back down to Shelby's lips, and she licked them in response. Her senses did that woo-woo thing where everything zoomed in on the man in front of her and how he made an ugly sweater stretched across those broad shoulders look fetching. Maybe she could reach up and straighten his neckline. But as she lifted her hand, she realized it wasn't crooked, just knitted that way. John's hand on her arm, softened as he slid it up to—

A couple exited the Stitch-and-Thyme, destroying the electric pulses that had nothing to do with Christmas decorations.

"We should go before my family starts texting me," John said, gesturing toward the pavilion at the end of Main Street. Magnolia Bend had been built around two streets—Main Street and Front Street. In between the two sat a string of old businesses, including an ancient general store, a Western Auto straight out of the 1950s, a jewelry store, hair salon, resale shop and a small art gallery. Outside of each business was a table with refreshments. Passersby tugged children down the main drag and carolers clumped on street corners, heralding the season the town would launch with the lighting of the Christmas tree.

As they walked toward the small park, people stared. A few stopped to greet John, taking in Shelby with interest, smiling politely when he introduced her. It took them a lot longer than it should to reach where his family stood because John seemed to know everyone.

"Shelby," Fancy said, patting an older woman on the shoulder before breaking away and taking Shelby's hand. "You look precious. I love your hair down like that with those bouncy curls. How do you get them?"

"Um, curling iron," Shelby said, pasting on a smile as Fancy moved her toward the older woman.

"Of course," Fancy crowed, nodding like a bobblehead. "I want you to meet Hilda Brunet, she's a councilwoman and my first cousin."

The older woman wearing a St. John sweater and

Alexander McQueen flats regarded Fancy with tolerant affection...and Shelby with suspicion.

"So you're Shelby," the woman said, inclining a quite regal mane of silver, diamonds flashing at her ears. She swept Shelby with a discerning glance, lingering on her shoes. Shelby would bet her nonexistent paycheck the woman recognized Louboutin.

"Guilty," Shelby said, extending her hand, wincing at the older woman's bruising handshake.

Reverend Beauchamp talked to an older man she thought was Uncle Carney, but couldn't be sure because they stood in the shadows. A priest talked to John's oldest brother and his wife while their boys frolicked, playing tag or football or something little boys did when they were bored and a plot of grass was available. Abigail and Birdie stood nearby— Abigail talked to a woman wearing a costume and Birdie tapped on her phone. Big happy family moment.

"So, John has skipped dating and gone straight to shacking up," Hilda said.

"Shacking up?" Shelby asked.

"Yes, I know it's not as frowned upon these days, but his father is a man of God."

Shelby dropped the woman's cold hand and looked at Fancy, who'd turned the color of a radish. "What does that have to do with my staying in his spare room?"

Hilda fake-chuckled, but her eyes remained granite chips. "Not a thing other than people do talk.

Such a shame to have aspersions cast on the Beau-champ family for no good reason."

"Well, do you have a spare bedroom?" Shelby asked, unwilling to let the judgmental councilwoman make her look like a freaking whore because she stayed at Breezy Hill. Sure, she had a few fantasies about the man, but she hadn't straddled him…yet.

"I beg your pardon," Hilda said, her condescending attitude deflating a bit.

"I can stay with you if you have room," Shelby said with a smile. "Unless you're afraid of people talking? I don't swing that way, but you might not want people to asperse."

Fancy clapped a hand over her mouth, her eyes the size of Texas. Finally, a laugh escaped. "See, Hildy, I told you you'd love her. She dresses and acts just like you."

Hilda snorted. "Yeah, she's pretty good."

Weird. Cousin Hildy obviously played the role of ball-busting family matriarch who demanded feistiness from an, uh…well, hell, Shelby didn't know who she was to the family. At present it was soon-to-be mother of a Beauchamp. Not that any of them knew.

"Thank you," Shelby said, "I think."

Hilda Brunet gave her a shark smile. "Oh, honey, it's definitely a compliment. We Beauchamps don't suffer our men pairing off with weak women. Dilutes the gene pool."

Shelby nearly choked, but was saved from further

awkwardness by John's father. "Evening, Shelby. Nice of you to come with John to the lighting."

"I appreciate the invitation. I haven't seen much of the town. Very pretty when dressed up for the holidays."

"Isn't it?" The man regarded the town sparkling before him. "Nothing like a small town Christmas."

"I wouldn't know."

"Are you staying through Christmas, dear?" Fancy asked, casting an indecipherable glance to her husband, making Shelby wonder about Hilda's earlier words. John's father *was* a pastor. Did they disapprove of her staying with John?

"Depends," Shelby replied, looking over at John. "I need to make some decisions about my career."

"Matt, come over here and talk to Miss Mackey about teaching jobs," Hilda drawled, reminding Shelby of Olympia Dukakis's role in *Steel Magnolias*. Bored droll Empress of the town.

Matt excused himself from speaking to Father Whoever He Was and stepped over. "A teaching job?"

"Shelby's a teacher in…in…I can't remember what you told me," Reverend Beauchamp said.

"Math," John finished.

"Oh, I must have missed that at Thanksgiving dinner," Matt said. "So you're a secondary teacher?"

Shelby nodded. "I've taught everything but Calculus."

A smile appeared on the man's rather severe features. "This is too good to be true."

Shelby must have looked confused.

"Our Algebra I teacher had surgery earlier this month and suffered complications. She had planned to be back in the classroom after Thanksgiving, but can't come back until after Christmas break. You'd be helping us out if you'd come sub."

"Oh," Shelby said, taken aback by the opportunity tossed in her lap. "I wasn't expecting to find something so soon."

Matt frowned. "So you're not looking for a position?"

"I am," she rectified, something inside her waffling over making her stay so permanent. She had moved in with John, telling herself she could leave within a few weeks if it didn't work out. Taking a job in Magnolia Bend would make it a bit harder to bail. But teaching would give her something to occupy her time, something to give her purpose.

"It's not permanent. Much depends on Mrs. Fox's recovery. You can work as a substitute for the next month and perhaps the following one. At the very least, subbing would give you time to look around for a permanent position within our district."

John glanced at her, awaiting her answer.

"Sounds perfect," Shelby said with a little shrug, agreeing before anything inside her could toss up a reason not to help John's brother. Since finding out she was pregnant, she'd felt lost. Snatching at the opportunity to stay with John and teach in Magnolia Bend felt a little desperate, a little unreasonable, but at the same time it felt meant to be. Maybe she'd been brought to this exact place and time for a larger purpose. Or maybe she wanted to believe that in order to justify her rash decisions.

"Father Finnegan, come meet the answer to our problem," Matt said, calling to the priest who had stopped to chat with Birdie. Shelby noted Birdie looked a bit guilt-stricken at conversing with a man of the cloth. Peeping at naked men had a way of making a girl feel…oh, who was Shelby kidding? She'd seen the ass on their neighbor. Couldn't fault the kid for admiring a work of art.

Father Finnegan fit every image she'd ever had of Friar Tuck down to the fringe above his ears and flushed cheeks. "The devil you say."

Oh, and he was Irish and said Old English–sounding things. Totally adorable.

"This is Miss—"

"Mackey," Shelby filled in, extending her hand. "I'm new to Magnolia Bend and will be here until Christmas—"

"Or longer," John interjected, which made his family's collective ears perk up. She'd never seen something like that actually happen, but apparently ear-perking was a real thing.

"Or longer," she agreed. "I'm certified in secondary Math and can pitch in to help out."

The priest clapped his hands together. "This is fantastic."

She'd been hoping for *jolly good* or *smashing,* but *fantastic* worked.

"You can start…Monday?" Matt asked.

"As long as her doctor gives her the all clear," John said, setting a hand on her shoulder, making her feel protected. She shouldn't like that feeling, but she did. She craved someone to care.

Pathetic.

"Doctor?" Fancy repeated, her eyes narrowing. "Are you sick?"

"Not anymore," Shelby clarified. "I can start Monday."

She smiled through the questioning looks from John's family, but was saved from having to explain further by the screech of the microphone.

Like salmon, the crowds skirting the darkened park streamed toward the charming white platform with the gingerbread trim and the rotund man clad in red and white fussing with the microphone. The silent Christmas tree, gold tinsel glinting occasionally, waited to be set ablaze.

"Whew," John breathed, moving to stand beside her.

Shelby looked up at him as everyone fell into a small semicircle, facing the mayor and the choir clad in festive red robes assembling onstage. Not bad for a first da—whatever this was. She wasn't going to try and label her and John's evening…just enjoy it.

The microphone screeched again. "Sorry, folks," the mayor said, cupping the mic and giving a sheepish grin. A few men catcalled and everyone laughed, seemingly in good spirits.

"Are we good, Jimbo?" the mayor said into the mic. A plump man wearing candy cane suspenders gave him a thumbs-up. "Good, now let me try this again."

He extended his hands. "I'm Mayor Richard Burnside, and I want to welcome kith, kin and those of you who found your way here by accident to the thirty-second Magnolia Bend Candy Cane Festival."

A cheer went up and John leaned close. "Bet you never thought you'd be here on a Saturday night."

Shelby whispered, "It's cute. I like it."

"You say that now, but wait until the cloggers take the stage."

"What are cloggers?"

"You'll find out, but walk with me for a minute." John jerked his head toward the wide space behind the gathered crowd. As unobtrusively as possible, Shelby faded into the darkness with him. Behind the pavilion, a few kids, including John's nephews, ran around tossing a football. A few teens clumped together, faces aglow in the light of their cell phones, around benches circling a huge live oak. Beyond this area sat a small playground.

"Sometimes being with my family is like being underwater holding your breath. Gotta come up for air."

Shelby matched his stride on the brick pathway leading to the playground. "They don't bother me, though I think they're all confused by my moving in with you. I'm afraid your father doesn't approve, your mother has false expectations of romance and your sister will figure the baby thing out soon. Or Hilda. This secret might not be a secret long."

"You think I should tell them about the baby?"

Shelby shook her head. "Not for me to decide."

John said nothing, merely headed toward the bank of swings. He sank onto the curved blue plastic, digging his boots into the worn dirt beneath. Shelby took the swing beside him.

"I'll wait a bit longer I guess," he said, releasing his feet and allowing the swing to fall forward. "I don't know what the hell I'm doing here."

"Neither do I," she said, following his motion, careful to lift her shoes above any mud that might be present. "I don't think there are rules, John."

For a moment he said nothing, just kicked the swing into motion, the creak of metal against metal a keening moan in the darkness.

"I want you," he said matter-of-factly as if he might have said "might rain tomorrow."

Shelby planted her feet, slipping a bit in the high heels, and the swing hit the back of her thighs. He wanted her.

John, however, didn't stop swinging. For a few seconds, she stood wondering what to say to him, feeling something warm slip around her heart and squeeze it. Not to mention how the tinderbox of her loins fired at the raw statement. The sexy night folded around them, intimate despite the celebration going on a football field length away.

"I don't want to want you. I shouldn't," he said, still not looking at her, still swinging.

Shelby sank back into the swing, regarding the lonely, tortured man, who was able to address his desire only in the cloak of darkness. After a moment, she reached out and caught the chain of his swing, bringing him toward her. John stood, still clutching the chains of the swing.

"Why are you so afraid?" she asked. "Don't you know everyone carries fear? Everyone hurts?"

He stared at her, his eyes shrouded in the night. Still she could feel them move over her, weighing her words. "I don't want to feel that way again," he said. "I lost Rebecca and it took a piece of me. I'll never get that back."

His words sliced at her and she didn't know why. Why should she care? She didn't love John. Her need to have him beneath her, above her, inside her was nothing more than a product of nature. She felt bad for him, liked him most of the time, but nothing else. So why did it feel like he'd punched her when he said he didn't want to want her?

"Well, I'm not Rebecca. You don't know me."

He let go of the swing and lifted a hand, cupping her face, tilting it up to the glow of the moon peeking from behind the darkened clouds. His calloused thumb stroked her cheek. "I know who you are."

"No, you don't."

His gaze moved over her, caressing the stubborn chin she lifted to him, perhaps yearning for the mouth she'd colored rum raisin. "Shelby, you're so damn pretty."

The tinderbox exploded at the need shining in his eyes, and flames licked her body. She swallowed hard, seeking his firm mouth with eyes she knew reflected the desire welling inside her. God help her, but she wanted to heal him, wanted to show him that heartache could be healed…if only with her touch.

With her lips.

"All I can think about is how good you tasted that night," he said, his gaze still on her mouth.

"I thought you didn't remember that night."

"I remember some things. Like how you tasted of wine, like something so good I had to have just one kiss," he murmured, lowering his head, his thumb tracing her lower lip just before his mouth covered hers.

A moan escaped her as his arm curved around her back, bringing her against him. She tilted her head, opening her mouth enough to taste him. He tasted like mint, warm and good. She lifted a hand to his jaw, thrilling at the feel of his body hard against the softness of hers. Being held by John felt too damn good.

He broke off the kiss and studied her in the moonlight. "See? I can't seem to help myself."

Shelby licked her lips. "I know."

And then he lowered his head again, this time sliding his hand into her curls, tugging her hair gently, making her open to him. His mouth was hungry, moving over hers, nipping her lower lip. His tongue dipped into the heat of her mouth, stroking her, amping the liquid heat pooling in her pelvis. Her breasts, tender from the pregnancy hormones surging through her body, ached for his touch. She felt aflame and devoured his mouth with equal enthusiasm.

Finally, breathing hard, John broke the kiss and stepped back, his breath little puffs in the cool night air. Shelby, matching the rhythm of his breaths, lifted a hand to her mouth, turning away.

"I'm sorry," John said.

Shelby shook her head. Why did he apologize after every kiss? But, of course, this was the way it had been from the beginning. John with his guilt and tears and regret standing in the bathroom of Boots Grocery. Apologizing for wanting her had become a habit.

She stepped away, sinking onto the swing she'd abandoned. The creak of the metal hinges might as well have been a scream in the night. John looked guilt-stricken standing beneath the low branch of the oak bowing over the climbing structure. At that moment she wanted to punch him as much as she wanted to kiss him again.

"Know what?" she said.

He turned to her. "What?"

"Don't kiss me again. Don't touch me again."

He stretched out his hands. "Shelby, I'm—"

"No." She held up a finger. "Every time you touch me you apologize. Like I'm a goddamn disease. How do you think that makes me feel?"

"I'm sorry. I—"

"There it is again—the apology," she snapped. Nothing made a gal feel worse than a man being sorry for kissing her. Okay. Crying after sex was worse. "Just go. I want to be alone for a little while, and I'm sure your family wonders where you are."

"No," he said, shaking his head. "Look, I screwed up."

"And that's your lot in life, isn't it? Messing up, apologizing for it and, what? Expecting everyone to say 'poor John, his wife died' and then accepting you being a shit?"

"Don't go there."

"Why? Because you like being the walking wounded? Do you think you're the only person who has ever survived a spouse dying?"

"Shut up," he said, pointing a finger at her.

"No," she said, turning her head from him. "You need to hear something besides 'poor John.'"

"Stop it, Shelby."

"You don't have the right to tell me to stop it. I'm the woman you knocked up and apologized to for feeling something besides grief. How do you think that makes me feel?"

He said nothing.

"It makes me feel like I need to go back to Seattle and forget trying to do whatever the hell we're doing. You don't want to stop grieving. You don't feel anything for me." Her words made her chest ache. She was angry and crushed at the same time.

"You know that's not true. You know I want you here. I care about you."

"Because I carry your child. If that wasn't an issue, you wouldn't be standing here with me."

Shelby inhaled, trying to keep the tears at bay. She did *not* feel sorry for herself and she wasn't begging John for anything. He needed to hear the truth.

"Of course not," he said. "Because you wouldn't be here. You'd be back in Seattle, forgetting about me and the dumb-ass thing you did in a bathroom one night. And, I really don't want to hear you talk about my grief. You have no right."

Shelby stood, hands clenched, so she wouldn't smack him. "I may not have any right, but I'm obviously the only person who will tell you to snap the hell out of it and stop feeling guilty because you're here and she's not."

His face froze, anger flashing in his eyes. "You don't know what you're talking about. You don't know anything about me or Rebecca."

"No, I don't. But I'm not stupid. I see what you're doing, hiding from life, running from everyone, apologizing for feeling desire. Who lives like that, John?"

He grabbed her arm, dragging her and the swing to him. "Who do you think you are? A shrink? I've had counseling. I know what I feel. I know what I'm doing."

She stuck her chin out and glared at him. "So why are you still clinging to death? Why won't you let yourself feel something?"

His breath came fast, just like before, but this time it was fueled by a new emotion. "Because you scare me."

His words slammed into her and at that moment

she got it. She understood. The attraction he had for her had knocked him down and dragged him along for the ride, and now he was running, searching for a way to get back to something he could control.

For a moment, they both faced off against one another, intense, angry and wary.

Shelby lifted her hand and patted John's cheek. "Good. Because that means you're running from something you can actually do something about rather than something you can't."

Then she walked away, heading back to where the First Presbyterian Church choir sang "Silent Night."

"Hey," John called, his voice still pissed. "What are you doing?"

"Going back to the festival," she called over her shoulder, not slowing. She'd punched him in the face with her words, and he needed time to think about them. She needed time to think about them.

Her heels clicked on the brick, and rightness settled between her shoulder blades. Or maybe John shot daggers at her with his glower and that was the cause of the sensation. Still, she knew the words she'd thrown at him had been necessary if they were going to, well, she couldn't say move forward in their relationship because there were no definitions on what they had.

"Shelby," Abigail said, catching her out of the corner of her eye just as the crowd applauded the choir exiting the stage. A horde of girls in fluffy red skirts with ribbons wound around their calves trotted on stage. "Where have you been?"

"John and I stepped away for a moment," Shelby said, shifting away from the suspicious inn owner. She didn't want any lectures or warnings about pursuing something with John. Instead, Shelby fell into place beside Hilda, who watched the kids clacking around the stage to "Rockin' Around the Christmas Tree." She turned to Shelby. "Our John needs to step away more often if you ask me. He needs some lagniappe in his life."

"What's land yap?"

"French for a 'little something extra,'" Hilda said, returning her eyes to the girls making an inordinate amount of noise. "Our John needs something extra."

"Or he needs a kick in the ass," Jake said, sidling up to Shelby and giving her a smile that on anyone less handsome would be deemed slimy. "You're looking lovely this evening, Shelby."

"Mmm," Shelby said, not wanting to encourage John's brother, who looked more interested in the buttons on Shelby's blouse than his brother's need for something extra…and that bothered her. Not Jake being overconfident in his sexual prowess. He was hot and deserving of the ego, but the fact Jake hadn't gotten the message she belonged to John.

No, wait. She did not belong to John. The dense man she now lived with, who had just kissed her senseless, would not make a claim so she'd have to deal with Jake herself.

"Aunt Hildy, you look just as delicious," Jake said, bestowing a kiss on the older woman's cheek.

Hilda pinched Jake's cheek. "Save it for the whores at Ray-Ray's."

Jake laughed. "I don't need flattery at Ray-Ray's, Aunt Hildy. Just money for drinks."

Hilda snorted.

"What about you, Shelby? Wanna come check out the scene at Ray-Ray's?"

"Sounds like a load of fun, but I'll pass," Shelby said, watching one little girl miss a few steps and look as if she might cry. Shelby knew that little girl all too well.

Keep stompin', sister. You can do it.

"Come on," Jake said, his minty breath caressing her ear.

"Look, Jake, you're not my type."

He laughed. "Ah, you like the strong, silent and grump-ass type, huh? I get it, and actually, I'm relieved."

Shelby turned to John's younger brother, who wore tight jeans and a long-sleeved polo shirt. The ugly holiday sweater looped about his neck, proving Jake Beauchamp didn't march to anyone's beat but his own. And, Lord, was he gorgeous. Rugged and rangy, Jake had dimples, baby-blues and *that* look. *That* look had no actual name, but it signified the fact Jake could likely get a gal out of her panties, screw her silly, never call again and the gal would still be grateful because he'd been so damn good. Jake was a modern-day Paul Newman. Dangerous.

"Why?"

"'Cause you're waking him up."

"John and I are friends."

"So that's why he can't keep his eyes off you."

Shelby made a face. "You don't know what you're talking about."

"Oh, I know," he said with a secret smile. "And you do, too. John, however, is clueless, but give him time."

Shelby ignored Jake, instead clapping as the Creole Cutie Cloggers bowed, wiggling little fingers at their parents. She didn't have to turn around to know John stood behind her. She could smell his clean scent, sense his presence. Something inside her went still even as her pulse increased.

Damn Jake Beauchamp. How could he see what John couldn't?

John's fingers were light as they brushed her arm, almost an apology. She jerked away.

He leaned forward, but she hissed under her breath, "Don't you dare say it."

John stepped back, solidifying their festive night as a disaster.

It had begun with perfume, French lace and great expectation, and had ended like a dog turd on a blanket of white snow.

CHAPTER TWELVE

JOHN SAT AT the table sipping coffee that could strip furniture, wondering if Shelby would emerge from the bedroom. He glanced at his watch: 10:00 a.m. If she didn't hurry, he'd be late for church. He'd invited her to attend services at his father's church last night despite the anger and regret that still spun in his gut.

She'd poked him with a stick, saying hard things. Mean things. He hadn't wanted to hear them, but she didn't seem to take that into consideration.

So different from Rebecca.

His wife and his new roommate weren't merely polar opposites physically—their personalities were night and day.

Rebecca's rebukes had been like Novocain. She'd carefully place the criticism and give it time to work. Her gentle corrections likely came from her interaction with children who had special needs, but Shelby struck hard and fast with her accusations. She was the Bruce Lee of argument.

Yet Shelby had been breathtaking to behold—blue eyes narrowed, lush mouth pressed into a stubborn line and those magnificent breasts heaving. Even if his first inclination was to smack her silly for the hateful words she'd thrown at him, his next inclination was to slam her up against the oak tree, rip off her blouse that hinted at puckered nipples and shut her up in the most delicious of ways. She infuriated him. She tempted him. She made him feel.

Church probably wasn't a good place for him at the moment.

Her footfalls on the back stairs, which led directly into the kitchen, jarred him from his thoughts. Anticipation fluttered in his gut.

First came bare feet, then the curve of her gorgeous legs, and then a fluffy pink robe. Finally, a mussed and makeup-free Shelby alighted in the kitchen. "Oh, you're still here," she said.

"I take it you're not going to church with me?"

"You take it right," she said, opening a cabinet before closing it and opening another.

"Why not?"

"If you must know, I need some space."

"Space," he repeated, relieved it wasn't about church. John wasn't a Bible thumper and had spent a year blaming God for what had happened to Rebecca, but he was also the quintessential preacher's kid, a streak of rebellion twined around beliefs instilled when he was knee-high.

"Besides I'm not feeling so hot this morning," she said, frowning at the cabinets. "Where are the mugs?"

He stood so quickly his own coffee sloshed. "Are you okay? Are you bleeding again?"

She pressed a hand toward him. "Sit. I'm fine. I'm just really, really tired. Since I'm starting at St. George's tomorrow as a substitute, I wanted to sleep in. Feel like I have a sleep hangover is all."

"Oh," he said, sinking back into the chair. "Mugs are over the coffeemaker."

"Makes sense," she said, starting the kettle, presumably for tea. She leaned against the sink, watching him the way a blackbird would regard a scarecrow.

He didn't say anything for a moment, just became very aware of how pretty she looked barefoot and pregnant. Her breasts strained against the robe, and her curvy hips were magnified by the tight belt at her waist. With her golden hair and lips stained pink from the lipstick she'd worn last night, she looked like Marilyn Monroe. And God help him, but he wanted to pick her up, take her upstairs and go back to bed. And not sleep.

She kept the stare steady and it made him uncomfortable.

"What?" he said finally.

"You look nice," she said, turning and digging out another expired tea bag from the Orchard tea tin.

He wore a Southern Tide gingham plaid shirt, a navy sweater vest and khaki trousers with oxford bucks peeking out from the cuff. Little too frat boy, but his mother always shopped at Perlis in Uptown New Orleans when she shopped at Christmas. Rebecca had always rolled her eyes at the preppiness of his dress clothes. "Thank you."

"Like a Southern planter," she said, not quite smiling.

"If the bucks fit," he said, wiggling a foot before rising. "I'll be back later. We always have Sunday lunch at my parents and then I'll have to go back out in the fields this afternoon."

"I don't want to go to lunch. I told you—I need space."

"Shelby, I don't want things to be awkward between us. Last night I—" He stopped because he didn't know what to say. She'd gotten pissed when he apologized to her, so he couldn't come out and say he was sorry for ruining everything between them by being horny.

Shelby watched him struggle. "Hard to come up with something other than *I'm sorry,* isn't it?"

He made a face.

"Here's the deal, John. You and I are two people who are in limbo right now. You're coming out of something I can't imagine going through, and I'm coming off getting dumped. We're attracted to one another and about to become parents, so I think we should give each other a break for not knowing what to say sometimes. So don't sweat it, but also know this—"

He swallowed because he knew what she was going to say.

"Don't touch me, don't kiss me, don't screw me again until you can do so without apologizing for it. I'm worth more than that."

Not what he thought she was going to say.

She turned around, effectively dismissing him, humming "Walking in a Winter Wonderland."

For a few seconds he stood there like an idiot, watching her, wondering if he should respond to that particular statement.

Did that mean she wanted him to touch her? Kiss her? Rip her clothes off and do it right this time?

Swallowing, he picked up his Bible, looked at the gilded words and tucked it beneath his arm, hoping smoke didn't erupt when it touched his skin.

You already messed up that night at Boots, John. Let's not go any further with this. You can control your passions. You can control your feelings. Shelby is a friend and not a sex object. Shelby is the mother of your child, and you feel nothing for her other than the care and concern you would feel for any fellow human being.

He scooted the chair back underneath the table and picked up his keys. "I'll bring you a plate from Mama's."

"Okay," she said, tossing the tea bag into the trash and petting Bart, who'd finally risen from his foam bed in the corner.

Thou shall not lie echoed in his head as he pushed out the back door.

Yeah, he was a big ol' fat liar because he could profess all he wanted to himself, but fact was he

wanted Shelby in a most carnal way and no good
intentions would take that away.

Either way—lust or lie—John Beauchamp was a
Sunday sinner.

SHELBY TOOK A long hot shower, scrubbing her body
with a loofah she found in a drawer. By the time
she got out she was the color of a Louisiana craw-
fish and smelled like lilacs. After pulling on her
nightgown because she wasn't ready to get dressed
yet, she sank onto the bed and tried to leaf through
the magazines she'd already looked through the day
John brought them to her. Maybe she should have
gone to church with John.

No, she wasn't ready to make that sort of commitment. Staying with John seemed intimate enough,
but insinuating herself into his faith, into the very
fabric of his life, was too much too fast.

Sighing, she tossed the *People* magazine onto the
soft quilt folded at the foot of the bed and looked
around the room. Soft blush paint covered the
walls, and an old window twined with grapevine
hung above the bed. It had a mid-1990s feel, a sort
of folksy shabby chic rather than clean lines, but it
suited the house with its high ceilings and warm
honey hardwood floors. But the best part of the room
was the window seat with an overstuffed blue ticking cushion and plump pillows. A stack of books sat
forgotten in one corner.

Shelby went over and sat, tilting back so the sunshine warmed her shoulders. Tucking her bare feet under one pillow, she riffled through the books. The top one was a book of Emily Dickinson poems, which didn't interest her at all. Love, death and birds. Blah. The next book made her lift her eyebrows. *Kama Sutra?* She scanned it to see if there were any pages marked—there weren't—and then set it aside separate from the poetry. She went through the rest quickly, relegating the literary books along with self-help and Bible study books into the not-interested pile. When she finished, all that was left in her pile was the *Kama Sutra* and a journal.

She picked up the journal with the beautiful tan leather, bound with a braided cord that wrapped around a silver vintage button. Unwrapping the cord, she opened it to the first page.

To my sweet Rebecca. May you find yourself in these pages and may you chart the journey of a lifetime. Love, Mother.

Shelby flipped to the first page, which bore the date January 1, 2002. She read the first page written in sloping, almost boyish cursive.

So my mother says I should keep a journal of my thoughts the way she did as a new bride. She says it will help me understand who I am and mark the way I change as I grow into the woman I'm meant to be. So first question—are mothers always right?

Shelby closed the journal quick as a cat, the snap echoing in the silence of the house where the woman who'd penned those words had lived, loved and then surrendered to death. Sudden tears pricked Shelby's eyes.

These were Rebecca Beauchamp's private thoughts. No, not just her thoughts, but her dreams, her doubts, her very essence. So did John know his wife's journal sat among a random stack of books? If he had, wouldn't he have tucked it away somewhere, someplace in his room away from random prying eyes?

Shelby stroked the cover before winding the leather strap around the pretty button. She wanted to read more, but knew it wasn't right to pry into the intimate thoughts of John's dead wife.

But it was so very tempting.

In between the covers was the key to knowing the enigmatic man who ran hot one moment, but cold the next. If she read Rebecca's words, she might know how to better handle the situation she found herself in, but that would be totally, emphatically wrong.

As soon as John got home, she'd address the issue with him.

Her phone vibrated on the antique dresser and Shelby scooped it up.

Her own mother.

"Hello," Shelby said, wondering what fresh hell she'd invited by answering the call.

"Shelby?"

"Yes, Mother. You dialed my number."

"Didn't sound like you. Good heavens, you've already picked up a Southern accent." Marilyn Mackey didn't sound amused. Rather critical.

"Not yet," Shelby said, setting the journal back on top of the stack she'd separated as poor reading material. The lonely *Kama Sutra* stared back at her, reminding her it was a rather kinky reading choice for a woman who had the hots for the man down the hall.

"Good," Marilyn said. In the background Shelby could hear her mother leafing through some papers. She glanced at her watch and realized it was eight o'clock in Seattle. Her mother had slept in, and after reading the paper, would head to the club for a light brunch and a round of golf with Shelby's father. Sunday was their together day. "Now tell me why you requested Carol send your things? I thought you planned to stay in Seattle while Darby completed his MBA?"

"I never said Darby was going to get his MBA."

"So why are you staying in Mississippi?"

"Louisiana."

"Yes. Wherever."

"I like it here, and there is nothing to keep me in Seattle."

"Other than your family and the fact this is your home."

Shelby wanted to say something snide like "Really?" but didn't because being a smart-ass never worked with her mother. The woman dealt with egocentric male executives all day long and never blinked. A pissy daughter was a piece of cake. "I've always enjoyed traveling, Mother, and I never planned on living in Washington State. I'm going to stay here for a while." *With a man I met in a bar. Oh, and by the way, I'm pregnant.*

She didn't say that, of course.

Maybe she should. Then her mother would cut ties and turn the "Shelby is such a disappointment" into "Shelby? Who is she?"

"Well, do what you wish. We missed you for Thanksgiving. Uncle Thad flew in from Glasgow and you missed seeing him."

"Oh, sorry to have missed him."

"So what about Darby?"

"What about him?"

The silence hung, answer enough.

Shelby sighed. "Okay. Fine. I didn't come down here to spend the holiday with him. We're no longer together."

"Oh?"

She just couldn't say it. Telling her mother Darby had been married made her feel like the stupid girl who'd given her heart and virginity away years before. Fool me once and all that. "Time apart didn't make us fonder."

"So why are you in Louisiana?"

Shelby heard the turn of the page and wondered how much attention her mother gave her. "I had some unfinished business here. That's all."

Silence again. Was her mother waiting for an explanation?

"I'm actually taking a temporary teaching job. A school needs a sub for Algebra."

"You're interviewing for jobs down there? Why in the world would you be interested if you and Darby are no longer together? Doesn't compute." Her mother's voice didn't hold displeasure, merely befuddlement.

"Sometimes decisions don't compute, but that doesn't mean they shouldn't be made. I'm not making any definitive decisions. Just weighing options."

"Well, your father's waiting on me to dress. The Carlisles are meeting us for brunch. Their son Carter is home for the next few weeks while he applies for residencies. You always liked Carter."

"Sure. He's a nice guy." If a gal was into dudes who picked their noses when they thought no one was looking and argued about things he knew nothing about. Oh, and liked to talk about skin disease, but that could be because he'd always wanted to be a dermatologist.

"I heard his mother mention you as a possible date for Christmas Around the Clock…if you were here." Shelby heard no more rustling of papers and knew her mother had folded the *New York Times* and placed it on the glass table next to her chair in the morning room. Yes, her mother called it the morning room.

"I'm not interested in Carter or a snooty charity ball for that matter. Besides he's too young for me. I babysat him once."

"He's four years younger…and a doctor," her mother said.

"That doesn't make him any more appetizing. Degrees don't matter to me, remember?" Shelby said, tossing back the words her mother had thrown at her more than twice in her life.

Elaborate sigh. "Fine, Shelby, it's your life. You've always made it crystal clear you will go your own way. I wish you the best even if living thousands of miles away and teaching Algebra is what you choose for yourself."

"Thank you, Mother."

"Have to run now. Let me know if you will be home for Christmas. I have to give the caterers a head count."

"What about Mosa?"

"Saved her vacation time so she could go home to South Africa for a month. At the worst time of the year, too."

Of course her mother would see Mosa wanting to be with her family at Christmas for the first time in twenty years an inconvenience. Shelby started to point out how incredibly selfish it was to resent their housekeeper for taking the vacation she more than earned looking after the Mackeys for two decades. But she didn't. Instead, the devil prodded her to do something awfully immature. Something almost evil for a Sunday morning. "Oh, by the way, I meant to tell you I'm pregnant. You'll be a grandmother in June. Tell Daddy I said hello. The Carlisles, too."

"Ah," her mother said. "Ah, what? Did you—"

"Gotta go," Shelby chirped. "Talk to you next Sunday."

She pressed the end button.

"Oh, my God," she said into the empty room. Then she tossed the phone on the bed and flopped down beside it, causing the do-not-read stack of books to landslide toward her. Rebecca's journal landed on her stomach.

Her phone vibrated insistently.

Shelby giggled, pressing her hand over her mouth. Yep, in true Shelby fashion she'd shocked her mom right out of her Gucci slippers. And no matter what, she wasn't going to answer the ringing phone.

But then her phone chirped.

Holy cow poop. Her mother had texted her. Marilyn never texted because she considered it tasteless as a form of conversation.

Call me back. Now.

Not on your life, Mother.

Shelby picked up the journal and studied it against the bright light haloing her hands. The phone on the bed stopped vibrating, magnifying the stillness of the house. Running a finger around the slightly frayed edge of the leather, Shelby laid the journal on her chest.

Looking up, she could see the ceiling fan needed dusting, but she could also picture Rebecca as a girl lying on the bed, looking up at the same gray ceiling trimmed with white molding. What had Rebecca dreamed about?

John?

Or had she dreamed of being a fashion designer? Or maybe she'd prayed to make cheerleader? Or hoped to get the prized solo in the choir? Dreams, prayers, hopes…that's what being a girl entailed.

A sudden warmth grew in Shelby's stomach, radiating throughout her body. She often received the same sort of peaceful intuitiveness when she practiced Shavasana in her yoga class, when she connected to herself. Strange to feel so reflective and at peace after a difficult conversation with her mother.

Yet, lying in the small space with nothing but the warm sun shining in and the wind tangling the chimes on the porch, Shelby felt touched by something she couldn't begin to describe.

Her fingers fanned the pages still held tight between the cover of the journal. Lifting the journal off her chest, she slowly unwound the cord looped round the button and touched the first entry.

Dear journal (or Becca! Ha-ha)
Today I went to Mama and Daddy's new house

to take a few things they left behind. Still can't believe they let John and me have Breezy Hill all to ourselves. I think it broke Daddy's heart to leave the place he loves so, but Mama swears it will be good for him to live somewhere else, and she loves their neighborhood with the walking trails and small pond. She said it was time to change the guard and let Daddy rest. I guess she's right. He's always worked so hard.

I've put away all of our wedding gifts and asked Susi Evans to sew some new curtains for the breakfast nook. Sounds boring, but I'll be back at work soon. John is already making improvements on the barn. He's so funny, like a kid in a candy store, picking out this and that. He's so proud to be running Breezy Hill (though he tries really hard not to show it in front of Daddy.) Tonight I'm making pork chops which is John's favorite. Maybe an apple pie, too. Or not since he didn't remember to pick up the dry cleaning.

Maybe I'll get the hang of this writing stuff and not be so boring. Ha!
Becca

Closing the journal, Shelby set it away from her, knowing she shouldn't have read any of Rebecca's thoughts even if she'd felt compelled by some woo-woo moment that felt ordained.

She wasn't living in a made-for-TV movie where the ghost of John's wife gave her permission to be nosy so she could send a message from another realm.

Shelby rewrapped the cord and righted the stack of books. "No more snooping, Nancy Drew."

Turning on her side, Shelby looked out the window at the blue Louisiana sky...and then closed her eyes.

And fell asleep.

CHAPTER THIRTEEN

"JOHN, WAIT UP," Matt called across the church parking lot.

John turned and waited on his brother, who jogged toward him in a perfectly tailored charcoal suit. Matt felt being the headmaster of St. George's Episcopal called for a certain amount of pomp. The man had rules in his head and he lived by them.

"I have the Algebra teacher's edition for Shelby in my car along with forms the payroll office will need."

"I'll take them to her," John said. "Where're Mary Jane and the kids?"

"Just me today. Mary Jane's taking the boys to her parents' for the afternoon. Something about going to the zoo. So are you going to Mom's for lunch?"

John followed his brother to the Chevy Impala. Sturdy car for a sturdy brother. "Not sure."

"So this Shelby thing? You going to talk about it?"

John didn't say anything.

"She's living with you."

John shook his head. "We're not sleeping together if that's what you're implying."

Matt waved at someone over John's shoulder before zeroing in on John. "I'm not implying anything. Just an odd situation. Can't expect people not to comment."

"I don't," John said, watching as Matt moved his gym bag and lifted the box filled with a binder, book and a folder and passed it to him.

"But you're not being forthcoming?"

"Do I need to?"

"This isn't like you."

Exasperation rose inside John. "Maybe I'm tired of grieving, tired of feeling guilty over the circumstances around Rebecca's death." If he said it, maybe he'd believe it. He had to want to heal. He had to give himself a break.

Matt closed the door. "You should be tired of it. Still, this new woman came out of the blue. Mom swears she's just what you need, but the rest of us are worried. We don't know Shelby. What if she's—"

"What? After my money? Then she'll be disappointed. Almost everything I've made these years has been reinvested in the farm."

"You got insurance money. There are some people who follow that kind of thing and they take advantage."

John felt like Matt had punched him. No one had asked him about the beneficiary money he received once Rebecca's death had been ruled an accident. "Are you serious?"

"You know the kind of world we live in."

"Shelby's not like that. And so you know, I gave the money to the school."

"Avondale?"

"Every penny. Rebecca would have wanted something good to have come from something so terrible."

Matt stared at him, a strange look on his face. "I always wondered."

"Now you know." John started for his truck.

"John?"

"What now?"

Matt jogged behind him. "Let me get the truck door."

"I don't need help."

Matt's hand stopped him, turning him slightly as his brother stepped in front of him. "You never let anyone help you, but if you need me, I'll be at the fishing camp."

"The camp?"

His brother made a face. "Thing is, Mary Jane and I are having some issues. Nothing major, just some growing pains in our marriage. For the time being, I'm staying at the camp." His brother averted his eyes and looked flustered. Embarrassed.

"God, Matt," John said, shifting the box to his hip and stretching out a hand to his brother's shoulder. "Is there something I can do?"

"Nah. I'm offering to help you. Don't worry. Mary Jane and I will be fine. We both need some time to think about what we want."

"She's not happy?"

Matt shook his head. "No, and honestly, neither am I. Raising kids is hard, and since I took over as the principal of St. George's, I've been way too busy. And there are other things."

"Another woman? Or another man?"

"God, no." Matt looked insulted. "Nothing like that. But remember the stress you faced with Rebecca? All the fertility treatments, hormonal surges and grief? Remember how you left some nights and came over just to get away? It's that kind of thing."

"Mary Jane wants another baby?"

"No. The opposite. She wants to move to New Orleans to run an art gallery." Matt shook his head, staring at the cars filing out of the lot. "I shouldn't be going into this right now, and I wasn't trying to make you feel weird about the fact you're living with… Well, Shelby's pretty nice to look at."

Yeah, she was. Everyone seemed to notice her beauty. So if Shelby weren't hotter than a two-dollar pistol, would people even care they were shacking up? Not that they were shacking up in the literal sense. But if Shelby were unattractive, would anyone doubt the reason John gave Shelby a place to stay? "Yeah, she's pretty, but that doesn't figure into it."

Matt hooked a dark brow.

John sighed.

"Fine," his brother said, swiping a weary hand over his face. John looked hard at Matt, noting the lines in his face, the worry ringing his gray-green eyes. In the span of a few months, his brother had aged. So how bad were things between him and

Mary Jane? Not good if they were no longer living in the same house.

"What time should I tell Shelby to be at school tomorrow?"

"We open the doors at seven o'clock. Since she'll likely want to settle into the classroom, I'd suggest getting there at that time. Ms. Fox said she marked the chapter they were on and included some handouts. I'm sure she can figure it out, but if there are questions, give her my cell phone number."

"Okay. Have a good one, Matt. I'm sorry about... the thing."

His brother nodded, and with a slight wave, walked away, his shoulders heavy as his footfalls.

Damn.

John hadn't seen trouble between Matt and Mary Jane coming, but then again he'd never seen Shelby coming, either.

John climbed inside his truck and set the box on the passenger seat. He'd spent the past year alone in this truck. Over the past few days, it felt good to have Shelby beside him, someone to point out two deer perched on the side of the road or the old Tomlinson house that had burned down two weeks ago. Not that the house burning was a good thing...it was just nice not to be alone.

He'd wanted her to come to church with him. Stand beside him and sing hymns and smile at the kids when they ran down the aisle for children's church. He missed having someone beside him. Missed the smell of floral perfume and the clack of high heels. But he understood Shelby's reluctance to come to First Pres with him. Lots of looky loos in his father's congregation.

Maybe he could talk her into coming to his parents' house for lunch. She'd already been there before so it wouldn't be intimidating, and she could grill Matt about St. George's and all the school stuff teachers had to deal with. Besides, who passed up a good old-fashioned Sunday dinner?

When he entered the house at Breezy Hill, it was eerily quiet, making his mind jump to the worst possible conclusion. He circled through the downstairs and double-checked that her car still sat in the drive before taking the stairs two at a time calling Shelby's name. She didn't answer, but the door to the guest room was slightly ajar.

John's throat tightened, his mind tripping back to that horrible evening when he stumbled over his wife's blood-soaked body on the back steps.

Dear God, please let Shelby be okay.

He sucked in a deep breath and pushed the door open.

Shelby lay sound asleep on the bed, flopped onto her back, mouth slightly open, lightly snoring. She still wore her nightgown, a short light purple silky thing bunched at the hip, revealing a pair of polka-dot lacy panties. Her blond hair spilled across the bed, and her rather large and quite possibly perfect breasts rose and fell with each breath.

Desire fired straight to his groin, causing an erection to stir in those pressed khaki pants his mother had ordered from J. Crew.

If Shelby had a bow tied around her, she wouldn't have been any more of a gift.

But she wasn't his to open, was she?

Her words from the night before still echoed in his mind. *Don't touch me, don't kiss me, don't screw me until you can do so without apologizing.*

John wasn't sure he could do as asked. If he slipped into her bedroom and took what he was certain the sleepy, responsive Shelby would likely give him, after it was over, he'd feel regret. He wasn't ready to own the desire he had for Shelby. She'd been right—regretting every time he gave in to lust wasn't fair to her. Making love to Shelby would be pleasurable, but the intimacy would still feel like a betrayal of Rebecca. So waking sweet Shelby with a kiss wouldn't happen no matter how much he craved sinking inside her, losing himself inside a vortex of desire, owning the craving, marking Shelby as his.

Slowly and carefully, he closed the door.

"John?"

Her voice, raspy with sleep, sounded like pure seduction.

He opened the door enough to pop his head inside and said, "Sorry to wake you."

Struggling to sit up, Shelby pushed hair out of her eyes, nearly exposing one breast, before righting the gown to cover her absolutely delicious plump flesh. John swallowed and tried to look away as she pushed the hem of the gown past her thighs and stretched.

The motion caused her breasts to sway against the material pulled taut. "What time is it?"

"Twelve-thirty." He somehow managed to not squeak.

She rubbed a hand over her face, yawning. "Oh, I've been so tired lately. Can't believe I conked out like that. You called for me?"

"Yeah, and I got worried when you didn't answer."

"Oh," she said, before stiffening as if she realized what her not answering had done to him. "Oh. Sorry I worried you."

"I came back to see if I could talk you into lunch at my parents' house," he said, changing the subject from the fear he'd experienced. He'd hated feeling so helpless, hated the dread knitted inside him.

Swinging her legs over the bed, she stood and the gown slid down her legs, clinging to all the right places. She reached for her robe and her breasts fell forward, the sunlight illuminating her figure within the thin fabric.

Temptation wrapped round him, digging in its fangs. Desire, raw and wicked, invaded. John pulled the door tighter against him. He could control himself. He could. Had to.

Knuckles white, he clung to the door as if it could prevent him from going to her, peeling off that robe, sliding down the straps of the silky gown and then reveling in the healing power of a sexy, hotter-than-hell woman.

She tugged on the robe, tying it emphatically around her waist as if she sensed his thoughts and knew his conflict. "I'd rather stay here. Like I told you before."

"Of course," he said, stepping back, pulling the knob to him. "I'll be back later. Matt sent some stuff for you. I'll put the box on the kitchen table."

"Thanks," she said, withdrawing a book from the top of a stack sitting on the end of the bed. "I found this. It's a journal your wife kept." She pushed it toward him.

Tan leather with a silver button, the journal bobbed in her hand. "Rebecca?"

"You didn't have another wife, did you?" she said with a small smile.

He didn't want to cross the room because he still had a semierection going. "No. Just put it with the other books. I should have cleaned this room out before I offered it to you."

"But don't you want the journal?" she asked, drawing the book back to her, looking at him with puzzlement.

"Sure," he said, still holding the door between them. "I'll come back in here at an appointed time and take out the stuff that's in your way. Carla may want some of the things—I think there are some scrapbooks and even an old doll in the top of the closet."

Slowly, Shelby turned, setting the journal on the dresser.

"I don't have to go to my parents' house. I can stay here and we can watch a movie?"

"I thought you had to work this afternoon."

"I decided against it. My men like to go to church or sleep in one day a week. We only miss if we're running way behind." *Or want to avoid things in our lives.*

She shook her head. "Go to your parents'. I need to go through the box your brother sent. I haven't taught Algebra in a while so I need to get some lesson plans together for the week."

"Oh, sounds good," he said, not believing his own words, wishing she would have asked him to stay. Why would she, though? She'd made herself perfectly clear. And shouldn't he still harbor anger over the way she'd lashed out the night before, saying things she'd had no right to say for a woman who'd known him for only a week? Of course, he likely needed to hear those things—to remember he still lived in a world where others had grieved and moved on to find happiness in life.

"Bye," she said, watching him stand there like a moron.

"Oh, right. I'll be back later. Make your—"

"—self at home," she finished. "Got it."

He closed the door, wanting to immediately bang his head against it. But he didn't. He turned toward the stairs intent to soldier on.

Or what had Matt called it? Growing pains?

Living with someone always took time and patience. Even when he and Rebecca first got married, they struggled over space and time constraints, bickering about clothes left in the bathroom or who ate the last protein bar. And they had been emphatically in love with one another.

He and Shelby were still essentially strangers.

Giving her space after their argument last night was necessary. He wanted her to stay, to feel like he could be an asset to her and the baby, so if she wanted to spend the afternoon alone, he'd respect her wish.

Onward, soldier.

CARLA STANTON LIKED sleeping in. Her ideal wake-up time was around 9:00 a.m. followed by a half hour of coffee, newspaper and Bible study. She rarely went out before lunch and never without teased hair, painted-on eyebrows and Think Bronze lipstick in place.

But Monday morning she rose before the sun peeked over the river levee. Before *Good Morning America* came on, she was out the door, heading for Magnolia Bend wearing her newest scarf.

First she'd breakfast with a few of her dearest friends, ladies who held plenty of influence in the small town. She'd made a point to leave John's mother out. Fancy always looked at the glass half-full and notoriously did things like adopt raggedy ol' tomcats and buy the most expensive popcorn packs from local Boy Scouts. Fancy would be relieved John had found someone else, so she hadn't been invited for waffles, lattes and well-placed gossip at PattyAnn's Café.

After doing something she'd likely have to ask the

Lord forgiveness for, Carla headed to her attorney's office to review instructions for the Stanton trust and to amend her last will and testament.

Sad, really, that she had to take such drastic measures, especially when John hadn't done anything more than seek the comfort of a woman. Perhaps finding a little side of something could have been overlooked, but to allow the hussy to live in Breezy Hill, to sleep in sheets Carla's own mother had embroidered before her death? Not a chance. A whore would have better luck at getting through the pearly gates than she'd have living in the house that belonged to the Stanton trust.

When Rebecca and John had married, she and Hal had decided to allow the couple to manage Breezy Hill and all of its properties, keeping all earnings for themselves after taxes. Hal's will stipulated Carla retain control of the trust upon his death, allowing John and Rebecca to continue as before. Upon Carla's death, control and ownership of the trust would revert to Rebecca. If for some reason both Carla and Rebecca died, ownership would pass to Rebecca's beneficiary to manage until any heirs came of age.

But now there was no one left.

And with John behaving so irrationally, Carla had to act.

A flash of shame seared her gut as she pulled into Remy Broussard's office building. She'd told John nothing would change. Did that make her a liar?

Maybe.

But what choice did she have? She'd not thought

hard enough about her words that day so long ago. Driven by emotion, she'd made a promise to John.

It had been a Wednesday, two days after the worst day of her life, and Carla had driven out to Breezy Hill to pick a dress for her daughter to be buried in. The shotgun had done so much damage to Rebecca that open casket wasn't possible, but Carla couldn't stand the thought of her precious girl being buried in something other than full clothing. She'd found the house unlocked and dark…and her son-in-law in his bedroom fully dressed and curled up on the bed, clutching Rebecca's nightgown. His gut-wrenching sobs had robbed her of breath.

"John," she'd said, laying a hand on his shoulder.

He'd turned, his eyes so confused, looking through her. "Becca?"

"No, honey. It's Carla."

"Oh, God, Carla. Oh, God," he'd moaned. She had never seen a man so crippled with grief and hadn't known what to do. She had patted him as he rocked and cried out in anguish.

After what seemed like hours, she had shaken him. "John, I know you're hurting, but it's time to get ahold of yourself."

His hand had clamped over hers, squeezing it until she whimpered, but he didn't let go. She bore it because her hand couldn't possibly hurt as badly as his heart. "My life's gone. What am I going to do, Carla? What am I going to do? I killed her. That goddamned gun. That goddamned gun."

Carla pulled his hand off hers and sank onto the

bed. "You're going to go on just like before. You have Breezy Hill. She loved this place and now you have to keep it alive for her."

Eventually his sobs had subsided and he sat up, still clutching her hand. "I can't."

"You can and you will. You told Hal you'd take care of his daughter, you'd take care of his legacy. Did you lie?"

"God, no."

"Then don't say you don't have anything left. You have this land and the legacy my husband entrusted to you. Rebecca would have wanted this. She always said the first day you stepped in the field you became part of the history of Breezy Hill. She said you looked as comfortable here as a pair of worn-out jeans. You belong here."

He'd released her hand, wiped the tears from his face and straightened. "I'll keep my word, Carla, and I'll put one foot in front of the other because Rebecca would have expected me to press on."

"Yes, she would. We'll both have to press on, broken, but still moving."

He'd looked at her then, his green eyes so grief-stricken, but his gaze also resolute. "I won't let you down."

Carla blinked away the sudden tears as the memory of that day and the promise she'd made slipped back into the past where it belonged.

John hadn't let her down in regards to the plantation. Last year she'd met with Remy and Duke Hassell at the bank and reviewed the profits and losses of the trust. John had increased production in one short year and the projections for this year predicted more than marginal growth. Every day, the man who'd loved her daughter, who'd unwillingly caused her death, worked himself to the bone in the Stanton fields, planting, growing and harvesting Louisiana sugar.

But today wasn't about profits or promises.

Today was about choices.

Carla owed it to Hal to protect the Stanton trust.

And she owed it to her daughter to see that John Beauchamp never had what Rebecca couldn't.

CHAPTER FOURTEEN

SHELBY JANGLED THE key in the classroom door while balancing the box Matt had sent her yesterday, but she couldn't get the stupid lock to pop.

"Here, let me help," a man said behind her.

Shelby straightened, letting the keys dangle. "Thanks, it's stuck."

"Nah, you just have to have the right touch," he said, stepping in front of her, jiggling the key until a small metal click sounded. "There you go."

Shelby sighed. "Whew, thanks."

"Here, let me get that for you," he said, taking the box from her hand.

Shelby stepped inside the classroom and flipped on the lights, stepping back to let the man pass. Her Good Samaritan stood about six foot three inches with burly shoulders, silver-peppered hair and a white beard.

"I'm Shelby Mackey," she said as he set the box on the desk. "I'm substituting for Ms. Fox until she returns."

"David Hyatt," he said, a smile breaking the hard planes of his face. "I teach American history right next door and I'm happy to show you the ropes."

"Good to know."

"You're obviously not from around here. West Coast?"

"Seattle."

He smiled. "I'm from Oregon."

"Really? I went to Oregon State."

"Well, hello, fellow Beaver," he said, his smile even larger.

For the next few minutes, Shelby chatted with David, but he seemed to sense her need to get the classroom set up and departed with a wave and an invitation to sit at the cool teachers' table at lunch.

Shelby took a 360-degree turn around the room, taking in the placid blue walls, decorated bulletin board, subdued posters and clean whiteboard. Neat, tidy, minimalist. Perfect room, nice desk and as she slid the filing cabinet open, perfect filing system.

Yay, Ms. Fox.

Time to work. This morning, she'd review the last chapter the kids had completed and give them a small quiz to ascertain mastery since the chapter had been taught by a parent substitute who had honestly stated she had no clue what to teach.

At eight o'clock a few students strolled in, shifting their eyes nervously, straightening their green-and-navy plaid skirts or tucking their shirts into belted khaki uniform pants. At five after eight, the bell rang and the room filled, every student casting puzzled looks at her, a few of the boys cracking jokes, no doubt about the way Shelby looked.

Which was totally professional in a pencil charcoal skirt and black sweater. A red scarf draped across her neckline and the black boots, though designer, were conservative. She could do nothing about her curviness or the enormous pregnancy boobs, but she'd tried to dial down the boomchickawowwow thing she always seemed to have going as best she could.

Another bell sounded and the students slid into their desks.

Shelby closed the classroom door, the sound of her boots loud to her own ears. Turning, she smiled. "Hi, everyone, I'm Miss Mackey, and I'm going to be your teacher for the next few weeks."

Twenty-one gazes met hers. One boy in the back row raised his hand. "So are you married?"

Right. Shelby had been dealing with these sorts of comments her entire teaching career. "Why? Are you available?"

The class tittered and the boy turned red.

"I'm joking, of course," Shelby said, giving the boy a no-hard-feelings smile. His lips twitched as the boy next to him gave him a fist bump. "I'm not married and I'm a certified high school math teacher who has taught everything from Algebra I to Trig."

She saw several front row students nod, their eyes shining in relief.

She discussed her expectations and gathered information about their past few weeks under a substitute before getting started on a review of previous material. The fifty-five-minute class flew by as did the next few classes. Before she could blink, David stuck his head in and cried, "Lunch!"

Shelby jumped at the boom of his voice.

"Sorry, I'm the official announcer of my favorite time of day," he joked, waiting while Shelby grabbed the lunch she'd made for herself that morning in the empty kitchen of Breezy Hill. John had left the coffeepot on, no doubt forgetting she couldn't imbibe caffeine. Strangely enough, as uncomfortable as she'd been at times with him, she'd felt lonely having her breakfast with only Bart. The dog had been some company, though, lolling out his tongue, staring at her with adoring eyes. Now she understood why people had dogs...they made you feel a whole lot better about yourself.

Shelby followed David down the hall to the door marked teachers' lounge. When he opened the door, laughter met her ears.

David held up a hand. "Folks, folks, we got a new one here."

The educators, in all shapes and sexes, turned with smiles. One overweight woman in a horrid purple jumper called out, "God help you."

They all laughed, several standing to shake her hand, before David cleared her a seat at one of the tables. Shelby sank into the spot a little overwhelmed, but glad of the camaraderie. Being welcomed into the fold always made being a substitute easier.

The door behind her opened and a Greek god walked in. No, more like a Norse god with his chiseled face. Golden locks brushed his natural-hewn hoodie. His trousers were linen and he wore Toms. A hippie Norse god with icy-blue eyes and a slightly crooked nose.

"Leif," David cried, "come meet Shelby."

His name was Leif—the old Scandinavian name meaning "heir," and Shelby didn't know how she knew that. Probably from some celebrity couple who'd chosen the name.

Leif's eyes moved over her before he cracked a smile. "Well, things are looking up around here."

Shelby tried not to blush, but she felt the heat in her cheeks anyhow. Leif seemed a natural born charmer with his rambling loose gait and flirty smile. Good gracious, he was pretty. She extended a hand. "Hi, I'm subbing for Ms. Fox."

"Enchanté," he said, arching one eyebrow. "Leif Lively."

It should have sounded absolutely cheesy, like something Austin Powers would say, but it didn't. His voice was smooth as scotch and his demeanor unassuming.

Lively? Where had she heard that?

"Leif's the art department head, as if you couldn't tell," David said. "And he drives those poor sixteen-year-old girls to write bad poetry and sigh every time he walks by. Swear my hair blows from all the 'ahs' and 'ohs.'"

Oh. My. God. Leif was the dude Birdie had been spying on. He turned around to grab something from the teachers' boxes attached to the far wall. Yep. Fine-assed Leif in the flesh...but covered.

He whirled back. "You still have hair left to blow. Be glad. Look at ol' Bobby over here." He winked at the grumpy-looking man with a mustache, large glasses and a small ring of brown hair around his scalp.

"Watch it, sissy boy."

Leif settled across from her, setting down a weird-looking container. "That's what they love to call me. Hey, I'm a lover not a fighter." He pulled off the lid revealing a lunch of bean sprouts, tofu and kale along with a funky smell. Shelby's stomach rolled.

And then she knew she was about to throw up.

"Oh, God. Bathroom?" she squeaked.

"Right through there." Leif pointed behind her left shoulder.

Shelby's chair made a huge screech as she bolted for the bathroom door, praying it wasn't occupied. God answered, and she made it in the nick of time.

She emerged a few minutes later, shaky and pale, but better.

"You okay?" purple jumper asked, her brow furrowed, concern in her eyes. "Here, come sit with us."

"Thank you. Uh, sorry, everyone," she said, giving a weak smile. "I'm a bit nervous and that smell…" She nodded toward Leif's disgusting-looking lunch.

"Sorry about that. It's probably the curry sauce. Or the anchovies," he said.

"Come on," purple jumper said, her earrings jingling a merry tune. "I'm Anne. I teach English and

I'm always nice to the math people even if I don't understand you all."

Another lady who looked pretty much normal grabbed Shelby's lunch and sat it in front of her. "And I'm Susan. I teach Latin. You sure you're okay?"

"Yeah, much better." Shelby untied the plastic tabs on the bag she'd grabbed out of John's kitchen pantry this morning. "Hey, at least I know how to make an impression, right?"

The two women smiled, easing Shelby's paranoia that someone would suspect she had morning sickness. She'd agreed to substitute at St. George's, but knew she could never stay employed there as an unmarried woman expecting a baby. Small town religious institutions usually frowned on such. Better to hide that little fact as long as possible and look for a public teaching gig where one's personal life belonged to her.

She nibbled at her sandwich, thankfully experiencing no more nausea. The other teachers were nice, and even the artsy-fartsy hunk apologized again for the smell of his lunch. By the end of the hour, Shelby felt more comfortable in her role as Ms. Fox's substitute.

And by the end of the day, she felt as if she had a firm hand on what each class needed in terms of getting caught up and prepared for semester tests. The students had challenged her at times, but soon discovered she had more classroom experience and authority than they did. No student had been sent out for disciplinary reasons, and Shelby could still smile at the end of the day. Mission accomplished.

Now if only she could manage the personal life she tried to hide, as well.

CARLA HATED GOING to the grocery store in Gonzales, where she forgot where things were located and sometimes didn't know a soul, so after meeting with Duke Hassell over the dissolution of the trust, she decided to stop by Schwartz's Economical Grocery in Magnolia Bend. The family run grocery story had escaped buyout from a big name competitor and managed to supply the small town with decent prices and quality products. Carla especially liked the produce manager and knew all the checkout gals. So walking into Schwartz's was like walking into home.

After conversing with the associate manager Jimmy about the upcoming cold front, Carla pushed her buggy toward the produce section. Even as the familiarity soothed her, her stomach still burned with aggravation at Duke.

Blasted man wanted her to think about things before doing anything rash.

Didn't he know she had thought about this? The future of Breezy Hill and the legacy of the Stantons sat on Carla's shoulders. She didn't take her responsibility lightly...even if she had put off thinking about the business for the past year. Grieving had a way of bleeding into every aspect of life. Hell, getting out of bed and deciding on breakfast were struggles, so dealing with the trust Hal had established and deciding the fate of the land, house and John had been easy to ignore.

So when she told Duke and Remy she contemplated dissolving and selling Breezy Hill if John progressed with the relationship with Shelby, they'd looked alarmed, saying things like "Let's not be too hasty, Carla."

Hadn't those two morons already suggested the same thing shortly after Rebecca's death?

Men were fools.

Carla was the only heir. Since Rebecca died without having a child, Louisiana communal law should entitle her heir, aka John, to her part of the trust, but Hal hadn't been born yesterday. He made sure the trust couldn't be divided, circumnavigating John with a clause in the case of death or divorce. Carla now held all the cards. With the trustee's permission, she could petition for dissolution of the trust.

Which meant John Beauchamp could choose— Breezy Hill or the bimbo?

But Duke, who served as trustee, didn't want Carla to move quickly. With cane still standing in the field, he made a valid point—if she were to dissolve the trust and try to sell Breezy Hill, the value wouldn't be as high as it would after harvest.

Carla picked up a winter squash and then set it back down, rolling her cart over to the bananas, trying to calm the ire still scratching around inside her.

Duke wasn't wrong. All Carla had to do was wait

until mid-January when the cane was in the mill. Then if John hadn't come to his senses, she could fire him and sell Breezy Hill.

The thought of signing away her husband's pride and joy made her heart ache, but she'd rather sell the house and lands and all it had meant to her family than let John continue as he was.

She supposed she could find someone else to manage the farm. Still, what would happen when she died? She wasn't leaving the house and land to some distant cousin who knew squat about farming sugarcane.

No, better to proceed with her plan.

Carla was almost certain that when faced with losing all he'd known or that girl, John would be reasonable.

But if he chose a piece of ass over Breezy Hill, Carla could use the proceeds from the sale to travel, help build a wing at the new cancer center in Baton Rouge or create scholarships for the underprivileged. Anything was better than...

"Mrs. Stanton?"

She turned, holding a cluster of ripe bananas. Well, slap her sideways, there stood the very woman who'd set this all in motion.

Shelby.

Carla stood a moment looking at the girl in her trim skirt and boots. Shelby didn't look like a bimbo, but Carla knew the type. Deceitful. A woman didn't have to wear see-through shirts and hoochie skirts to be a whore.

"Uh, you're Mrs. Stanton, aren't you?" the girl prodded, giving a small smile.

"That's right." Ice hung on her words.

"I thought so," Shelby said, setting a bag of fresh green beans into her cart. "Uh, do you have a minute?"

"No, I do not," Carla said, seeing an older lady she didn't know crane her head around the scales dangling in the aisle, eyes wide. Her frosty words had drawn attention. "If you'll move your cart."

"Mrs. Stanton, I know how this whole thing looks, but John and I aren't together. He's merely giving me a hand by—"

"I know what he's giving you. I know men and I'm not blind. I saw you on Thanksgiving and it wasn't innocent."

Shelby frowned, her blue eyes contrite. "I think you've misunderstood the situation. John still loves Rebecca. I know that."

Carla went still, her dead heart thunking hollow with each pulse of blood. The world slowed down; the store faded around her. All that existed was this stupid, stupid girl talking about her Rebecca. "You don't know anything. You don't have the right to say her name, much less sleep in the house she lived in her entire life. Now get your cart out of my way before I cause a huge scene by knocking your head off."

The woman drew back, her pretty blue eyes as round as the discounted cantaloupes sitting beyond her shoulder. "But I found something of your daughter's you might want."

A terrible impulse to hurt the woman invaded Carla. She clenched the cart. "I took everything I wanted and stop speaking her name," Carla said, ramming Shelby's cart out of the way. The clash of metal on metal caused the woman weighing a bag of apples to squeak.

Shelby gasped, stumbling backward, nearly colliding with a rack of raw nuts sitting beside the banana bin. Jimmy, apparently catching the melee out of the corner of his eye, hurried over.

"Everything okay, ladies?" he asked.

"Fine. I'm ready to check out," Carla said, reversing direction, heading for the front, away from the horrible woman who thought she could smooth things over. Probably knew all about Carla and the trust. Probably thought she could smile and look innocent, all the while wheedling her way into a life that didn't belong to her. Into a house and money that belonged to the Stantons.

Carla didn't look back, kept rolling toward the checkout even though she could hear Jimmy inquiring if Shelby was okay. Typical dumb sheep. All Shelby had to do was bat those thick eyelashes and wiggle that tight rump and men jumped to do her bidding, jumped to make sure the mean ol' witch hadn't hurt her widdle self.

Pure hate coursed through her at the thought of Shelby…what was her last name?

Mackey.

Shelby Mackey didn't belong in John's bed…or Breezy Hill…or Magnolia Bend. John had belonged to Rebecca and so had this town, a place she'd loved from the moment she'd toddled into the post office and the Head over Heels shoe store and the First National Bank. This had been the Stantons' home for generations, and she would be damned if she let Shelby make a place for herself in the town her daughter had loved so well.

CHAPTER FIFTEEN

JOHN WALKED FROM the barn, the twilight a descending curtain on opening night. Jolly stars winked at him as Freddy stood silent on the back stoop waiting for him to give him a scratch under the chin. Unlike every other night for the past year and three months, his kitchen glowed like coals in the hearth, warm with potential.

"Evening, Fred," John said, bending and giving the ragged-eared Tom a scratch.

Shelby appeared at the kitchen door. "Hey."

"Hey," he said, feeling the immediate intimacy, the instantaneous firing of his blood at the sight of her curvy shadow against the screen door. The scent of food permeated the air. "You cooking?"

"No, I'm *trying* to cook. There's a difference, trust me," she said, pushing the door open and stepping back so he could enter. He toed off his work boots leaving them on the stoop and stepped inside. So normal. Like he did this every day.

Of course when he saw the kitchen, he nearly backed out the door. The counter was a colossal disaster with open egg cartons, a gallon of milk and a spray of white flour across the backsplash. Bowls of every shape and size sat along the counter along with apple peels, bottles of oil and a pack of butter. And—

"Is something burning?" he asked, eyeing the stove.

"Oh, my God," Shelby squeaked, racing to the pan where gray smoke had started to billow. "I forgot about the green beans."

Grabbing a spoon, she stirred the blackening beans and shoved the sizzling pan to the back burner, twisting the knob to extinguish the fire.

"Shit," she said, dropping her forehead into her hands.

A buzzer sounded on the double ovens and she spun and grabbed the oven mitt and opened the oven. Carefully pulling the pan out, she set it on the burner she'd just extinguished...and then frowned at it. "It doesn't look cooked."

He walked over and peered over her shoulder at the pork chops sitting in the pan. She'd covered them with flour and breadcrumbs, but they hadn't baked.

Glancing back at the ovens, he noted she had taken the chops from the top oven, which hadn't been turned on. The bottom oven, however, radiated heat. "I think you turned on the bottom oven and not the top."

He turned to smile at her and tell her it was okay, but it wasn't.

Poor Shelby swayed, lip trembling, wiping tears from her eyes. She wore an apron he'd never seen before, and she'd gathered her hair into a low knot from which several strands escaped to hang in her face. "I suck at this. I wanted to be… Ugh. I'm so stupid."

John walked over and grasped her shoulders. "Hey, it was a nice gesture—one of the nicest things anyone has done for me in a while."

She still wouldn't look at him, sniffling, her hands hanging at her side. "I thought I could cook something healthy for us. I knew you'd be hungry, and I'm starving. Look at this crap. We can't eat it."

He pulled her to him, giving her a hug, before releasing her. "I'll help you clean up the mess. Put the chops in the bottom oven to cook, and we'll have them in sandwiches tomorrow. Have you ever had a pork chop sandwich? They're delicious."

"I don't eat meat," she said, still frowning at the pan. "But what about tonight?"

"We'll toss the green beans, and I'll make you a John Beauchamp omelet that will make you slap your mama."

"My mother's in Seattle."

"Yeah, but my omelets are so good you might be tempted to fly up there just to slap her," he joked, really wanting to kiss his sad Shelby until she smiled again, but not daring because he knew he might not be able to stop once he started. Besides she wasn't his. She was his bona fide roommate. That was it, even if he fantasized about her in the shower, beneath the patchwork quilt wearing pink polka-dot panties and in the barn wearing a pair of cutoff shorts that showed the curve of her ass.

Shelby's lips twitched. "Guess my mom will have to risk it. An omelet sounds good. Besides, my apple cobbler will be okay. We can have that for dessert."

"Apple cobbler?" he asked, his stomach growling appropriately. Apple pie or cobbler was his absolute favorite. "I hope I have some vanilla ice cream in the freezer."

"I bought some," she said.

"Oh, woman, you will have me fat and happy in no time."

Her expression shifted. "Would that be so bad? For you to have a little happiness?"

John's heart skipped a beat at her earnestness, at her longing to make him a little bit happy. "Wouldn't be bad at all, Shelby. Thank you."

"You're welcome. I'll clean up the dishes while you make the omelet." She spun toward the stove and lifted the pan with the charred green beans. "I'll start by dumping these in the trash."

John cleared off a space on the counter and plucked out the five eggs left in the carton. Bart's tail thumped a content beat on the old wood floors as John and Shelby worked rhythmically to restore order and create dinner. He found some shrimp that his sister had put in the freezer in late September and made his special gravy. Luckily, he had some green onions that weren't too wilted and some mild cheese to add flavor. If he'd had some Andouille sausage, it would have been better, but he hadn't had time to go to the butcher last week.

Fifteen minutes later, he and Shelby sat down at

the table with omelets, a garden salad and the promise of apple cobbler.

"This is amazing," Shelby said, stabbing a piece of omelet and swirling it in the sauce. She looked pretty happy to be digging into something after having a small breakdown earlier. She ate with appreciation, even making a small "mmm" sound in her throat when she first tasted the sauce.

"Yeah," he said, making short work of his salad.

"You can cook. I eat a little fish and some shellfish, but I've never had it prepared this way."

"I'm a Louisiana man. I'm great on the grill and I'm good with Louisiana dishes like étouffée and jambalaya. I don't bake."

"My housekeeper, Mosa, made the best dishes. She's from South Africa and would infuse exotic spices into her cooking. I hold her fully responsible for my teenage fat years. I couldn't say no to her cooking." Affection shadowed her voice, telling him more than how she was raised...more like who had raised her.

"So you grew up with a housekeeper? Live-in?"

"Yeah. My parents were rarely home, so they wanted a full-time housekeeper and nanny. I'm the youngest, sort of a surprise to parents who wanted only two children. A mistake. Guess the apple doesn't fall far from the tree, huh?" She said it with a laugh, but he could hear the pain in her voice. His Playboy Bunny had been raised in the shadows, far from the sunshine she projected. No wonder she used humor to deflect unpleasantness.

"I don't think you were a mistake any more than I think the child growing inside you is a mistake. Maybe he or she stemmed from our being irresponsible, though I still can't figure out how the pregnancy happened in the first place. Bad condom, I suppose. But it was meant to be."

Shelby set her fork on her plate and stared at the saltshakers for a moment before lifting her gaze to his. "Do you truly believe that?"

Something inside him moved. He'd already devoured his omelet, so it could have been some residual air in his gut, but he was fairly certain the movement was something else, something he hadn't felt in a while. Not desire, but something deeper and more satisfying. "Yeah, I do. This thing between us, this whole experience that unites us, happened for a reason. Two people who had no good reason for being at Boots Grocery shared a laugh, shared more than a few drinks and leaned on each other in an effort to lessen what hurt them. From that need to feel something more than pain, a child was created. He's not a mistake."

"Or she."

"Or she," he conceded, grappling at the idea of a daughter with blond hair, blue eyes and a sweet voice that called "daddy." Something inside him moved again, clamping down on his heart, making his throat scratchy. "You and I were strangers, but we aren't strangers anymore. You came to move me from the horrible place I'd been stuck. And maybe you've found where you're meant to be, too."

"Here?"

John hesitated for a moment before nodding. "Maybe so."

He watched as her throat worked to swallow whatever had crept up on her. Tears sheened her eyes again, and he felt like she wanted to believe him, wanted to think they'd been brought together for a bigger purpose. And Lord help him, he wanted her to believe that.

Finally, she said, "Do you believe in fate?"

"I believe in goodness. I believe you and I deserve some good in our life. Maybe fate brought you here for more than a baby. Maybe you're home." This time his words weren't about slanting things so she'd stay. They were true. He'd place his hand on the Bible he'd left sitting on the counter yesterday and swear as much. Shelby in Magnolia Bend was meant to be.

"So much is uncertain in my life," she said. "I feel like I'm from nowhere and everywhere at the same time. Half of me loves the idea of staying here—the other half feels as if I'm a fraud, trying to play at something I'm not suited to play."

He thought about that, about being where she was in life, and understood. "One day at a time is a good strategy."

Shelby nodded. "Yeah, it is, but eventually my stomach will grow. Eventually, we'll have to tell your family about, well, not the mistake we made, but about the child we made. Eventually, I'll have to find a real teaching job and it won't be at St. George's. And eventually, I'll have to decide whether I will stay in Louisiana and make a life here, where the father of my child lives, or go back to Seattle and establish a life for me and the baby. Once everyone knows I'm pregnant with our baby, decisions will have to be made."

Shelby was unequivocally correct. Once they broke the seal on the secret, the gig was up. Carla popped into his mind, along with the anger she'd demonstrated a few days ago. Some would not understand; some would think he dishonored Rebecca.

But at one time, he thought the same way.

Holding Shelby, laughing, sinking into her, losing himself had felt so freeing, but afterward, he'd felt like he'd destroyed his vows to Rebecca. Didn't matter her body lay in Field of Memories Cemetery four miles down the road. Their love transcended death, and he'd stomped on it because he'd wanted to feel a woman's arms around him again. Because he had wanted to feel like a man again.

But as he'd said those words about "meant to be" earlier, he had believed them. So when had he stopped viewing Shelby as a mistake? When had he stopped resenting the trouble she'd laid at his door? Maybe it was when he'd pictured himself chasing a small toddler around the living room, playing rodeo. Or maybe the vision of himself teaching a blond ponytailed seven-year-old how to ride her bike down the gravel road? Or maybe it was realizing he needed to concrete the drive so there was a place to ride a bike? Didn't matter. Thing was, John had changed in less than a week.

Felt like a miracle.

Felt like a gift.

John couldn't overthink it. If he thought too much about the way he felt, he'd stifle what he had growing inside him.

Trouble would come. He knew this, but he wasn't willing to forsake the next few weeks of getting to know Shelby better, of hiding their secret from the world for a bit longer.

"You're right," he said. "Things will get rocky for us when we tell the world about our child, but we can prepare better by knowing each other. I'll tell my mom and dad soon. And Carla—"

"Who hates me," Shelby interrupted.

"She doesn't hate you," he said.

"Oh, I beg to differ."

"She's been hurt and she's angry at me. Doesn't matter that what she thinks about us is wrong. In her eyes, I let go of Rebecca when I let you move in."

"A baby won't make that better. It'll make it worse." Shelby pushed the remainder of her salad around her plate. "What can she do to you?"

"Well, essentially I'm an employee of the trust. Carla controls the trust."

"Can she fire you?"

"Yeah, she could. She could make me leave Breezy Hill, but I don't think it will come to that. She needs me to run the place. It would be irresponsible and irrational to send me packing. I'm still her family."

Shelby arched an eyebrow.

John couldn't imagine Carla taking Breezy Hill from him merely because he no longer rambled about the place, haunted by misery. The woman he knew wouldn't punish him for wanting to feel something besides regret, would she? "And then everyone else will find out. We might face potential censure from a few folks in the town but—"

"You sure you don't work for Magnolia Bend tourism? Suddenly I so want to stay here," Shelby drawled.

John gave a wry smile. "Sounds like fun, huh?"

"A blast."

"I'm just ticking off what might be coming down the pipe with the main point being we need this time to learn about each other, to become a solid front."

"A team?"

"Exactly. We're about to become parents, and no matter what happens between us, we need to put the baby first and treat one another and each decision made with respect. The best way to do that is to do exactly what we're doing here tonight."

"Eating?"

"Working together, giving each other a break, caring about each other. For example, even though it was a bit of a disaster, it was kind of you to fix me dinner."

Shelby smiled and it filled up some of the empty places in his heart. The woman made *pretty* merely an adjective. Her face lit when she smiled, that sparkling thing happened with her blue eyes. "I wish dinner would have turned out better, though it smells like the chops are cooking. Maybe not a total disaster."

John scooted back his chair, lifting his empty plate. "See? Even disasters can be salvaged, and I'll enjoy the hell out of my pork chop sandwich tomorrow."

"This positive spin you put on things seems atypical to your character. The man I met months ago was so...so not apt to see a positive side of anything."

He stilled at those words. They were true. Even Shelby could see the metamorphosis of his spirit. "I'm trying."

She placed one hand on her stomach. "A baby changes everything."

"That's what they say in commercials," he said, turning his back to her so she couldn't see how vulnerable his admission made him.

"So for the next month, we're taking it one day at a time, filling in the lines on our coloring sheet?" Shelby said, picking up her own plate and cleaning it.

Interesting way to put it. "And finding out what colors work best. If we make a mistake, we'll change crayons and figure it out. Whatever comes once we announce the pregnancy, we'll handle as best we can, relying on the fact we respect each other."

"Sounds so simple," she muttered, setting the plate on the counter and sliding the cobbler off the shelf of the baking rack. "Like apple pie."

"Sometimes the simplest of things are the best of things."

Shelby popped a walnut from the top of the cobbler into her mouth and looked at him. At that moment, John knew nothing was as simple as he wished it. How he felt about Shelby and the child she carried was ten times more complex than anything he'd ever felt in his life. He could talk about one day at a time and simplicity, but he knew that as each day, each hour, each minute ticked by, he wanted Shelby Mackey.

Not just in his life as the mother of his child, but in his bed and by his side.

And that complex thought scared the hell out of him.

FOR THE NEXT few weeks, Shelby's life settled into a pattern. She got up and did some yoga stretches recommended for pregnant women, took a nice not-too-hot shower and had breakfast with Bart. After letting the dog out for a romp, she locked up Breezy Hill, hopped in her car and was behind her desk before the other teachers arrived. Matt sometimes came by to check on her, and the other teachers treated her as one of the gang, even inviting her to participate in their Christmas song and dance they performed every year for the Christmas assembly.

Shelby bowed out because dancing in a Christmas mouse costume wasn't her cup of tea, but she helped make props for the stage and even helped David track down mouse ears. The students adapted well to her teaching style, and preparation for midterms progressed nicely.

Every evening when the sun went down, she and

John prepared something for dinner, made their sack lunches for the next day and watched TV. They pretended family, Carla and repercussions didn't exist.

One evening when Shelby asked about a Christmas tree, John climbed up into the attic and started bringing boxes down. "I never thought I'd use these again."

"Why not? They're pretty," Shelby said, unpacking the antique glass ornaments from the bubble wrap.

"These were Rebecca's grandmother's. The old bat, ahem, lady used to collect them. Some are priceless, but last year the thought of dragging this out made me feel sick. Couldn't do it."

"I understand. Grief is a powerful wall. Hard to get around."

"Have you ever lost anyone close to you?"

"Well, my grandfather passed away when I was four. I barely remember him, but what I do remember is that he was a kind man and always had a peppermint in his pocket for me—the soft chalky kind. I loved when I got to visit him at the office."

"What sort of business was he in?"

"Lumber and some other stuff. They made furniture, too," she said, not wanting to flat-out admit her family held a lion's share of stock in a Fortune 500 company. Her mother still sat at the helm of Inabnet Industries. "What about your family? Have they always lived here in Louisiana?"

"Pretty much. My great-great-great-grandfather settled here back in the early 1800s on land granted to him by the governor for his service in the War of 1812. Of course, ol' Burnsides immediately sold half to pay off gambling debts. The family moved to Chicago and George's grandson became a minor railroad baron. He sold his shares in the railroad company, bought the plantation house from the woman who became his mistress and settled into building the town. Beauchamps and Burnsides have been here ever since. At one time my family was the wealthiest sugar family in the South. But that's all gone away. Today we're merely the guardians of our history. Sugar collapsed and land was sold to corporations."

"And the Stantons?"

"Been here since after the war. This house was actually rebuilt back in the 1920s after a kitchen fire destroyed much of the main house. This mantel was in the original, though," John said, running a hand over the mahogany and marble before hanging the garland from the small hooks beneath.

"Fascinating. I visited tons of plantations this past fall. I had just come from Hermitage when I stopped at Boots. You know, I turned into the parking lot at the last minute only because I didn't want to go back to the Dufrenes' house."

He adjusted the garland and plugged in the white Christmas lights twined throughout. "Dufrenes?"

"The family of the guy who dumped me," Shelby said, picking up two pewter candelabras shaped like reindeer.

"The man is a dumb-ass for letting you get away."

"Ha. This from a man who ran out of Boots like I'd turned into a man-eating alligator?" Shelby joked, passing him the reindeer so they could anchor either end of the mantel.

"I wasn't in good shape that night."

Shelby didn't say anything, merely walked over to the tree they'd just put up and touched one of the ornaments. "Might as well share my bad history with men since we're…becoming a team."

John turned. "How about some hot chocolate even if it's turned warm for December?"

Shelby nodded. After grabbing a mug and taking one himself, John sat down amid the boxes and bubble wrap and said, "So tell me your sordid past."

Shelby sank onto the sofa, tucking her leg beneath her. "Well, remember how I told you I couldn't say no to my housekeeper's cooking?"

He smiled.

"My siblings were older by twelve and nine years, so I was basically an only child. I didn't want to go to the private schools my brother and sister had attended. I insisted on public school because I wanted to be normal, like the kids on TV. Anyway, I was a chubby nonentity at public school. I had friends, but I wasn't popular and I only went to prom because all the science geeks asked me and my friends. Quintessential ugly duckling until the end of my senior year when the weight fell off. Sela took me to NYC over spring break and hired a stylist. Under those shapeless flannel shirts was a gal I never knew existed. I mean, I had these boobs and a waist and pretty kick-ass long legs. When I got back to Seattle a week later, boys were all over me."

"Yeah, I get that," he said, leaning back on his elbows. "Who's Sela?"

"My sister." Shelby didn't have time to explain that complex hate-hate relationship. Sela had never cared for Shelby beyond the standard sister obligation her parents had drilled into her. Besides, Sela had only taken Shelby because their father had refused to pay for Sela's trip if she didn't take her sister.

"So anyway, I had no clue how to deal with these guys flirting with me. It embarrassed me, and my social skills were crap. But at my dad's office, there was this junior attorney from California. He was thirty years old and pretty hot. The kind of guy all the secretaries fluttered about. I didn't feel awkward around him because I had known him for a few years, but suddenly he started paying more attention to me. Started innocently enough, but it ended pretty much the way things started with us."

"In a bathroom?"

"No, his office," Shelby said, averting her eyes. It still hurt to think about what a rube she'd been, how she'd fallen for all his lines and then allowed him to take her virginity next to the copier. Seriously. "And it was complicated. Kurt was married."

John lifted off his elbows, his brow crinkling. "Married?"

"Technically. His wife had been in a serious car accident, and I know this sounds like a bad movie plot, but she was in an induced coma for an entire month. The doctors thought she wouldn't make it, and Kurt seemed devastated and lost. I thought I was helping him by being a good friend to lean on. In my naïveté, I didn't realize he exploited my feelings in order to seduce me."

And just like that, anger sluiced off John. "If I could get my hands on that son of a bitch…"

"Yeah, he's a real turd, but thing was I was really stupid."

"You were a kid."

"But I should have known better. Should have seen the writing on the wall. He used me, and one of the firm's partners caught us having sex in Kurt's office."

"Yikes."

Shelby gave a hard laugh. "Wasn't pretty. My father's a hard man and scandal is something he doesn't tolerate in his firm. He fired Kurt and finally embraced the concept of me going to Oregon State. But dumb bunny I am, I declared Kurt loved me and showed up at his house ready to sacrifice everything for him. Of course, Kurt told me it was over, but I didn't believe it until I saw him a week later at the hospital kissing his wife, tears streaming down his face, for the media's benefit I might add. His wife had emerged from the coma. I packed my bags and headed to college."

"That's a pretty rough introduction to being an adult."

"No shit," she cracked. "So I had a few on-again

off-again guys in my life my first few years of teaching, but when my father hired Kurt again as if what he had done didn't matter more than the clients he could bring to Mackey and Associates, I signed up to teach in a naval base school. I got sent to Rota, Spain, where I met a JAG corp attorney from Louisiana."

"This Dufrene guy?"

"Yeah. He's from Bayou Bridge and seemed perfect for me. He was interested in moving to Seattle because he didn't want to come back here. Thing was, he didn't realize it, but the marriage he thought null and void from his past was legitimate. While waiting for the divorce, he fell back in love with his wife."

"Another made-for-TV movie?"

"I'm a walking Lifetime movie." Shelby picked up the wreath with the crushed bow and straightened the wired fabric. "Saying it out loud only makes it sound crazier, but that particular event led me to Boots and a sad cowboy who laughed at my lame jokes."

John's face softened. "I'm a sucker for bad jokes."

Shelby eyed the tree. "I think the tree looks a little crooked."

John stood and closed one eye and then the other. "Maybe. Are you changing the subject?"

"This conversation feels a little heavy. Saying all my past screwups out loud makes me feel naive. Stupid."

He moved toward her and brushed back the hair

on her shoulder. "Nothing wrong with making mistakes. No one's perfect. No one makes the right decision all the time. Look at me."

So Shelby looked at him. At his hard jaw with the five o'clock whiskers emerging, the green eyes she could dive into, the firm mouth she wanted to kiss but wouldn't. She'd meant it when she said no more kissing until he wasn't sorry about it.

"Just because you were unlucky a few times, doesn't mean you always will be."

Shelby shook her head. "I'm pretty sure you're the wrong guy to tell me this."

"Why?"

"Because you very likely will be my next 'you won't believe this' story," she said, turning from him.

"You think I'm going to hurt you?" His voice was soft. Serious.

Shelby knew the possibility of falling for John was there and creeping ever closer. On one hand, she wanted to keep what they had between them—an easy camaraderie, ever since she'd burned the pork chops—but on the other hand, she didn't want to live so safely. In her mind, the question *what if* kept circulating.

What if they gave into the ever-present sexual desire pulsing between them?

What if they were unified by more than the baby growing inside her?

What if they took a chance and went for broke?

What if?

"I don't know," she said, turning away so he

couldn't see the uncertainty in her gaze. "I think you could have that power. After all, you just heard me admit how much of a sucker I am for guys who are already committed."

"I'm not committed."

"Yeah, you are. Maybe not physically, but emotionally you're still in love with your wife."

For a moment, he didn't answer. "To be in love, there have to be two people present, and Rebecca is no longer here. Part of me will always love her. I'm working on the other part," he said. His eyes illuminated by the glow of the white lights crisscrossing the tree looked like bottle glass. Truly beautiful. So easy to lose herself in eyes filled with the intent to move past grief. But could he let that part of himself go? Could he truly stop wishing his life were different? And even if he did, would she even be an option?

Shelby gave herself a mental shake and stepped back from the intimacy. She had waited for weeks for John to open up about where he was in regards to his grief, in regards to her. But now it felt too vulnerable to open herself to that hope, especially after lifting the veil to reveal the warts and bruises beneath her sunny exterior. It was likely safer for her and John to remain what they were—friends who cared for one another.

Friends who wanted to rip the clothes off each other.

"What's wrong?" he asked.

"Nothing." She shrugged, picking up a box they hadn't opened. "It's fine to grow closer, but we can't cross that line. We have to stay friends. Easier that way."

He watched her as she opened the box, which held two embroidered stockings. One had a jolly St. Nick sitting in a sleigh full of gifts, the beading and sequins catching the light of the tree. John's name was written at the top. The other depicted an angel in white, golden beading glowing around her head. Rebecca's stocking.

"Let me take those. We don't need stockings." John folded the stockings and put them back inside the box with the foam liner.

Something in the way he moved so quickly, something in the sadness that ripped across his face, made her heart ache.

"Yep, Santa is passing you up 'cause you've been a bad boy," Shelby teased, trying to draw them back to the easiness they'd had before she'd admitted her sordid past. "Knocking up girls in roadside bars and then inviting them to live with you. Some preacher's boy you are."

Easier to joke than cry.

Rebecca's stocking had made her want to cry.

An angel.

After Carla had rammed her cart into Shelby's at Schwartz's a few weeks ago, Shelby had set Rebecca's journal on the top shelf next to the porcelain china doll. Every time she opened the closet to find something to wear, her eyes went up to where it sat.

An angel…but was that who Rebecca truly was?

Shelby's perception of John's late wife was based

on everyone else's grief, but she didn't know who the woman had been. Maybe she wasn't supposed to know the woman John had loved. But the fact she could know more if she opened the journal tempted her. All she had to do was lift her arm and grab the story of Rebecca.

John folded the flaps of the box, interrupting her thoughts. "Guess I should expect a lump of coal, huh?"

"Well, you can use coal for a lot of things. To keep warm and draw. You can even make a diamond out of coal." Shelby took the box and set it atop the ones John would return to storage. They'd finished decorating the house, and the living room looked different with the holly, greenery and red velvet bows. The trappings of Christmas had brought life to the room, making it feel like a home.

"I'm glad we did this," he said, standing back and folding his arms. The gesture made his shoulders broader, his jaw harder. Well, it actually didn't, but to Shelby, he seemed more masculine than seconds before.

"I've never decorated a Christmas tree before," she said. "My parents had decorators put up our holiday decorations. In Spain I just hung a wreath."

The look he gave her said enough.

"Yeah, I'm pitiful."

"No, you're beautiful, and I'm glad you stayed here."

Shelby looked back at the sparkling world spread before her. "I'm glad I stayed, too."

Later, Shelby went up to her room the way she did each night. Using the stairs. And very much alone.

Until an hour ago, John had refused to move into any other realm than friendship. During the past few weeks, they'd been decent roommates, agreeable pals, mutual fans of *The Walking Dead*—who wasn't?—and that was all. Well, John wanted her physically, of course. Shelby hadn't climbed off the boat yesterday and knew that much.

So why when he finally moved toward something more intimate than "pass the salt" had she pulled back?

Perhaps because ticking off all the shitty decisions she'd made over the guys in her past reminded her she couldn't trust her heart. Wanting John and something more than a platonic relationship scared her, because now she couldn't walk away and never see him again. Their child would link them forever.

So wouldn't it be better to ignore the unspoken attraction between them and settle for friendship rather than risk their hearts? Probably.

But then again, when had Shelby ever done what she was supposed to do?

Only on the fourth of never.

"You can't be so irresponsible anymore, chickadee," she said to herself as she closed the door and switched on the bedside lamp. Rubbing the stomach that had finally started getting poochy, she pulled her Oregon State sweatshirt over her head. With a yawn, she went to the closet and hung it up, glancing at the journal on the top shelf the way she did every day.

No one wanted the journal…it was forgotten.

Shelby had tried to give it to John, and then Carla hadn't even given her a chance to tell her about her daughter's journal. So maybe fate or whatever one wanted to call it had left Rebecca's journal to Shelby.

What had John said earlier? Meant to be? Maybe this was the same thing. Maybe Shelby was meant to read Rebecca's journal for whatever reason, which was definitely a higher purpose than Shelby being nosy.

Sliding a glance at the unlocked door as if she were about to sneak a copy of *Playgirl,* she pulled the journal off the shelf.

Don't be silly, Shelby. He's not coming in to catch you reading his dead wife's journal.

She tossed Rebecca's journal on her pillow and quickly pulled on her gown, scrubbed her face and brushed her teeth. When she settled into bed, piling up the goose-down pillows behind her, the alarm clock read 9:47 p.m.

When she finished reading the entries constituting Rebecca's first year of marriage with John, the clock read 12:13 a.m.

Switching off the lamp, Shelby stared up at the shadows, her head full of too much. She now knew Rebecca had dreamed about being a photojournalist, had sex for the first time with someone other than John and grew tired of the way John made decisions for her without consulting her. She also knew that despite hating the way John snored, the constant talk of sugarcane and the way her husband always agreed with her father, Rebecca had loved John.

The picture sitting in the bathroom had been taken at Destin on their first wedding anniversary. Rebecca had bought John a funny Hawaiian shirt and some Ray-Ban aviator glasses. He'd bought her a diamond tennis bracelet. They'd had sex on the beach… not the drink and John had cut his butt on a shell.

Shelby felt dirty for having read the journal. She'd had no right, and now she knew things she wasn't supposed to know. But even as guilt assuaged her, she knew one thing had changed.

Rebecca was real to her…and she liked the woman despite the fact she didn't want to, despite the fact she was jealous as hell of her.

Closing her eyes, Shelby murmured a small prayer. "Please don't let this be so wrong. Please don't let me make a terrible mistake."

When she opened her eyes again, nothing had changed. The ceiling fan still turned, the shadows still swayed against the pale walls and Rebecca's journal still sat beside her, fat and guilty, holding the key to loving John or hurting him more.

CHAPTER SIXTEEN

CHRISTMAS EVE HAD always been a big deal for John's family. After the Christmas Eve service ended, the entire clan went back to the big house on Front Street to drink wassail, eat Aunt Fran's sour cream pound cake and hear John's father read *The Night Before Christmas*. In between, there was plenty of merriment, and if Matt felt like it, he set up karaoke in the living room and everyone took turns singing. Uncle Carlton usually got as toasted as any Christmas chestnut and did his version of "It's Raining Men," which explained without him having to extend a toe out of the closet why he'd never married.

Even last year in the midst of despair over losing Rebecca, John had relished the sacredness of the Christmas candlelight service in the church where he'd once ridden his tricycle down the aisle. The soft glow combined with the smell of evergreen and wax comforted him, and finally after three weeks of begging off of attending church, Shelby sat beside him on the pew. He'd noticed her black dress looked a little snug at her waist, the first sign of the impending bump that would soon emerge. She wore those black boots that had made an appearance in a couple of the fantasies he'd allowed to play out in his mind each night, and even dressed somberly, she looked chic and festive with a red velvet bow holding her hair back. She shifted on the pew. "Everyone's looking at me."

"Well, you look beautiful. I like the red ribbon."

"I need a haircut. This was the best I could do."

He smiled and winked at Birdie who, for once, looked less sulky and more amiable. His sister, Abigail, wore a sweater dress that really didn't flatter her thin frame. She needed to stop worrying about him and Birdie and the fact their mother's mammogram looked off. Abigail took on the world every day and it showed on her.

"I can ask Abigail who she uses."

"I already got a name from your Aunt Hilda. Where is she, by the way?"

"She'll be here later. She spends part of the evening with her late husband's family in New Orleans."

The service began with traditional hymns and girls in white lighting candles. His father preached a short sermon on the true gift of Christmas and then small individual candles were passed out, each neighbor lighting the candle of the other while "Silent Night" made the rounds.

"I'm glad you came," he whispered to Shelby as she lit his candle with hers.

"I am, too. Lots of firsts for me at Christmas, but sharing your family traditions is important."

For the baby.

The words were unspoken, and right then and

there, he didn't want it to be about the baby. He wanted it to be about him. This revelation startled him. He'd told himself for the past month that everything he'd done had been for his unborn child. He'd convinced himself the only thing he and Shelby could have between them was the child they'd made. He'd tried to ignore his burgeoning feelings for her, telling himself he wanted her the way any man would want a beautiful, sexy woman. He'd lied to himself because every day he grew closer and closer to something more with Shelby and further and further away from the man he'd been.

He tilted his candle to his brother Jake's. Jake had showed up looking like sin, claiming the church would fall in on him. Of course, even though Jake could raise hell, he got still and solemn when he sank onto a church pew.

"Shelby looks good," Jake said, leaning slightly forward. "If you're not going to do anything with that, I'm going to make a move—"

"To the graveyard if you think about laying a finger on her luscious body," John finished.

"Luscious body?" Jake whispered before giving John a grin. "That's what I'm talking about, bro."

John scowled at Jake, even as inside he acknowledged his brother was right. He needed to show Shelby he wanted something more than what they now had. If he didn't, the interest he suspected she had in him would wane. That's the way things went with attraction. A woman would only wait for so long, and Shelby had been extraordinarily patient with him. Hesitation equaled lost opportunity.

Or masturbation.

Eh, both.

Over the past four weeks, he'd moved through many stages and gone through things he hadn't been prepared to tackle so soon after Rebecca's death. He thought it would take years before he could feel something in the caverns of his heart. But over the course of a month, he'd learned his life could be more…and it was okay to want another woman. But this wasn't just about sex. No, he held a deep warmth for the woman who fed Bart when he forgot, who watered plants that were near death and double-checked the locks before trudging up to bed. Such a city girl, but a city girl he'd grown more and more fond of day after day. The thought of her ever leaving Magnolia Bend made his heart lurch against his ribs.

She wanted him, or at least he was almost certain she did, even if she'd pulled back a few nights ago when she'd told him about her past mistakes. He'd been thinking about the way she'd felt in his arms since that night in the park, and the night they decorated the Christmas tree, he'd wanted to kiss her. And not apologize for it.

"Why aren't you singing?" she asked, turning her eyes to where the choir director robustly belted out the Christmas song.

"I'm a horrible singer."

"So am I, but that choir guy is giving you the stink eye."

John moved his lips, faking the chorus.

"Cheater pants," she whispered.

Abigail shot John the same evil eye when John laughed. But he didn't care how many people looked at him and Shelby. A couple of old bats who were Carla's bosom buddies had stared coldly and whispered behind their programs, but he didn't give a rip-roaring damn. God strike him dead in church, but he liked having Shelby beside him. Lately, he'd been thinking about what Rebecca would think about Shelby, and he knew she would have wanted him to move on and love again.

Wait…love?

He wasn't ready for love yet. But he was ready to move away from grief and claim a future not as bleak as it had seemed months ago.

On impulse, he curved an arm around Shelby and pulled her to him, giving her a good squeeze, and then he belted out the last verse in a very off-key baritone. Jake winced, Abigail rolled her eyes and his father made a funny face from the pulpit.

But Shelby…Shelby smiled.

And then and there, John decided he had to find some dang mistletoe.

THE BEAUCHAMP HOUSE looked like a spread for *Good Housekeeping*. White lights lined the eaves and huge urns with evergreens anchored the front door. Inside a huge tree with large old-fashioned bulbs cast a festive glow over the crowded living room. Matt stood in the corner fussing with electrical cords and something that looked like—

Oh, no. Karaoke.

Shelby inched back toward the open front door, but John blocked her path. Oh, well, guess she'd hide in the kitchen if she had to. Happy chatter swelled around her as she slid off her black velvet jacket and turned to John.

"Please tell me you're not going to sing," she said.

His green eyes glinted. "Why? I killed that last verse of *Silent Night*."

"Killed is right," Abigail said, sliding in behind them.

Shelby grinned. "You know, the carol becomes a total oxymoron when you sing it."

"*Moron* being the key word," Abigail drawled, tempering her barb with a smile.

"This is what it's like having her as a sister. It's a wonder I have any self-esteem."

"Ha," Abigail said, stripping the little girl wool coat off Birdie, who bobbed her head to the song playing through her earbuds.

"God, Mom. I'm not a little kid. Stop," Birdie said, jerking the coat from her mother and dumping it on the bench by the front door. Then she stomped off, obviously abandoning the little bit of joy she had shown earlier.

"Don't use the Lord's name in vain," Abigail called after her before turning back to Shelby and

John. "I swear I don't know what I'm going to do with her. She tried to invite that art teacher tonight."

"Leif?" Shelby asked.

"Yes. Ever since I walked her over to apologize for spying, she's struck up an unhealthy friendship with him. He plays the bongos like that Matthew McConaughey. Strange fellow."

"But he has an ass you could bounce a quarter off and dreamy blue eyes. You're not blind, are you?" Shelby asked.

Abigail looked at Shelby like she'd squawked and laid an egg right in the foyer.

"Tight ass?" John repeated, a frown marring the handsome span of his brow. The two siblings looked appalled at her comment…obviously for two different reasons. Something sweet blanketed Shelby as she noted the jealous glint in John's eyes.

"Oooh, jealousy?" Abigail purred, abandoning her puzzlement for torturing her brother.

"I'm getting a drink," John said, hanging his corduroy blazer on the hooks anchored above the bench. "Shelby?"

"What?"

"You want something?"

"Nothing for me," she said, wondering why he'd even asked. He knew she couldn't imbibe.

"You don't drink?" Abigail said, moving farther into the warmth of the house. "Odd for a city girl. I thought y'all loved cosmopolitans and gin tonics."

"Oh, of course, and I attend every opening art

show, shop sample sales and tell Charlotte, Samantha and Miranda all about my favorite sex positions."

Abigail smiled. "Okay, okay. I shouldn't stereotype. Are you a recovering alcoholic? You can tell me."

Shelby snorted. She liked bitchy Abigail. "You'd be fun if you let yourself."

"I'm fun. I'm a blast when I don't have a mortgage the size of the *Titanic,* a daughter with a shitty attitude and no batteries for my vibrator. Thank you very much."

Shelby didn't have time to respond to those little nuggets because Fancy descended in the only way she seemed to know how—with a squeal and a hug.

"Merry Christmas, Shelby. And, Abigail, fetch me another brandy cocktail. We've got a little shindig to put on tonight."

"Jesus, Mother."

"Don't take the Lord's name in vain, Abi," Fancy said, shooting her daughter the same look Abigail had employed earlier at the church. "Now, Shelby, Hilda just got here and wants you to come sit with her. She said she wants to talk bad about people, and you're the only one who will do. She's joking, of course. I think."

For the next few hours, Shelby soaked in the zany, sometimes exasperating celebration in a way she never had—as a participant. John sang old Garth Brooks' songs with his brothers, of which only Matt had a decent voice. Mary Jane was noticeably absent. Hilda said Matt's wife had to spend the evening with her father, who was in hospice, but the two boys were there, teasing Birdie and being pretty much obnoxious the way boys were. Assorted aunts and uncles and Jake showed up much later with a date who looked to be playing the part of sexually frustrated librarian with a severe bun, studious glasses and barely restrained breasts. The party was almost as irreverent as the Candlelight ceremony was reverent. Shelby had never experienced such a Christmas Eve.

Afterward, she and John headed back to Breezy Hill. Moonlight lay across the half-cut cane fields, softening the ruts and tangles. Silent as the night, John kept his eyes on the road, hand slung across the wheel as the miles sped by.

Looking at him, she couldn't help but think of Rebecca's words scrawled in the journal. She knew so much more about him now—like how he'd cried when Fancy had been diagnosed with breast cancer and how he didn't like sci-fi movies—all through the eyes of a woman who'd known his flaws, but loved him in spite of them.

Did that distort her own vision of John?

"So what did you think?" he asked.

His words jolted her, zapping her with guilt. She should tell him she'd read some of the journal. "About what?"

"Beauchamp Christmas Eve."

Shelby smiled. "It was like being in a TV show. Nothing like what I'm accustomed to."

"So can you handle it?"

"You mean as in from now on?"

He turned to her, his gaze intent, prying the lid off her emotions. His assumption she'd be a part of every family Christmas startled her, filled her with hope. And reservation. She didn't want to stumble here, relying on holiday cheer to color her decision. "I know you're feeling good after that rendition of 'Friends in Low Places,' but I'm not ready to make a big decision like staying in Magnolia Bend permanently. It's only been a month."

"But it's been a good month," he said, slowing the truck as they neared the entrance to Breezy Hill. "We get along and you like teaching here. Sure, people are still curious, but no one has turned a finger on you and screamed 'harlot.' So with that in mind—"

"Yikes," she yelped, grabbing the door handle as he took the turn too fast, grateful for the interruption.

She didn't want to have this conversation tonight. The service and party had given her what she'd always wanted as a girl—an old-fashioned TV-esque Christmas—and she didn't want to destroy the fantasy by having John, who was high on eggnog, propose something he wished he hadn't the next day.

John tapped the brakes. "Sorry."

"John, what are you really asking me?" Okay, obviously she *did* want to have the conversation.

His face tightened. "I guess I'm asking you to stay in Magnolia Bend until the baby is born.

Maybe even longer. I'm asking you if you'll make this more official."

"Make what official? My living with you? That's pretty much official, uh, 'cause I am."

"You said you'd stay for a while, but you never defined 'a while.' I'm trying to figure out how much more I need to do to—" He snapped his mouth shut and shook his head as the truck ground to a halt. John shifted into Park, and they sat there, truck idling, the headlights casting light onto the porch where the cat waited.

Shelby unbuckled her seat belt. "Need to what? Be nice to me? Give me just enough of yourself, just enough hope for something more so I'll stay?"

He whipped his head around. "You make it sound like I have motives other than—"

"Don't you? You wanted me to stay because of the baby. Don't create something false in order to string me along. Don't lead me to think there's a possibility of a future with you when you're not willing to let yourself feel anything."

"I'm not doing that. I want you to stay for a lot of reasons."

"Name one other than the fact I'm carrying your child."

"Are you shitting me?"

Shelby shook her head slowly. "No, I'm not shitting you."

John hooked a hand around her neck, and his lips covered hers, hot and hungry. She hadn't expected the assault, and her mouth fell open. He took advantage, deepening the kiss, tightening his grip.

He tasted so good. A little like bourbon, a little like the chocolate icing on the cupcakes and a lot like pent-up, horny man.

Shelby dissolved into liquid, melting against him, starved for the man she'd wanted ever since he'd bought her a drink and told her she made him feel like sunshine on that bar stool.

John's hand moved down and the next thing she knew, he'd hooked her under her arms and dragged her into his lap, never ceasing to keep his mouth moving over hers. His tongue stroked, teased, revved her engine to full-on purr. She wound her arms around his neck, drawing him to her, and kissed him back.

Her fingers raked through his hair, making him moan.

He pulled back, his pupils dilated, his breathing erratic. "Because I want you," he said, dropping kisses along her jaw, moving his lips toward her ear. "All I want to do is touch you, taste you, sink inside of you. I think about it all day long. All night long. I can't stop. You make me crazy."

His mouth found her earlobe, and he nipped her while his free hand ran up and down her side, cupping her ass, cupping her breast.

"Sweet—" he murmured when he molded his hand to her breast. "I want to—"

He couldn't talk because he couldn't stop devouring her, and Shelby didn't want him to stop. His reason for wanting her in Magnolia Bend sounded good enough at the moment. She grabbed him by his hair and dragged his mouth back to hers, shifting in his arms so she could get closer. He crushed her to him, his mouth and hands everywhere at once.

For several minutes, Shelby was content to receive his touch, reveling in the heat of his kiss. John, however, wasn't as satisfied and wrenched his mouth from hers, tugging at the neckline of her dress, sliding the stretchy fabric over one shoulder.

"Please," he said, pulling the bra strap, too. "I didn't get to see them before, and all I can think about is the way they'll fill my hands."

His words bathed her in pleasure and her breasts so heavy and full from pregnancy literally ached. She tugged the dress over her other shoulder and reached around and unhooked her bra. The black lace barely contained them and the bra flew out of her hands landing somewhere that didn't matter at the moment.

"Oh, sweet mother of—" John groaned, cupping each breast and lifting them, lowering his head to nestle his face between them. Then he caught one pink tip, closing his mouth around it. Her head dropped back.

"Ahhh…" she groaned.

And then her shoulder blade caught the horn.

The sound jolted both of them. John lifted his head and looked at her leaning back across his steering wheel. He looked struck dumb at the sight of her half-naked in his lap.

Shelby lifted her hands to cover her naked breasts and for a good ten seconds, they stared at one another, each panting, each taken aback about how quickly it went from a simple kiss to second base.

"I swear to God if you apologize to me, I'm going to punch you in the nose," she said finally.

A sharp bark of laughter escaped John. "Apologize? For the sweetest moment I've had since September? Not on your life."

Shelby slid off his lap while simultaneously searching for her bra. Losing her underthings had become a habit around John. "Um, have you seen my bra?"

"Like I'd give it to you. If I had breasts like that, I'd never cover them."

"If you had breasts like these we wouldn't be having this conversation."

"True," he said, dangling her black bra from his fingertips.

She plucked the lace offering with one hand, carefully containing her flesh with one arm. She'd have to drop her arm and reveal herself to put the bra back on. Moments ago, she'd not hesitated to unhook it, but the honk of the horn had been like a glass of water in the face, cooling the ardor, reminding her that physical pleasure wasn't the only thing she wanted from John.

Somehow she wanted more.

He unbuckled his seat belt, tilting his shoulder forward, giving his gaze to Freddy, who twined around the porch column meowing for attention.

John Beauchamp was a Southern gentleman, averting his eyes, giving her a piece of privacy. So frickin' sweet.

Shelby hurriedly pulled on her bra and tugged up her dress.

"Ready?" he asked.

"Ready. I think."

John paused and glanced back at her in the weak cab light. "I'm not sorry for kissing you, but I didn't mean to attack you, either. Obviously, you weren't ready for that."

"I'm pretty sure I was. You just got to second base without even trying hard. If that horn hadn't honked, you'd probably be sliding into home about now."

"Oh, don't tempt me," he groaned, making a pained face. "But I didn't mean attack in a physical sense, I meant emotionally. I think both of us are more than ready on a physical level."

"Well, that *is* how we started."

"But I've moved past the horny-for-you stage."

At her arched brow, he backpedaled. "Don't get me wrong, I'm horny as a fourteen-year-old boy the day the *Victoria's Secret* magazine arrives." He laughed at that thought before growing serious. "But I want more than sex, Shelby."

"You want more than being roommates? Because then we go from you giving me a place to stay to living together. That's a big step."

John pressed his lips together. "I know."

"If we're really going to move on to something else, we need to rethink our living situation. There's much to consider, like your image in the community and your job here at Breezy Hill. If we sleep together then everything you've professed about us becomes a lie," Shelby said, climbing from the cab and closing the door, grateful for the cloak of darkness so he couldn't see how much she wanted him to want her.

Ever since she was old enough for lipstick, she wanted a man to love her. Why was that so important?

Okay, she knew. She'd had some therapy after the scandal at her dad's law firm and knew the lack of parental attention, combined with the feeling of being unwanted by her siblings, had colored her relationships with men. Beyond everything, she desired to feel normal, to be valued, loved and accepted for who she was. Yeah, pretty much what everyone on God's green earth wanted. She merely happened to be overly focused on it.

John cleared his throat, waiting for her to round the truck. So she did, falling into step with him, wishing she'd kept her mouth shut…before the kiss and after. This vulnerability thing she had going on embarrassed her. Even if she did want to screw him up one wall and down the other, she shouldn't be so eager to put everything out there. Hadn't the past taught her as much?

"It's not a lie," he said. "And just to clarify, I'm not stringing you along so you'll stay in Louisiana with the baby. I want to move forward with you," he said, climbing the steps, "but I can't promise love and a future with a bow on it."

"Who can ever really promise happily ever after?"

"I guess I learned the hard way nothing is certain, but I no longer want to be the man you met in that bar. I don't want to run."

Hope flooded her. "You don't?"

"No. You make me want to be better. For you. And you've done it by giving me a space to heal. For the first time since I lost her, I can think about Rebecca and our past without guilt and sadness. If you and I are never more than friends and parents, I'll always be thankful for meeting you, Shelby."

"Wow, that might be the coolest thing anyone has ever said to me." She climbed the steps, stooping to give the purring Freddy a scratch. "Thank you."

"I don't think anyone has ever called me cool."

"A monumental night for both of us," Shelby joked before jabbing a finger into his chest. "And I didn't say you were cool, I said what you said was cool. There's a difference."

John drew her into his arms, nudging the purring feline away from his feet. Brushing away a piece of hair that had loosened during their earlier kiss, he glanced down at her, the planes of his face in sharp relief in the orange glow of the porch light.

He dropped his head and caught her lips in the sweetest of kisses. Breaking it, he cupped her chin and tilted her face to his.

"Shelby?"

The kiss made her all woozy again. "Hmm?"

"Will you go out with me?"

"I just did."

"No, an official date. Dressed up for a nice dinner, maybe a bottle of wine."

"I can't drink because you already knocked me up," she said, rising onto her toes and brushing a kiss across his mouth. "But I'd love to go on a date with you."

"Good," he said, giving her another kiss as the cat twined around their ankles as unrelenting as the desire clinging to them. "I have a good feeling about this new year."

"Yeah?"

"Yeah. Something good is on the horizon. Finally."

CHAPTER SEVENTEEN

CHRISTMAS MORNING DAWNED clear and cold. Frost covered the lawn, crystalline in the rising sun. John puttered around the kitchen in his blue robe and moccasin slippers looking for the coffee he bought a few weeks back.

"It's on the shelf next to the tea caddy," Shelby said, peering over his shoulder.

"Tea caddy? What's that?"

"Right here," Shelby said, reaching over his shoulder and tapping the shelf. Sure enough, the red-and-gold Community Coffee bag sat right next to some organizer thing. He was happy to find the coffee and even happier to feel the brush of Shelby's unbound breasts against his back.

He'd gone to bed hard as a poker, making do with recalling the weight of her breasts cradled in his hands along with the taste of her sweet, sweet—

"Can you move?" she asked, poking his shoulder.

Right. He turned around. "Are you feeling okay today? Seem grumpy."

She made a contrite face. "Sorry. I didn't sleep well."

"Well, you could have slept very, very well

after a satisfying night in my bed…so that's your own fault."

Her eyes widened, and he decided he liked shocking her.

"Yeah?" she said, poking his chest this time. "If I remember Boots Grocery bathroom correctly, I would say there's a fifty-fifty chance I could have slept well."

"Wait a sec, are you suggesting I'm a bad lover?"

"If the boot fits, lace that bitch up and wear it," she said with a grin, pushing him aside and grabbing the box of herbal tea.

"I know you didn't just say that." He caught her hand and pulled her back to him.

Shelby grinned, her face makeup free, her blond hair tangled, the robe belted around her expanding waist. He pulled her to him and she looped her arms about his neck, leaning back. "I guess you got some convincing to do."

"I guess I do, but what man doesn't love a challenge?"

Shelby rose on her toes and brushed her lips against his before slipping from his arms. "I like being your challenge."

John set about making coffee, keeping one eye on the woman sliding a foil-covered casserole dish from the fridge and delivering it to the waiting oven. John may have spent long days in the fields, but since Shelby's substitute teaching gig ended with the start of Christmas vacation, she'd spent the previous five days doing Christmasy stuff like wrapping presents, trying Pinterest—whatever that was—recipes and cooking. So she couldn't complain about the love-making skills he hadn't had a chance to practice on her if he couldn't complain about some truly awful dinners he'd consumed over the past week. "What's that?"

"Breakfast casserole."

"Yum," he said unconvincingly.

"No, it's good. I followed every step and made sure I cooked the sausage *before* I put it together. It's going to be perfect because this is our first Christmas together."

He stiffened at her words. Their first Christmas together. Sounded so strange to think they'd made a commitment of sorts. Or maybe they hadn't so much as made a commitment as caused the commitment back in September. But either way, they were about to find out what they might have together.

Last night when he'd asked her to take their relationship to the next level, she'd been cautious, which had surprised him. Passion was a positive quality of this new woman in his life, and after the way they'd nearly gone up in smoke from their encounter in the truck, he thought she'd be more willing to move from friends to lovers.

Presently, he was tired of moving slowly, but dating sounded good…even if they'd already had sex, made a baby and moved in together. Already the flirting and kissing thrilled him, and something about walking backward before they could walk forward again made sense.

"Did you call your parents to wish them a Merry Christmas?" he asked.

"Not yet. Still early in Seattle, besides Mother isn't talking to me at the moment, though she did send me a polite note thanking me for her gift." Shelby pulled orange juice out of the fridge and poured some into two glasses. Already she knew what he liked to drink and that thought warmed him.

"Oh, well, at least she's communicating in some way."

"I guess. She refuses to believe I'm having a baby and can't figure out why I would want to stay in Mississippi to have it."

"Mississippi?"

"To mother, all Southern states are alike. Except Texas. She likes Texas for whatever reason."

Just as the coffee finished brewing, the doorbell rang.

"I say someone must be delivering the prize Christmas goose," Shelby joked in her best British voice. They'd watched George C. Scott's version of *A Christmas Carol* last night instead of indulging in other pleasurable activities. Shelby had kept the popcorn bowl firmly between them and had given him a chaste kiss right before midnight.

John walked to the front door, trying not to smile like a fool. There was something so wonderful about a cold Christmas morning and a sexy woman flirting with him in the kitchen.

When he opened the door, he found Carla Stanton wrapped in a long wool coat standing on the doorstep.

His joy shriveled, and at that moment he absolutely knew he'd screwed up. Carla looked brittle, despite the high color in her cheeks.

Bart barked and bounded toward the woman. John caught the dog's collar just as he rose up to plant his paws on Carla. "Down, Bart."

He reined in the beast and added, "Hey, Merry Christmas, Carla."

"Merry Christmas," the woman said, her face pinched. She brushed a hand down at Bart who leaped against the restraint.

"Won't you come in?"

"Why wouldn't I? This is my house after all," she said with a lift of her chin.

At those words, John's stomach pitched. Why in the hell hadn't he already visited Carla and smoothed her ruffled feathers? But, of course, he knew why—after long days in the fields, he hadn't wanted to give up any time with Shelby. For the past month, he'd ignored anything that might jeopardize their getting to know each other…and Carla was a major boat rocker. But he should have sucked it up and made sure his mother-in-law understood about Shelby.

Carla stepped inside and John closed the door. "Good to see you. We missed you last night at Mom and Dad's."

Her look withered. "I'm sure you did."

Whoa. He'd never seen Carla Stanton so cold and angry. This was a woman he didn't know. "Uh, what brings you out today?"

"Business," she said.

"It's Christmas Day, Carla. Even I don't do business on Christmas."

"Well, it's just another day to me."

"Carla," he said, softening his voice. "Rebecca and Hal aren't here, but that doesn't mean the day isn't—"

"What? A day of rejoicing? Damn. I forgot to be joyful. Sue me."

John cast a glance at the kitchen, praying Shelby wouldn't come traipsing out in her robe. All he needed was for Carla to see the intimacy and grow even angrier. If he needed a bit of time to accustom himself to a possible new life, Carla needed an eternity. She'd clung to her grief over her daughter even harder than he had. "This isn't like you, Carla. You love Christmas."

"Correction. Loved. Not any longer," Carla said, eyeing the tree and the gifts beneath. He could see her thoughts.

"Would you like a cup of coffee?" he asked, motioning her toward the couch with the throw tossed carelessly from last night. The coffee table held the empty popcorn bowl and two glasses. The house looked very lived-in, unlike the past few months where he'd barely existed in the rooms at all.

"No, thank you," she said, sinking onto the wingback chair and pursing her lips. "I've come for a specific reason."

John sank onto the couch. "Yes?"

"I'm here to ask you to do what is right."

"What is right?" he repeated.

"To stop living in sin with that woman."

"I'm not living in sin," he said. Of course, if Shelby hadn't stopped him last night, he would have had to consider the possibility.

"You're living with that woman."

"I have a name," Shelby said from the doorway of the kitchen.

Oh, no. Not good.

Carla turned toward Shelby, her eyes narrowing, taking in her mussed hair and robe. "I don't care what your name is. I care only that you leave Breezy Hill. You don't belong here."

Shelby moved into the room, a steaming cup of tea in hand. "Why is that?"

"Because this house belongs to the Stanton trust. I'm the beneficiary and guardian of that trust. I don't want you here. I thought John would get the hint a few weeks ago, but here you still are."

Shelby looked hard at Carla.

Carla looked back equally hard.

John wondered if he could create a distraction. Maybe a fire? Okay, that would be cowardly. "Carla, Shelby and I have not—" he stopped himself from explaining. Carla had no business trying to control his personal life. "Did you think I would mourn Rebecca forever? That I would live alone for the rest of my life?"

His former mother-in-law snapped her head around, zeroing in on him with eyes so like Rebecca's, except way angrier than his wife's had ever been. "I thought you'd wait until my daughter was cold in the grave."

Her words slapped him. "Jesus, Carla, it's been over a year since Rebecca died—a miserable, horrible year."

"But it didn't take you long to find someone to ease your pain, did it?"

"Wait a minute," Shelby said, moving toward Carla. "You think there's a time limit on grief? Or are you so selfish you'd want him to waste away, pining for your daughter? Do you think Rebecca would have wanted that for the man she loved?"

Carla stood and aimed a finger at Shelby. "Don't talk about my daughter like you knew her. She was—"

"An angel," Shelby finished. "Yeah, I get it. And if she was so good, would she have wanted this between you two? I don't think so."

"You don't get an opinion, missy," Carla said, breathing hard. In her dark eyes, John saw a hurt so deep it might never be healed. Turning away from Shelby, Carla jabbed her finger at him. "I came to warn you that there are repercussions to actions."

"Warn me?"

"You remember the day I told you that you could stay at Breezy Hill? I meant it that day. You've proven a good caretaker of the land, but if you persist in shacking up with this two-bit hussy—"

"I'm at least three bits," Shelby shouted, her cheeks flushed. Dread knotted inside him, but that didn't stop him from noticing her breasts moving up and down with her quickened breaths. The woman was magnificent when angry.

Carla's gave a bitter laugh. "Fine, have it your way…a three-bit whore."

Shelby crossed her arms, spilling a little of her tea, and nodded. "Thanks. Three bits is better, and honestly, I'd rather be a whore than a miserable, broken old woman who can't see past the end of her own nose. At least whores aren't selfish cows."

Carla opened and shut her mouth several times before ripping her gaze from Shelby and fixing it on him. "You understand, don't you, John? This land, this house, all you have loved for well over a decade is at risk. You have a choice to make."

"Don't do this, Carla," he said. "Let's talk next week. Don't go off half-cocked, making assumptions. Moving forward is always hard. It's been hard on me, too."

The older woman's eyes flicked from him to Shelby, as icy as the December morning outside the door. "Doesn't look so hard for you. My eyes work rather well."

"But not your heart," Shelby said, her words falling like hot lead on a cold battlefront.

Carla made a noise in the back of her throat and spun toward the front door. "I shouldn't have come. Should have left well enough alone, leaving the cards to fall where they may. I was trying to be generous and give you another chance. My little Christmas gift to you."

"Wait, Carla," he said, not knowing what to do to

make the situation better. He'd never thought Carla would take Breezy Hill from him. The place had been essentially his since Hal had passed away eight years ago. Of course, essentially wasn't the same as legally. And that's all that mattered in the courts. He'd actually thought that once Carla got past the shock of Shelby, she'd be happy for him. But he'd been way off base, and in the time he'd spent getting to know Shelby, Carla's initial anger had knitted into something ugly. Instead of accepting, she'd put her energy into making him pay for wanting to love again. "Think about what you're doing. This isn't like you."

She whirled, tears in her eyes. "You think about what you're doing. This is Stanton land. This is the house where Rebecca grew up." Carla pointed at the stairs. "The third step is where she fell and cracked her tooth, and that piano is where she sat and picked out the first strands of 'The Entertainer,' and that coffee table is where she stood and danced to 'N Sync when she was fifteen. So don't tell me to think. You're desecrating her memory by screwing that woman in the bed you shared with my daughter, you bastard."

She paused, taking a deep, steadying breath. "I'll dissolve the trust and sell this place before I let you be happy here with her." She didn't say more. Just clamped her mouth shout, stalked to the door and walked out. She didn't even bother to close the door behind her.

For several seconds John stared at the empty

space. Finally, Shelby walked over and closed the door, the snick of the latch like thunder in the room.

John sank back on the couch. "Well, Merry Christmas to me."

"Wow, she's really mad," Shelby said, leaning against the door with a sigh. "When I told her I was living here, I poked her with a stick."

"I never thought she'd go to such lengths. I knew being with you would be hard for her, but I didn't think it would make her want to destroy me."

"We've got a lot stacked against us," Shelby said, her hand shaking as she lifted the cup of tea to her lips. "You want to trash the idea of dating? Maybe I should find a place in town…or go back to Seattle for a while."

"No. I'm not letting Carla or anyone else keep me in the past. Last year was the worst year of my life, and Carla's anger isn't destroying what I've found with you. Rebecca would have wanted me to be happy."

"I think so, too," Shelby said with a strange look on her face. "You know, everybody remembers Rebecca as such an angel, but the grieving heart looks on lost loved ones with forgiving eyes. They forget they were once human. Rebecca wasn't perfect, but she loved you. And when you love someone, you want them to be happy. So whatever that is, John, you will have to decide. But your wife wouldn't have begrudged you happiness. I know her a little."

John turned Shelby's words over in his mind, weighing if they were said with any intent to sway him. They weren't. Even if Shelby weren't in the picture, the words would be true. Rebecca wasn't perfect, but she'd been a good person, who'd loved him enough to want his happiness. "How do you know her a little?"

"Well, for one thing, she's very much a part of this house. I find little notes she's written, like the recipe for blackening seasoning taped to the inside of a cabinet door, and there are certain ways things are organized, but most of all I know because I read some of her journal."

"Read her journal?"

Shelby's face turned red. "I tried to give it to you, and then when I saw Carla at the market, I tried to tell her about it. But no one wanted it, and I was lonely and…it was wrong of me, but I'm not sorry."

He didn't know what to say. He remembered Shelby trying to give him the journal the day he'd watched her sleeping in those polka-dot panties. Before that time, he'd never known Rebecca had kept a journal. Just how personal was it? "You shouldn't have—"

"I know. I can't unread it, but my point is Rebecca is no longer a phantom, an unknown entity I have to compete with—"

"Why would you think you have to compete?"

"Don't you remember my past? I've competed with unknown women two other times, and there was no way for me to know your wife beyond other people's memories. I know it was wrong. I tried to stop, but it was like hiding chocolate from myself when I'm on a diet."

He looked at her with no words. Part of him felt betrayed, the other half wondered if Rebecca had done for him what he could never do—teach Shelby about what a committed relationship looked like. Wasn't always sunshine and daisies.

"Rebecca wouldn't want you to be as miserable as you were. She loved you that much."

John leaned back and closed his eyes, wishing he could go back to flirting in the kitchen. Before Carla arrived to stomp on his happiness.

I'll dissolve the trust and sell this place before I let you be happy here.

Those words punched a hole in his resolve.

Lose Breezy Hill? The thought sickened him. He'd poured every ounce of energy and love into the land, not to mention most of the profits on upkeep, the new barn and a new harvester. If he didn't have Breezy Hill, who was he?

He rose and picked up the remnants of last night's stay-at-home date. "I think we should put worry on the back burner. Today is Christmas Day, a time for presents and my mom's pecan pie. I can do nothing about Carla today, and as for the journal…" He shrugged. He didn't know if he was ready to read Rebecca's words. Reading the journal could pull him back into that lonely painful place he'd occupied for too long.

Shelby tried to smile. "You wanna try my breakfast casserole?"

"The one made by a three-bit whore?"

Shelby threw a pillow at him. "I'm upping myself to a whole four bits."

Carla's warning had the opposite effect on him, solidifying how good Shelby was for him. He couldn't go back to the man he was last year. Too late. He'd moved toward Shelby.

But not all was lost.

Carla's grief may have made her irrational, but maybe he could convince her that letting go of the anger was the only chance she had to be happy again. "Four bits, huh? Guess I better start saving my pennies."

CHRISTMAS DINNER AT the Beauchamps was anticlimactic compared to the Christmas Eve bash with John's uncle booming out a Weather Girls' classic and Fancy getting a little sloshed and doing some dance she'd learned online with said uncle. The turkey was a little dry, according to the gassy aunt, and the sweet potatoes were delicious, even if there was a marshmallow topping. In Seattle, they called them yams, but in the South, things were different. No mashed potatoes or asparagus with a crown pork roast. No sparkling champagne, no light conversation about the latest in art nouveau cinema or Pulitzer-prize-winning documentaries.

In other words, Beauchamp Christmas dinner was fattening and enjoyable, even if they did yell a lot at the football game on TV.

After dinner, the family exchanged gifts, and Shelby received a hand-knitted scarf and book of poetry from Abigail, a teacher mug and gift card from Matt and Mary Jane, some body lotion and scrub from Jake and a lovely embroidered pillow with her initials from John's parents. She'd reciprocated with like gifts, the kind you get for people you really don't know well enough—candles, bath salts, cashmere gloves.

Even though he smiled throughout the time at his parents' house, John looked worried. Carla's visit that morning had complicated things. Maybe dating wasn't a good idea. Maybe it was time to stop putting her life on pause, nurturing hope she and John could be more, and look at the reality of the situation. If they continued on the path they walked, it was a real possibility John could lose all he'd known.

When they returned to Breezy Hill, John lit a fire and poured himself a glass of wine and Shelby a glass of sparkling cider. The logs crackled and hissed in the hearth.

"This is nice," he said, settling beside her, just as he had the night before.

"It is," she said, staring into the flames.

"Did you enjoy today?"

"I did…other than the visit from Carla Stanton this morning."

He grew still but said nothing.

"I don't want you to have to choose. It's not fair,

because you never asked for any of this. You've been kind—"

"I wanted you to stay. I needed you to stay. Don't you get that?" He attempted to smile through his worry.

"Even if I went back to Seattle I would never deny you access to your child."

"This is about more than the baby. You know that," he said as he rubbed her shoulder. "Hey, we still have a few hours left of Christmas Day and I don't want to talk about anything unpleasant. Here." John pulled a slender jeweler's box from his pocket.

"What is this?" she asked, letting go of the worry and embracing the concept of enjoying the moment.

"I didn't have time to go into town, so I ordered this for you," he said, handing her the box. Something about his uncertainty touched her.

"You didn't have to—" she began.

"I wanted to. You're far away from family. And you're important to me."

Shelby slid the red bow off and pulled the gold foil paper from the box. Lifting the lid, she found a beautiful gold charm bracelet. Three charms hung on the bracelet. One was an *S* chipped with diamond rhinestones, the other was a small gold pacifier and the final one was a heart with the word *Mother* written in script. "Oh, John, it's lovely."

"You can add to it as the baby grows," he said, his eyes searching hers. "I hope it's not too—"

Shelby silenced him with her mouth.

He gathered her to him, deepening the kiss, stroking his tongue against hers in an unhurried, thorough kiss.

Shelby drew back. "It's perfect, and I don't think I've ever received something so thoughtful."

"Good." He smiled, settling back on the couch, snuggling her against him as the fire caught and blazed. Pressing the remote on the table, *White Christmas* came on the satellite TV.

"I have a gift for you, too," she said, not moving because the warmth he lent allowed strange contentment to seep into her bones.

"Do you?" he asked, twining his finger in her hair, also seemingly relaxed for the first time since Carla's untimely visit.

"Let me get it," she said.

"Later," he murmured, not releasing his hold on her. "This feels too good."

She smiled, unwound his finger from her curl and went to the tree, pulling out the large flat box wrapped in brown paper. She set it in his lap. "Here."

The light from the hearth threw flickering shadows over his face. "This is a big gift."

"For a big man."

"Oh, you remembered," he said.

His naughty joke made her snort. In all honesty, she didn't remember much about that night in Boots. He could have been a gherkin for all she knew. "Keep talking and you'll be digging out that money."

He looked confused.

"The four bits," she teased.

"That's right. Your price went up," he said, pulling the string off the gift. Carefully unwrapping the paper, he lifted the framed picture.

"It's Breezy Hill," he said, incredulity in his voice.

She could see her gift hit the mark. One of her friends from college was an artist. One morning when the sky had been soft and the sun peeked out over the cane fields, she'd taken a few snapshots and sent them to him. The painting he'd done had a hazy quality that softened the picture with smudged edges. The house sat prominent against the gray-green of the cane, backlit by the emerging sunrise. "I call it 'A Breezy Morning.'"

He ran a hand over the line of the roof. "It's...I don't have words."

"Sometimes it's okay not to have words."

He placed the picture on the table and gathered her in his arms, dropping small kisses across her cheeks before covering her mouth with his. It was a good kiss.

A toe-curling kiss.

A kiss to build a future on.

But still there was so much between them.

When he let her go, she looked up at him and murmured, "I like how you don't use words."

"Thank you," he said, his voice thick with emotion. And then and there on the couch of Breezy Hill, she experienced something she'd felt only once before in her life.

She fell in love.

It wasn't an epiphany, bells didn't sound and an angelic chorus didn't sing. It just…was.

"You're welcome," she said, fighting back the sudden prick of tears.

He settled her back against him. "New Year's Eve is around the corner. Might be a good time for our first official date."

"Can you take the time off?"

"If I work hard this week, I can manage it."

Shelby smiled. "Good. I already made us a reservation."

"Oh?"

She hesitated for a moment. After this morning, she hadn't been sure they should take their relationship to the next level. Carla's ultimatum sat between them, and Shelby had meant what she said—she wouldn't make John choose—but she wasn't going to give up on John. "At August in New Orleans. I also booked a suite at Windsor Court in case we drink too much and don't want to drive back."

"I'm pretty sure you won't drink too much. You're pregnant."

"Even so I'm pretty sure you won't want to drive back," she said, underlining her words with suggestiveness.

He didn't say anything, but then he pushed her back as if to rise.

"What are you doing?"

"I'm going out to work right now. I'm going to

need a full twenty-four hours off if you mean what I think you mean."

Shelby pulled him back, settling herself again in his arms. "Silly man, but I expect you better bring those four bits. I foresee us having to look for my underwear at some point during the night."

John dropped a kiss atop her head.

CHAPTER EIGHTEEN

CARLA STOOD OUTSIDE her patio home in the cool wind, surveying the white narcissus that had sprung up too early.

She loved seeing them explode in the window boxes in February. Damn things were noncompliant. Just like everyone else in her life. Dim Sum frolicked under the pin oak, which still shed leaves and harbored a few frisky squirrels.

"Carla?"

She turned to find John standing behind her. "John."

No surprise there. She knew he'd come. He was a man who thought his words could sway.

"Hope I haven't caught you at a bad time?"

"No, just fussing at flowers that ignore the fact it's too early to sprout," she said, brushing the dirt from her hands and motioning toward her porch. "Let's get out of this wind."

John had come from the fields. She could smell the cane on him, and the scent brought back memories of Hal coming home smelling of a hard day's work laced with the pungent sweet scent of the cane. Like a gentleman, John allowed her to pass, and she climbed the stairs slower than she wished, and settled in the wicker rocker.

John took the corresponding rocker, clasping his big hands between his knees. His tanned face crinkled in thought. "You know why I'm here."

"I do. You think you can change my mind."

"This has been hard, Carla."

"I don't doubt that," she said, looking out at the dog circling the tree. "Come here, Dim Sum."

The dog ignored her. She should have gotten a bitch rather than a male. Stubborn and unyielding in nature, Dim Sum was a credit to his gender. The dog ignored Carla and did whatever the hell he wanted.

"Want me to get him?" John asked.

"No, he's determined to get a squirrel this year. Once they shake to death one squirrel, they're hooked."

"This past year has been bad for you, too."

"You think?" she drawled before catching hold of her bitterness and reeling it back. "Yes. I lost my only child to a senseless accident."

He stiffened, his eyes darkening. Perhaps she shouldn't have poured salt in that particular wound, but she'd put gentility behind her. John's damn shotgun had killed her Rebecca. *Senseless* was a compassionate word for what she felt about the accident.

"Yes," he said, his eye focused on Dim Sum, who stood still as a statue, head tilted up, focusing on the branches supporting the barking squirrel.

"I've hated you as much as I've loved you, John. What happened to Rebecca wounded me. There's no way to fix that. I felt grief when I lost Hal, but it was fifty-fifty on whether I'd go first or he'd go. But when Rebecca died…well, it's not right for a child to beat a parent to the grave. I had thought I'd have years of grandchildren, of watching you two grow the Stanton family, but it was a cruel figment of my imagination."

"I had thought the same thing, Carla."

"So why are you letting it go so easily?"

He turned his head, his gaze settling on her. "Listen to that question, Carla."

"You know what I mean."

"No. I don't. Rebecca's gone. There is no 'it' to hold on to, and I can't live in the dark anymore. Grief is a terrible place that can suck a person in and not let go."

"You replaced her," Carla said, her heart contracting in her chest, "with that woman."

"I didn't replace Rebecca. She's irreplaceable, but she would have liked Shelby."

"You don't know what Rebecca would have liked. The last year of your marriage wasn't good. You spent all your time in the fields and she spent all her time crying. She wanted a baby and you had given up on her."

Something on his face surpassed guilt. *Agony* was the right word. "Sure, things were tough," he said. "All those hormones made her too emotional, but I never asked for a break from our marriage, just a break from the fertility treatments. She agreed. We planned a week away in Mexico right after harvest.

That's why Rebecca went to Gonzales that day. She'd met with a travel agent."

Carla said nothing.

"Don't do this to me, Carla. Don't say our marriage wasn't good. Don't make me carry any more of a burden than what I already carry."

Carla closed her eyes. "I'm still so angry about what happened. There are so many what-ifs."

"Yeah, there are, but I can't live that way anymore. Every single day for the past year, I've lived thinking what-if. But thing is, I can't change what happened. All I can do is go on without Rebecca, grateful for the time I had loving her. She wouldn't want me to live hurt and alone, unable to ever love again. She wasn't that kind of person."

Carla's clutched her chest and rocked for a moment, soaking in the truthfulness of his words. But even as part of her knew he was right, another part of her heart hardened. How could he replace her daughter so easily, so quickly…and with someone who looked like she belonged in a tube top and Hooter shorts?

This wasn't about love…it was about lust.

Maybe it wouldn't have mattered who John moved on with, because it signified the true end—his letting go meant Rebecca was truly dead. Of course, Carla knew this, but the thought of John getting to love again while Rebecca lay cold in a grave felt like a hot poker sinking into her flesh. "But things have changed. I have changed."

"Enough to sell Breezy Hill?"

Carla barricaded her emotions, reminding herself John had motive to convince her otherwise. He wanted his cake and to eat it right in front of her, sharing it with Shelby. "You can't have Breezy Hill and Shelby, too. Sorry. If you want her, I'll petition to dissolve the trust. Actually, I'm doing that no matter what I decide to do with the land."

"Why?"

"Because there are no more Stantons."

"There are other Stantons."

"But none who want a farm. They'd sell it anyway so why should I hold on to something no one wants?"

"I want it."

She didn't say anything else for a few minutes. Part of her wanted to do as he asked. Just let John live and work the land. She could think about what to do with all of it later. When it was easier and didn't hurt so much. But the other part of her wanted to punish him, wanted to make him live where she lived—in the dark realm of loss. "You should go."

John stood. "The harvest will be finished by mid-January. Pray on this, Carla."

"Don't," she said.

"I hope your need to punish me for what happened to Rebecca will wane with the knowledge I loved Rebecca and I love Breezy Hill."

"This isn't about love," Carla snapped, angry he'd brought God into it, angry he sounded so rational.

"It *is* about love, and so you know, I won't give up the chance to feel that way again. That will always be my answer, Carla."

With those words, John walked across the small porch, down the steps and climbed into the pickup truck he'd bought when he and Rebecca married. The old work truck was dented and well-used, the hallmark of a serious farmer whose fields were more important than style. John tipped his hat and with a final wave drove away, no doubt heading back to the tractor Hal had breathed his last breath in.

Pragmatic.

John had always been even-keeled and focused on the land. He'd loved her daughter, that she knew, but he'd also benefited from marrying Rebecca.

So how could he set it aside so easily, losing his head over a woman like the one he shacked up with?

So unlike the son-in-law she'd once loved.

Carla didn't understand him anymore, and she damn sure didn't respect a man who would jeopardize all he was for a pair of big tits. And if she couldn't respect him, she couldn't let him continue at Breezy Hill, farming, managing, safeguarding something that didn't exist anymore. The farm that had once meant everything to Hal was no more. She'd given John a chance to make things right again, and he'd spouted some drivel about moving on.

Well, she *was* moving on.

Tomorrow she'd call Duke at the bank and convince him to sign off on the dissolution of the trust. And she'd call the attorney's office to have the paperwork filed and rushed through. Harvest would be over, the cane would be in the mill, and Breezy Hill would go on the block.

If John wanted Breezy Hill, he'd have to flippin' buy it.

That's how she was moving on.

"Get up here now, Dim Sum," she said, standing. Finally, the little dog abandoned his post and trotted toward her, tongue lolling out happily. "Well, at least you can be happy about not getting what you want."

SHELBY STOOD IN the middle of the hotel suite cursing at the red cocktail dress.

She couldn't zip it.

Mother fricker.

She tugged again and heard the telltale rip.

Closing her eyes, she unzipped the part she'd been able to zip, stepped out of her favorite dress and kicked it across the room. Standing in a garter belt, red lace bra and high stilettos, she looked exactly like what Carla had accused her of being—a two-bit whore.

No. She wore La Perla.

Definitely worth four bits.

She'd brought one other dress—a stretchy bit of red lace that curved against her body. It would fit a woman who weighed two hundred and fifty pounds or one who weighed under a hundred. Either way, it fit like liquid satin, hugging every curve and every flaw.

Shelby didn't feel like having every flaw highlighted, but it was the only option she had left. Her stomach pooched out. Well, she *was* pregnant, but the long-sleeved stretchy see-through dress made her look like the Commodores' hit song.

Come on, baby. You can rock this look. Boobs, ass, kicking curves. A little pooch couldn't take away from letting it all hang out.

Shelby tugged on the dress, deciding to own it. She gathered her hair and twisted it into a knot, pinned it up, and then slid on her drop diamond earrings. She finished with sultry red lipstick.

Yep. She looked like a walking ad for sex, and after a week of flirting, taking long showers and waking from erotic dreams featuring John, she was ready to deliver as advertised.

Taking a deep breath, she opened the bedroom door and walked out. John turned around, holding a glass of whiskey, looking dashing in a navy suit.

"Holy shit," he said, swallowing.

"Figured I'd give you your money's worth," she said with a little bit of purr in her voice.

He didn't answer because he was busy undressing her with his eyes. "Stop," she said.

"What?"

"Doing what you're doing. We're not going to make the reservation if you keep looking at me like you can see the red lace bra I'm wearing. And the panties I'm not."

He tossed back the entire drink. "Holy shit."

She laughed, and it sounded like an invitation, but not yet. Shelby liked foreplay. She liked drawing it out. After their first time in that disgusting bathroom, they both deserved to be driven crazy by desire. Slow and torturous.

She picked up her jacket. "Let's grab a cab. We can make out in the backseat."

John picked up the phone on the secretary and punched a button. "We need a cab out front, please." Hanging up, he turned and watched her ease into her jacket.

"I'd help you with that, but if I touch you, one of two things will occur. I'll either strip you naked and we won't see champagne and oysters until breakfast or I'll have to change my pants."

Shelby laughed, suddenly very happy the appropriate satin red dress hadn't fit her. "Well, then keep your distance because I'm eating for two. If you want any chance of me being able to stay awake all night to do delicious things to your body, I'll need sustenance."

"Quick. Talk about world poverty or sweaty gym socks or poison ivy, because if you keep dropping those little innuendos, I'm not going to make it."

"That wasn't an innuendo. It was a promise," she said.

John groaned, reached out and slid his hand behind her thigh, moving it up, cupping the naked flesh of her ass. "You weren't lying."

Shelby straightened his tie, intentionally brushing against the nice erection tenting his pants before drawling, "I never lie about sex."

His response had her doubting their ability to make it to the cab. If she'd had panties on, they'd be damp. Turned on wasn't the concept for what she felt. Her body hummed with anticipation. She wanted the man she woke up thinking about every morning...and not just because she lived with him.

But because she loved him.

Tonight her heart was in the game and there was no going back.

John's hand shook as he poured another shot of bourbon.

Shelby smiled. "We better go."

He killed the drink and grabbed the room key. "After you. I want to watch the action from behind."

Shelby smiled and walked with an exaggerated gait to the elevator.

"Good show, good show," he teased from behind her.

SO MUCH FOR moving slowly.

John watched Shelby sip her water and tried to focus on an image of his fourth grade math teacher with her googly eyes, frizzy hair and horrible coffee breath. Dressed in a bikini.

Yeah. That deflated his lust a little.

The restaurant buzzed around them, but the intimacy at their table kept them in their own world.

"Are we still planning on going to your sister's bed-and-breakfast for New Year's Day buffet or will you have to go back to the fields?"

"Abigail has a full house this year, so we're switching to Mom and Dad's. I managed to eke out some extra time off. We haven't run into any issues this harvest. With the rain staying away, there are no rut repairs or bogged-down machinery. We should have the last of the cane to the sugar mill by midmonth."

"I'm sure that will be a relief," she said, finishing off the last of her eggplant parmesan. "What do you do next?"

Find another job?

No. Not going to think about Carla or Breezy Hill tonight. Just Shelby and a potential future. "Usually we do repairs, reassess fields and plant some soybeans. In farming, the work never ends, just slows down a bit."

"Did you go to school to be a farmer?"

He nodded, warming to the thought of her wanting to know about him and his passion for the land. "Sorta. I started out like most kids—majoring in business—but when a lot of graduating friends went to work at rent-a-car places, I looked hard at what I wanted. I loved living in Magnolia Bend. Since Rebecca and I were pretty serious, Hal steered me toward agriculture. I ended up with a masters, thinking that if things didn't work out, I could work for an agriculture chemical company or do crop consulting."

"So different from teaching."

"Yeah, but I love being out there, love the challenge of trying new things. Farming is a science and a gamble. There's something about that I love."

"So you're a risk taker." She smiled.

"Most people think of farming as simplistic and benign, but at heart a farmer is a rebel, shaking his fist against nature while secretly on his knees praying. I love what I do."

Shelby's knees kept brushing his, reminding him that though they talked on the surface about generalities, underneath simmered a hunger he'd kept at bay far too long. The delicate turn of her wrist, the curve of her breast revealed in the snug dress and the way silken strands of hair caressed her neck at each turn of her head drove him to near distraction.

"So what will you do about Carla?"

That question threw ice water on his desire way more effectively than thinking about Mrs. Shipley and her bad breath.

"There's nothing I can do about Carla. If she wants to hate our guts for…for…"

"Everyone hates guts. Think about it. Intestines and internal organs aren't on the top ten list of things people like."

"Only you," he said, shaking his head. Again, she turned discomfort into amusement. "But she's wrong about you. And me. We're not going to allow her actions to color this new beginning."

Shelby shrugged. "I don't, but others will agree with her."

Her words were true, and that alarmed him because he wanted her to stay. Once the truth about the baby was out, it would be harder. But the event in the bathroom that had created their baby was something altogether different than what heated the air between them tonight. That long ago night was about desperation, a need to feel comfort, a need to feel not so alone. But tonight was about fulfillment, about the need to be together.

"Do you want dessert?" he asked, changing the subject. He'd rather dance around what they would eventually face in order to get to what they would indulge in tonight.

Wrong or not, he wanted tonight with Shelby. Both of them needed to erase the booze-soaked desperation in their first hookup with tender, healing lovemaking.

"Do you want me to want dessert?" she countered.

"No."

Shelby laughed. "Then get the check already."

John paused, taking another sip of the watered-down bourbon. "We're doing this."

Shelby, the beautiful woman half the room couldn't keep their eyes off, stilled. "Well, we can't keep in a holding pattern. Eventually, we have to find out if what we have is worth it. Time to roll the dice on us. If we crap out, we crap out. But there's a chance this could be something more than making do in bad circumstances. This could be…meant to be."

Her words were ones he needed to hear.

John raised his hand and gestured to the waiter for the check. "Let's grab the brass ring and go for broke."

She smiled and it wasn't the sassy, sexy grin she'd been giving him all evening. This one held warmth, perhaps even relief. "You have the money? 'Cause I ain't cheap."

He reached in his jacket pocket and pulled out a fifty-cent piece and flipped it to her.

Shelby turned it in her hand. "You actually brought it?"

"You know it's just a joke, right?"

"Of course I do. Because if my body were for sale, it would be a helluva lot more than half a buck."

"I'd take out a loan."

"Damn straight," she said, her eyes teasing him back.

He signed the check, pulled out her chair, inhaling the scent of her expensive perfume, and wondered about Shelby's heart. She'd given it away several times before only to have it shattered. If her heart was up for grabs, the gift would be priceless.

He could accept her friendship, accept she would be the mother of his firstborn and accept her delectable body would be his tonight, but could he charge himself with safeguarding her heart?

She'd hinted he had the power to hurt her and that weighed on him. He was ready to move past grief, but was he really ready to fall in love again?

He didn't know, and that itself was good reason enough to halt what was about to go down in the fancy suite at the Windsor Court Hotel.

But he'd rolled the dice, said he'd reach for the brass ring. The only way to know if he could love again was to move toward Shelby and pray he wasn't screwing up.

With that thought, he placed his hand on Shelby's waist and escorted her out of the restaurant.

CHAPTER NINETEEN

SHELBY FELT LIKE her dinner might make a reappearance. Not because she was sick. No, her nerves were going haywire. Somehow, John had gotten cold feet, or at least she felt he had. He'd grown still and thoughtful at the end of dinner and halfway into the cab ride, she wasn't sure her sexy plan of seduction could work.

She might be ready to try for something more, but John had recently emerged from the shadows of grief. He might need more time…even if his kisses had said differently.

"We don't have to do this," she said.

His eyes widened, though it was barely perceptible in the dark cab. "I know we don't."

"Being with someone else is new to you. We shouldn't rush it."

"I want you."

The cab driver nodded, obviously not shy about eavesdropping.

John gave the man a sharp look before continuing. "But I don't want to hurt you."

Shelby glanced at the busy streets filled with people wearing party hats, carrying drinks and laughing as they ushered in a new year.

Hurt her? She'd already given him that power because she'd already fallen in love with him. It had happened slowly—over one of her inedible dinners or maybe standing with him in church on Christmas hearing him belt out a carol in a horrible off-key baritone. But the night in front of the Christmas tree had sealed it. So it didn't really matter whether they made love all night or John slept on the suite sofa, the deed had been done. "I don't want you to hurt me, either, but I won't stand outside the fire because I'm afraid to get burned. Not a good way to live."

He reached for her hand. "You're a smart lady."

"No, I'm a sucker for damaged guys. This had to happen. You're my personal crack."

"I'm trying to be the man you need me to be, but I can't make promises."

The cab pulled into the courtyard of the hotel and the driver pressed a few buttons on the meter, looked back over the seat and said, "I fulfilled my promise and got you to the Windsor. Remember, sometimes it's not about the destination, it's about the ride. That'll be $8.50."

Shelby slid from the cab, waiting as John paid the driver for the ride and unsolicited advice. After closing the door, he pulled her to him. "Our cab driver's brilliant."

"Oh, yeah? Why's he driving a cab and not performing heart surgery down the road? He's a guy. He wants you to get laid."

John laughed. "I gave him an extra ten dollars to say that thing about the ride."

"You did not."

"Okay, I didn't, but it's not bad advice. Tonight, let's fix what happened in Boots Grocery."

Shelby couldn't help but smile. "So no more doubts? You're up for the challenge?"

"*Up* is the key word," he joked.

And just like that, the night went from uncertain to promising again. No more worrying about what the future would hold. "Then we better get upstairs."

He took her hand and pulled her into a kiss. His lips covering hers were a sweet invitation, telling her how much he wanted her.

"Hurry," he whispered after breaking the kiss. "It will be midnight in an hour, and I know the perfect way to welcome the new year."

Minutes later, they stood before the French doors framing the Mississippi River wrapped in each other's arms, dancing to jazz music filtered in through the expensive sound system. Champagne had awaited them, and Shelby had had a teeny sip, toasting the New Year that would ring in while she and John were busy doing other stuff.

The light in John's eyes as she clinked her glass against his promised good things.

"I'm so glad we did this, Shelby," he whispered into her ear, his breath soft and warm. He'd taken off his navy suit coat and rolled up the white shirt-sleeves, revealing strong, tanned arms. His untied tie hung forgotten around his neck, his shirt collar open to the pulse in his strong throat. He took her glass and set it next to his before gathering her in his arms again, swaying to the sensuous saxophone.

Shelby laid her head on his shoulder and John's mouth moved to the sweet spot just beneath her ear, sliding down to the curve of her neck.

"You taste good," he said, his hands rucking up the fabric as he teased the back of her thighs. Shelby fisted her hands in his shirt, holding him to her. Tilting her head, she gave him the access he demanded with the nudge of his head against her jaw.

Shelby opened her eyes and the Greater New Orleans Bridge spanning the city tilted as John lifted her into his arms. "Oh."

"No more waiting. I want you naked and spread out on that bed," he said, stepping through the double doors leading to the bedroom. She teetered a bit in her heels when he set her down, but his arms came around her. The room was dark, but the window framing the moon gave enough light to see the intensity on his face.

Shelby unbuttoned John's shirt, sliding her hands beneath the fabric to the T-shirt and warmth beneath, savoring the hard planes beneath her hands. "I never got to touch you that night."

"We have plenty of time to make up for what we missed," he whispered, catching her lips before easing the shirt from his shoulders, tossing it behind him. Next, he tugged off his T-shirt, revealing a torso hewn from long days in the fields. Muscled arms cradled her, as she ran her hands down his chest with the soft furring all the way down to the trim waist. She tugged at his belt.

"Not yet," he said, unpinning her hair. How he knew where the bobby pins were she didn't know, but seconds later her hair tumbled over her shoulders. "There." He sighed.

Shelby stepped back. Grasping the hem of her stretchy dress, she pulled the dress off, tossing it onto his discarded shirt, and stood before him in her demicup red lace bra, red garter and silk stockings. The rest of her was bared to him, including the neatly trimmed juncture his gaze zipped to.

"Oh, yes," he breathed, reaching toward the floor lamp and turning the knob. A soft glow filled the darkness. "You're incredible."

Shelby moved to toe off the high-heeled pumps, but he made a noise of opposition.

"Can you leave them on?" he asked.

"Fantasy?"

"You have no idea," he said, and unhooked her bra. Before she got pregnant, she was easily a D cup. Pregnant, she was absolutely a double D. Her breasts fell free, lush and tipped with hard nipples.

"Holy—"

"Shit?" she finished for him, with a smile. Cupping her breasts, she smiled. "They're sensitive so be nice to them."

His hands replaced hers, cupping each one as his eyes took her in. "Just gorgeous. So very gorgeous."

Shelby closed her eyes, swaying against him as

he lowered his head and sucked one breast into the heat of his mouth. Pleasure poured over her. "Oh."

"Mmm," he murmured back, his mouth causing liquid heat to flood her center. Her knees gave and she sagged against him.

He lifted her, maneuvering her toward the bed. When the back of her knees hit the mattress, she fell. He made a sound of displeasure as her breast popped free of his mouth. But since she fell gracelessly, sprawling with breasts jiggling and legs half-splayed, he didn't complain long.

"I've never seen anything as sexy as you, Shelby Mackey," he said, as his eyes traced every square inch of her body. She propped herself up on her elbows, but left herself wantonly splayed in her garter belt, stockings and heels, because here stood a man who'd not had a woman since that night in the bathroom…and that had been a disaster.

She knew the power of her body. She was made for sex, and if she hadn't been such a good girl and so dedicated to being a teacher, she could have made a killing as a lingerie model…or porn star. So, no, she lay just as she was, spread out on the uppity French silk bed, a kinky fantasy for a farm boy.

She heard the clink of his belt. He moved fast, kicking out of his pants and shucking tented boxers. Then, man oh man, she discovered the gherkin theory was shot. She dropped back and opened her arms to him and said, "Silver lining on the pregnancy thing? We don't need a condom."

And then he covered her, tugging her legs so they

fit on either side of his hips. His mouth found hers, his tongue insistent.

He made guttural sounds in the back of his throat that revved her blood. She thrust her hips upward, trying to establish the rhythm she so desperately craved, but he clasped her hips, holding her still.

"Not yet," he said as he broke the kiss and moved his mouth down her neck. Hot and wet, he seared a path to her breast, taking several minutes to worship the lushness.

"You're so beautiful," he murmured, sliding his mouth down her breastbone to the rounded belly. He dropped a dozen kisses there, even dipping his tongue into her belly button and making her squeal. "You're just what I need."

And then he moved down, sliding his hands beneath her bottom, nuzzling her pubic bone with his nose. His mouth dotted kisses across her pelvis before he lifted her bottom, using his shoulders to spread her legs wide. He lifted his head, eyes dilated. "I believe I owe you a little something for my bad manners that night at Boots."

Shelby opened her mouth, but it was too late because he lowered his head and she couldn't even think how to put words together much less speak as he did wonderful, magical things with his mouth. Before long, she shattered against him, hands fisted in his hair as she rode the sweetest orgasm she'd had in quite a while, and then damned if she didn't have another one so excruciatingly pleasurable she could hardly catch her breath.

"Enough," she said, tugging his hair.

He looked up, sex-drugged green eyes, that little white scar on his chin, a grin as big as the harvester he used to cut sugarcane. "Better than last time?"

Shelby struggled to sit up. "Total A game, farmer."

He shimmied up, dropping a kiss atop each breast before wedging himself between her legs. His mouth caught hers and he tasted like sex and determination. He didn't rush her, seemingly content to use his body as a tool to reawaken the need within her. His erection lay hard and heavy at the juncture of her thighs, and John rocked his hips so that he teased her slick entrance. Mission accomplished.

"Please, John," she said, looking up at him.

His eyes looked almost sleepy, as if he were lost in some other plane of consciousness, but his body responded. With the slightest dip of his hips, he slid inside, filling her. Shelby's head bucked, grinding into the pillows, in an immediate response to the pleasure of being claimed by him.

"Oh," she moaned, her hand snapping up to grab the pillow behind her.

"Mmm," he agreed.

He established a strong rhythm that increased in intensity as the seconds raced by, grasping her hips, tilting and lifting her so he hit that perfect spot.

Tension gathered again within her, building toward a huge crescendo. Shelby wrapped her arms around John's neck, opening her eyes so she could watch him. He moved above her, his muscles taut, his face screwed in concentration as he drove them toward climax. She'd never seen anything so sexy in her life. He was beautiful, long, lean, his hardness such contrast to her softness. Something about the thought of his sheer masculinity made her dizzy with desire. She arched her back and angled her hips so he went deeper and then…she exploded.

"Ahhh," she cried, arching back, her hands twisting in the sheet. John made a noise that sounded nearly as painful and then joined her, pumping into her body, head thrown back.

Seconds later, he collapsed atop her, breathing hard, sheened in the only perspiration that was remotely sexy. After a few seconds, he rolled over, taking her with him.

"Whoa, that was good," she whispered, her head snug against his throat. She kissed the racing pulse and melted into him, completely worthless for anything. For at least a good thirty minutes.

"Beyond good."

She smiled against his skin. "I'll have to give you that fifty-cent piece back."

The rumble of laughter in his chest warmed her. "I didn't even have to work for it."

She pinched him. "Are you saying I'm easy?"

"No, I'm saying that was all for me, baby."

For several seconds, they lay wrapped in each other's arms. Then she moved. "I really want to take my shoes off."

John lifted his head, looking down at her legs on either side of his body. "I forgot you were being my fantasy girl." He gently lifted her off, before rising and padding toward the bathroom. He brought her back a damp washcloth and then pulled on his boxers.

Shelby kicked off the pumps and made short work of postcoital cleanup, sliding off the silk hose and garter and tugging on the shirt John had abandoned. Turning, she caught him standing near the window, staring into the glittering night outside.

She tiptoed up behind him and looped her arms around his waist, following his gaze to the sparkling world gathered around the dark river. "It's not midnight yet. We can still go on the balcony and catch the fireworks."

"We've already had fireworks," he said, pulling her around and cradling her backside against him. He set his chin on the top of her head. "I'm so glad we did this."

"I am, too. Pregnancy does weird things to your body, and I've been strangely turned on in my dreams and at the strangest times of day. Weird urges. I needed that so I wouldn't go humping fence posts or buying multiple packs of personal massagers at the pharmacy in town."

He laughed and she liked the way it felt against her. "I can't even imagine the talk that would generate."

"About you," she teased, twisting in his arms. "People would be saying, 'Look at John Beauchamp. Got a loose woman up there at Breezy Hill and he can't even satisfy her.'"

John lowered his head, dropping a kiss on the bridge of her nose. "I managed."

"Oh, you more than managed," she said as she rose on her toes to kiss the sweet dip at the base of his throat.

He kissed her, wrapping her tight against him. Soon the gentle kiss sparked something deeper. He broke the kiss and looked down at her with a teasing grin. "Wanna make some more fireworks?"

"Don't you have a refractory period?"

"Are you kidding? I haven't had sex in forever, well, outside of the 'wham, bam, I'm sorry ma'am' we had a few months back. I've been ready to go for the last five minutes."

"Let me see," she whispered, dropping to her knees.

"Oh, no, you don't" he said, lifting her and hauling her up against him. "I have another fantasy I want to indulge in."

"Oh, you do?" she murmured around the kisses he kept dropping on her lips.

"You know all those showers you take…the ones where you use up all the hot water?"

"Mmm, hmm," she said, sliding her hands down his back, dipping into the elastic band of his boxer shorts, cupping his tight ass.

"I wanna watch you shower," he said, moving his lips down the column of her throat.

"Oh, you dirty preacher's boy."

He responded by lifting her in his arms and strolling toward the Italian marble bath in the distance.

AFTER A LONG, leisurely brunch served in their room, eaten while absolutely naked—other than Shelby wearing her garter and heels again—John pulled the truck onto the I-10 West entrance ramp and glanced over at the woman who'd moved him into a place he never thought he'd go again.

Her cheeks were still flushed from their morning lovemaking, and her jeans wouldn't button.

That little fact had pissed her off, but he'd loved it. He'd kissed the tummy rounding gently with their child and marveled at the miracle they'd created by happenstance.

Meant to be.

He'd once told her the baby wasn't a mistake, and he believed it. The unplanned pregnancy had moved him to a new place and gave him hope he could be happy again.

But what if his gift hadn't been the baby, but rather the gorgeous outspoken blonde who'd cracked jokes at the bar while her baby blues reflected the same pain he felt? What if Shelby had been sent to give him a second chance at love?

His potential second chance gave a heavy sigh. "I need to buy some ugly maternity clothes I suppose. Ugh."

John tried not to smile. "You'll look good in anything you wear, but you look best in nothing at all."

She pointed to her chest. "You just like these huge boobs."

"Well, yeah."

"But you don't have to wrangle them into submission every day."

"Don't keep talking about your generous assets unless you want me to pull into a rest stop and indulge in fantasy number four."

She'd been contemplating her unsnapped jeans, but at those words, her head shot up. "You have a rest stop fantasy?"

"No. But I could."

He spotted the exit for Causeway and knew the Lakeside Mall was close by. Maneuvering the truck toward the exit, he aimed the vehicle at the large mall. "Let's get you something that fits. It'll make you feel better."

Shelby sighed. "I'm not sure getting clothes that make me look like that Shannon chick I met at Doctor French's office is going to make me happy. You could have sailed that woman."

John merely smiled because that's what Shelby made him do—smile. Felt good to be human again. To have dreams. To look forward to the next day. Of course the things that had driven him months ago— developing a new hybrid of sugarcane and growing the Stanton family land trust—were likely lost to him now. When he thought about Carla and her ultimatum, it felt like someone dumped concrete into his gut.

What had the woman expected of him?

He wished Rebecca hadn't died, but she had. He'd learned to face the pain and the fact he couldn't change the past. Shelby had helped him see there was more than merely existing.

His smile fled.

Maternity clothes meant it was time to tell his parents…and the rest of the world. He'd almost told Carla about the baby a few days ago, but had held off because he felt his family deserved to know before Carla. The baby would seal the deal—Breezy Hill would no longer be his future.

He didn't know how to feel about that.

But he'd meant what he said to Carla. He wasn't going to choose Breezy Hill if it meant closing himself off to love.

Love.

He didn't know if that's what he felt for Shelby. Everything with her was so different than it had been with Rebecca. Maybe it was supposed to be different. After all, he was not the person he'd been fifteen years ago. He wasn't sure about being in love, but he knew choosing Shelby and the baby was the only way he could be the man he wanted to be.

For now, he'd savor the magic they'd created the night before and worry about Carla, Breezy Hill and everything else tomorrow.

He found a parking place and jogged around to open Shelby's door. She sucked in a deep breath and looked at him flatly. "Guess I have to do this, huh?"

He kissed her, rubbing a hand on her belly. "For the prince."

"Or princess."

"Or since you're the mother, the jester?"

That made her smile finally. "Okay, let's go buy me some stretchy pants."

CHAPTER TWENTY

SHELBY SCOOPED UP another handful of peanuts from the communal bowl on the coffee table in the Beauchamps' den. Football flashed on the big-screen TV, and the men of the family stared at it as if they belonged to a cult, wincing when the ball was dropped, whooping when someone got "lit up"—whatever that meant in football terms.

Shelby had spent much of the time watching John, trying to see if he had been as changed as much as she had during the past twenty-four hours.

He looked happier. More relaxed in spite of the trouble brewing with Carla Stanton.

Maybe she'd breached the wall he'd erected against the world. Or maybe he was a man sated by a sex marathon. Her libido had grown along with her waistline, something she'd read about in her pregnancy books. Yeah, those experts were, like, expert, 'cause she'd worked poor John out.

He hadn't complained.

But even though John looked more at peace, she knew the future nagged at him the way it did with her. A flash of guilt hit her. Carla's ultimatum had been issued because of Shelby. If Shelby weren't in the picture, John wouldn't have to worry about losing Breezy Hill.

So much to worry over, so much she had no control over.

Abigail plopped down next to her and stretched out a foot. Today Abigail wore jeans, but they weren't trendy in the least. Straight-up Lee jeans with the high Mom waist. The woman so needed a makeover, but then again who was Shelby to talk? She now wore maternity clothes. They didn't look bad or even like maternity wear. The sales associate said they would grow with her. Yippee.

"So I can see that your whole taking it slow thing has sped up."

Shelby stared at John's sister and said nothing.

"I know what a weekend of sex looks like."

"It's not the weekend."

Abigail rolled her eyes. "Semantics."

"Are you sure? 'Cause postcoital high looks similar to a postconstipation high, and dairy really stops me up," Shelby cracked.

Abigail couldn't hide the smile. "I like you."

"Thanks, I think."

"No, at first I wasn't sure about you. You're slick with all that expensive luggage and horrid taste in reading material. Britney Spears, Kanye West and the Jenners? Really?"

"I see you read the magazines I left behind."

Abigail ignored her. "But I've changed my mind. It's good to see John smile again."

"You know he can hear you. He's right over there."

Shelby pointed to where John sat in one of the recliners dotting the room. The Beauchamps were obviously serious about sports and La-Z-Boys.

"They're watching football. You could recite the codes to launch a nuclear war and they wouldn't hear them."

"I would," Jake said from his spot where he sprawled on the floor.

"He doesn't count," Abigail said.

"I'm sure John would be happy to know you approve," Shelby said, not tempering the sarcasm in her voice.

"Well, I've never had much experience approving John's dates. Before Rebecca, he never had anyone serious."

Something inside Shelby stilled when she heard that. Shelby wasn't merely the first woman he'd been with since his wife died…she might be the only one he'd been with. Something tender unwound within even as a warning buzzer went off.

Abigail waited for her to say something, But Shelby had nothing to give her. What could she say?

That she was afraid John only wanted her because she carried his child and looked good sprawled on his bed?

That she was scared beyond belief John still loved his dead wife and he might never grow to love her?

That in addition to John's postcoital glow was a layer of worry over Carla Stanton?

Too much uncertainty…no real answers.

"Guess sometimes you have to take a leap of faith.

Nothing about falling in love is sane," Shelby said finally. Sounded vague. Sounded sort of lame and—

"Falling in love?" Abigail asked.

John's head jerked toward the two women, but Shelby was saved from answering because Matt Beauchamp called out, "Halftime!"

All at once the four Beauchamp men rose, and like worker ants, filed out of the den heading for the kitchen and the promise of food. John tossed a curious glance at Shelby, but she waved him on.

Abigail stared out the window before turning to Shelby. "He still loves Rebecca."

Those words slammed into Shelby like a tractor trailer skidding on ice. Hard. "I know he does, and I accept it. But that's a love that will go nowhere. She's gone and John needs to move on. Maybe you should support his taking a chance even if it's on shaky legs."

Abigail turned her eyes away as Shelby rose, feeling a little shaky herself, but proud for having spoken the truth.

Thing was, she knew John would always love Rebecca.

"Shelby," Abigail called before she left the room. Shelby turned. "What do you want?"

"I'm not sure, Abigail, but I won't settle for anything less than something true." And she meant that. She knew John felt many things for her—concern, lust, and obligation—but she refused to be chosen for any other reason than love. She wanted John to want her not because of the baby or because she scratched an itch, but because he couldn't imagine his life without her.

She deserved that man.

No more second runner-up to another woman—not even the memory of one. She'd already lived there. Hell, maybe she still lived there. Maybe John would always want the baby first and her second. But after the night they'd spent together, loving one another, she gathered up hope and clung to the idea he could love her.

One day.

But did Abigail see something that Shelby couldn't?

Shelby walked into the kitchen where most of the family gathered.

"Shelby," Fancy crowed, ever intent on making her middle son's "friend" feel comfortable. "John said you had a wonderful time on your date last night."

It was a question.

"Dinner was delicious and the fireworks were incredible." She shifted a glance over to John, whose mouth curved in a secret smile.

"How nice. I'm so glad you're making John get out and enjoy something other than driving that old tractor." Fancy pulled something from the oven. Pies. Shelby's stomach growled.

"Driving the tractor is my job, Mom," John said, rolling his eyes.

"Hey, Shelby," Matt said. "I wanted to speak to you about Mrs. Fox." He sneaked a pecan off the top of one of the pies and received a slap on the hand from his mother.

Grabbing a water from the standing cooler in the corner, Shelby turned to John's brother. "What about her? I left a complete report on each class along with a copy of all the material covered."

"No, you did a remarkable job. I've had tons of compliments from the parents, claiming their kid understood Algebra better now because of the way you taught. Can't tell you how much of a relief it was to find a substitute who could step in and put the students at a better place than they were before. Thanks."

"You're welcome. I enjoyed the experience."

"That's exactly why I wanted to offer you the position for the remainder of the year if Mrs. Fox is unable to come back."

Shelby raised her eyebrows. "Why wouldn't she come back?"

"I talked to her today and she mentioned the doctor's worried about the strain of her going back in the classroom. She's had a lot of difficulty recovering so he's recommending a trial period. If she can't hold up, she's going to take a sabbatical through the end of the year. We'll need a certified teacher."

Shelby felt two things uncurl in her stomach—pride and regret. "Well, I haven't decided to stay here permanently."

She felt John's attention home in on her.

"Oh, I assumed..." Matt's words trailed off, and he looked at his brother with an "oh, shit" look.

Shelby noticed Fancy tried to pretend like she wasn't listening, and thankfully Reverend Beauchamp and Jake were more focused on eating sausages wrapped in dough, popping them like candy.

"Uh, Shelby, can you step outside for a sec?" John asked, jerking his head toward the back door.

Everyone in the kitchen watched her.

"Sure," she said, setting her water down, dread unwinding in her stomach because she knew what he was going to ask…knew what he'd propose in order to bind her to the town. She could see it in those pretty green eyes.

John held the door for her and they stepped out, once again, into the garden, which now seemed much more winter-weary than it had a month ago. Wind whipped through the backyard, making Shelby draw her hands into her sleeves.

The screen door slammed shut, and John walked down the steps to meet her on the path. In silent communication, they began to walk.

"You know I can't take that job," she said, crossing her arms against the cold.

"You could."

"No, I'm an unwed pregnant woman and St. George's is a Catholic school. I teach math. Do the addition."

"You could marry me."

Yeah, she knew that's where he would go. "No, I can't."

"Why not? That would solve a lot of things. Our baby would have my name."

"I may not want him to have your name."

He didn't say anything as they walked a few more feet. "*I* want him to have my name. Maybe both our names. Mackey-Beauchamp is a little long, but not horrible."

Shelby sighed because the rent had come due. The past twenty-four hours had been a break, a wonderful sexy break that had moved them to a new level in their relationship. But not so far as to don white and walk the aisle. Three months ago, she'd been willing to marry Darby with or without love because she thought that's how life went. Make do. But now something had changed her. She didn't know why, she only knew she wasn't that girl anymore. Shelby wouldn't settle for less than love.

She wouldn't marry John because "it would solve a lot of things."

"Regardless of the baby's name, marriage is not something to be done lightly. You should know this. You were married."

"I'm not doing it lightly."

"No, you're proposing it for all the wrong reasons. This isn't the 1950s. I don't need the protection of your name, and I don't need a job."

John stopped and faced her, his eyes enigmatic. "Fine. I get that, but it would make sense."

She mimicked a buzzer. "Wrong answer."

"Shelby, just think about it."

"No. I don't want to get married for either of those reasons."

John shoved his hands into his pockets and contemplated the brown magnolia leaves scattering the path. The unspoken words of what she would marry for hung between them. She waited for him to say something. To say anything other than I'll marry you to make things look tidy.

But he didn't say anything.

"Right," she said, spinning on her heel, moving back to the house. "I'm going to tell Matt I can't do it."

"Shelby," he said.

She waved a hand and kept trucking. No sense in wanting something neither of them was ready for— talk of the *L* word. "No big deal, John, just know I don't think that's a solution."

"Hey," he called, jogging to catch up.

Shelby swung the door open, stepping into the warmth. John's hand caught her elbow, spinning her back to him.

"Don't make this something it's not," he said. "Things have been good between us. I just messed up back there. I'm sorry."

"And I'm used to that response from you," she said, and she knew her voice sounded wobbly. She wasn't near tears, but still something scratchy hurt the back of her throat. "I told your mother I'd help her take the Christmas tree decorations off the tree."

John released her elbow, but his eyes looked worried. Like he knew he'd pushed her to a place he didn't want her to go, but had no clue of how to get her back.

Shelby slipped into the kitchen, donning a smile

even though she felt like curling up and reading a trashy magazine where the peoples' lives were so screwed up it made her look like a nominee for the Nobel Peace Prize. That was how she dealt with things that hurt. Made jokes or read about ridiculous Hollywood drama.

No one was in the kitchen, but Shelby found John's mother and sister in the living room, boxes open and tree half-naked. Telling Matt she couldn't take the job would have to wait.

"Oh, there you are," Fancy said, looking up from an ornament organizer. The older woman's eyes narrowed slightly, ascertaining what might have gone down in her backyard. "You okay, dear?"

"Fine," Shelby said, sinking onto the couch. Various ornaments littered the coffee table. "How can I help?"

Fancy paused, as if considering whether she should pry or just shut up and accept Shelby's reticence. She chose the latter and gave Shelby instructions. For the next half hour, they worked at taking down the Christmas tree, the conversation steered pointedly away from Shelby and John, though Abigail and Fancy kept giving her questioning glances.

Shelby didn't want to talk about John or their relationship or whether she might stay in Louisiana. She liked playing the role of ostrich. Felt easier than vomiting out her doubts or trying to wrap up her concerns in a bow of platitudes the way she'd done earlier with Abigail.

After they'd pulled off all the decorations and

wrapped the valuable glass ornaments in bubble wrap, Fancy loaded the boxes. "Darn, I forgot the packing tape."

She held down one of the box lids and looked helplessly at Abigail, but her daughter had layers of lights looped around her arms.

"Where do you keep it?" Shelby asked.

"Kitchen junk drawer beside the telephone desk."

Shelby found the drawer on the second try. The kitchen was still empty and the pecan pie called her name. She grabbed a knife and cut off a small little wedge and popped it into her mouth, finding temporary comfort in the sweetness, and grabbed the tape. She approached the door that would lead back to the living room, but the sound of a man's voice down the hall slowed her steps. She'd seen Jake and Matt out the window, tossing the football with the kids, so the only males left in the house were John and his father. They were in the pastor's study.

Feeling as guilty as she had when she read Rebecca's journal, she inched toward the other kitchen door.

"I was drunk and it just happened, Dad."

"Sex doesn't just happen, son."

Silence sat for a moment. Finally, John said, "That night I felt so alone, almost not human. All I could see was Rebecca on the steps, her eyes open and that goddamn gun lying there, blood like a lake beneath her. I sat in that house alone and at some point I felt like I might go crazy. I just wanted the pain to go away so I went to Boots. I went somewhere where people wouldn't know me and wouldn't feel sorry for me."

"You could have come to us. We could have helped you get through that day and night, but you never asked."

John didn't say anything for a few seconds. "I couldn't change the past and neither could you. There's no changing the fact Rebecca picked up my gun, the fact the gunsmith didn't check the chamber and the fact I got drunk the anniversary of her death and had sex with Shelby."

"No, you can't change all that, but you can make wise decisions regarding the mistake you made with Shelby. You could have come to me before now. Why didn't you?"

"Because…because I don't know why."

"You do."

"I didn't want you to be ashamed of me, and I wanted Shelby to stay here in Magnolia Bend because we needed time to get to know one another and figure out what to do. If everyone knew about the baby, well, you know this town…"

"So why did you want her to stay? You said she wanted to go home."

"Because it's my baby, Dad." A long pause. "I wanted her to stay because it's my baby. It was a stupid mistake, but I still want my child."

Silence again. Shelby heard a burst of laughter from the living room. Fancy. The woman loved to laugh, and the sound of it pricked at Shelby like laughter at a funeral because John's words weren't about professing, but rather confessing something he wished he'd never done.

"I asked her to marry me," John said.

No words from his father.

"She said no."

"Why?" Reverend Beauchamp asked.

"I don't know. Probably because she thinks having a baby isn't a good enough reason to marry. Or maybe she doesn't want to be tied down to me."

"What about love?"

Shelby felt her heart rise in her throat. Reverend Beauchamp asked what she had been unable to bring herself to ask John earlier.

"I don't know, Dad. I can't seem to stop comparing what I have with Shelby to what I had with Rebecca. Shelby's different."

"Different isn't bad."

"No." Another long pause. "I want to do the right thing. Not bring shame on the family or embarrass you and Mom because I had one bad night. That's not fair to you. Marrying Shelby would rectify that and she could take the job at the school. We could raise the baby together. Here in Magnolia Bend. Love doesn't figure into doing the right thing."

Bring shame on the family? Keep her in Magnolia Bend?

Shelby covered her mouth with her hand, not sure whether she wanted to scream or march in there and punch John Beauchamp in the chops.

The tenderness they'd shared, the hope she'd nurtured shriveled up like a paper in a fire.

Love doesn't figure into doing the right thing.

Shelby had hoped they could move toward love. Like some blooming idiot, she'd convinced herself she could make John love her, that she'd helped him heal. She'd envisioned them starting a life together. But John wanted, to quote the Southern phrase she'd heard last week at the post office, to make a silk purse out of a sow's ear. Martha Boudreaux had explained the expression meant to try to trick someone into thinking something not so great was mighty fine. Yeah. Shelby was a freaking pig's ear.

And it hurt.

Searing pain shot across her stomach. Or was it her heart? She'd been so, so stupid in agreeing to stay here in Magnolia Bend. She'd been chasing a pipe dream created by an eleven-year-old little girl alone in her room after her brother got married, hearing the words her mother had said to a friend. *Yes, I don't know where Shelby came from. She's not like any of us.*

In Magnolia Bend, she'd thought she found a place she could belong. Most of the people in town had been so nice. Oh, sure they may have been titillated she lived with John, and some of the old biddies who were Carla's friends had tried to stir up stuff, but Fancy had quickly quelled their attempt at running the whore outta town. Shelby had also grown to love Breezy Hill. Through Rebecca's journal she'd seen the old house in a new light—she knew the waffling the woman had done over the right paint color for the kitchen, the struggle to get John to put in the flower beds, and how Rebecca had secretly brought Freddy home, but told John he just wandered up. And after last night, she felt the final piece of the puzzle had snapped into place.

She'd wanted to stay, but the whole marriage to fix this thing had zinged in from right field and smacked her in the head. Because at that moment when John proposed marriage, she knew she couldn't make herself fit into his life if he didn't love her.

See? This was what eavesdropping and sneaking and reading journals got her—the truth. And sometimes the truth wasn't much fun.

"Shelby, where's the tape?" Fancy called.

Shelby jumped, swallowed down the emotion threatening to spill down her cheeks and scampered toward the other kitchen door. Pushing through, she donned a smile. "Sorry, I sneaked some pie."

And overheard the way your son really feels about me.

Both Fancy and Abigail sat on the coffee table with their feet holding the box flaps down. Fancy's hands rubbed Abigail's shoulders, massaging them from an awkward angle. The intimate scene hit Shelby just as hard.

This. This is what she'd never had.

"There you are," Fancy said, her green eyes smiling as she withdrew her hands, eliciting a groan from Abigail. "Eating pie, huh?"

"Yeah, here's the tape."

Fancy took it and handed it to Abigail. "Are you okay, Shelby? You look pale, sweetheart."

"Just tired. I need a nap."

Abigail snorted and gave her the "I know what you did last night" look.

"Well, go on up to the guest bedroom and take a nap," Fancy said.

"Actually I'll see if John can run me out to Breezy Hill instead. I'd like a shower, too," Shelby said, wanting to get away from all the touchy-feely family stuff, wanting to get away from John, but not seeing a way that could happen.

"I can give you a lift," Abigail said, and taped the box, glancing up, her dark eyes probing Shelby, seeing beneath the surface. Maybe she knew Shelby's earlier confidence lay in pieces. That's exactly how Shelby felt. Shattered.

"Perfect," Shelby said, helping Fancy with her box. "John can finish watching football with his dad and brothers."

Five minutes later, Shelby rode beside an oddly silent Abigail. She'd told Fancy to tell John she went back to Breezy Hill. She hadn't the fortitude to face him without betraying her emotions.

They'd just turned out on the highway, when Shelby's phone buzzed. She glanced at it thinking it was John, but it was a text from her mother.

Texting, again?

But there was also a picture.

Shelby clicked on the small bubble and it enlarged, showing a beautiful christening gown of antique white lace. Underneath the pic her mother had written:

Found your christening gown when the decorators went up to the attic. I'll keep it out for the baby.

And that's when Shelby lost it.

"Shelby?" Abigail said, swerving the car over the line as she reached over to cup Shelby's shoulder as she launched herself forward, deep sobs welling up within her.

But Shelby couldn't talk, the hurt and pain and something she couldn't name about her mother had erupted inside her and there was no way to stop the meltdown.

"Shelby, what is it?" Abigail persisted. "Bad news? Do I need to stop?"

Shelby shook her head, holding a hand over her mouth, wanting to stop the deluge, but unable. Rocking slightly, she managed to choke out "Just drive". Finally after several minutes, Shelby leaned her head back on the headrest and swiped at her face.

Abigail darted a worried glance at her.

"Sorry," Shelby managed, between sniffs. "I've been needing to do that for a while."

Abigail nodded as if she understood that sometimes the only thing that helped was a good cry. "Bad news?"

"No, just an unexpected note from my mother. We don't have a great relationship and she just—" Shelby's voice trembled "—extended an olive branch of sorts."

"Oh," Abigail said. "I was worried I had upset you earlier by saying John still loved Rebecca. I shouldn't have said that. I don't know why I try to control every situation. I overstepped."

Abigail made the turn into Breezy Hill and bumped up the road, slowing when she saw another car parked beside Shelby's leased car.

"Oh, it's Carla," Abigail said, pulling in behind the Lexus. "Wonder what she's doing here on New Year's Day?"

Shelby didn't think she could handle dealing with Carla today, but the sight of the woman nailing something on the frame of the door gave her pause. "Who does she think she is? Martin Luther?"

Abigail shifted into Park and killed the engine. They both climbed out, and Carla, holding a hammer, turned to face them.

"Hey, Carla," Abigail said with caution in her voice. "What's going on?"

"Nothing you need to worry over, Abigail," Carla said in a no-nonsense voice, climbing carefully down the porch steps, a little winded. "Just business with John."

Abigail brushed past Carla and jogged up the steps. "Wait a sec, an eviction order? Are you insane?"

Carla didn't stop walking. She passed Shelby without looking at her.

"Carla," Abigail called, parking her hands on her hips. "What is this all about?"

"Dissolving the trust and putting Breezy Hill on the market as soon as possible. I gave him two weeks' notice. I won't need him after the harvest."

"What?" Abigail looked back at the paper fluttering in the breeze and then at Carla. "Why would you do this to him?"

Shelby watched Carla carefully as she turned around. The older woman's face was ravaged with guilt and grief. "He knows the reason, Abi."

Carla glanced over to Shelby and then got into her car. Abigail looked at Shelby, her normally calm, placid features twisted into disbelief, anger and a sort of understanding of what Carla's words meant.

"Stop," Abigail called out as Carla started her car. "Don't you dare do this." She ran back down the steps, heading for Carla's car.

Shelby climbed the steps, her eyes on the paper. Eviction notice set for January 20. She pulled it down, her heart breaking all over again, and wadded it into a ball.

Carla had taken John's dream and crumpled it like the notice in her hand...all because of Shelby.

Anger flooded her, along with a deep-seated sadness for the grief poisoning Rebecca's mother.

Shelby stood in a no-win situation.

Abigail, having no success in stopping John's former mother-in-law, tripped back up to the porch, looking incredulous. "I can't believe she's doing this."

"I can. She hates me."

"That's crazy. John has been nothing but good to Carla. He's taken Breezy Hill in a profitable direction, and he's family, for goodness sake. What does she expect? For him to stay here alone for the rest of his life, clinging to a dead woman?"

"Yeah, that's about right," Shelby said, pulling out the key John had given her over a month ago.

"This is nuts."

"Yeah. Nuts," Shelby agreed, wanting Abigail to leave. The woman must have sensed it because she didn't cross the threshold.

"I need to call John and then I have to go back to Laurel Woods. We have a full house. I hate to leave you here after a tough afternoon. Will you be okay?"

"Of course," Shelby said, lying through her teeth. Nothing was okay about today. Like a house of cards in the wind, her life had toppled. No more hoping for the best.

"What about John and this whole eviction thing?"

"Nothing you or I can do. John will have to handle it."

Abigail nodded. "Well, he can call our family attorney and see what might be done legally. I don't know anything about trusts, but it doesn't seem fair she can do this."

Shelby shrugged, and with a final wave, shut the front door, sinking immediately against it, closing her eyes.

The solution sat in front of her, fat and full of tears.

John didn't love her, and even though they were amazing in bed, liked vanilla ice cream and would become parents in June, it wasn't enough for her to stay and destroy his life. He deserved to keep what he loved, not sacrifice it to "do the right thing."

Shelby sighed, looking around at the house she'd grown to love. Beautifully simplistic, wholly warm, worn by time and care, Breezy Hill was not where she belonged no matter how much she wanted to believe it. No matter how much she convinced herself Rebecca's spirit had intended it.

Bunch of hogwash and wishful thinking.

And now her mother's text had given her hope for a new start with her parents.

A baby changes everything. That's what the commercial said. Maybe the thought of a new sweet life had moved her parents' hearts. That could be amazing. But also a baby shouldn't change everything about John's life. He didn't have to give up the land to be a good father. The child didn't have to live here to know his or her father's love. She could make the separation work. Somehow.

It's not like she hadn't given staying in Magnolia Bend a try. She had. But things were too hard, and she wanted more than John could give her. She didn't want him to give up his dreams. She wanted his heart.

And that might never happen.

Shelby climbed the stairs with no more tears left to cry.

Sometimes life just sucked. She'd learned that long ago, and so she knew how to put one foot in front of the other.

CHAPTER TWENTY-ONE

JOHN SAT IN his father's study feeling much the way he had as a child, ready to explain his way out of trouble, hiding from the shame of his actions. Some things never changed.

His father sat in the cracked leather chair, Bible close at hand with volumes of discourse and stacks of legal pads holding down the desk corners. In the center was a framed picture of him and his siblings taken twenty years ago. This was the desk of a man who thought, worked and embraced his faith every day.

"The reasons you gave are not reason enough to wed. Marriage is a sacrament—a selfless pledge of love."

"I know what marriage is. I've been married," John said.

Dan Beauchamp leaned forward, the chair creaking as he propped his elbows on the desk. "So do you love Shelby?"

"I don't know. Maybe. She's funny and makes me happy. I want her." He cleared his throat. "I mean to say the chemistry's there."

His father's laugh made him straighten. "You act

like your mother and I don't have good sex. I'll have you know—"

"Please," John interrupted, focusing on a pewter candlestick beyond his father's head. "That's not something I want nor need to know."

"Any more than I needed to know about your having drunken monkey sex in a bar."

"Monkey sex?"

"A term I picked up from Jake."

"Good Lord," John said, sucking in a deep breath, shame spiraling inside him at the truth in his father's words—not about monkey sex, but about the drunken in a bar part. "I'm not proud of myself."

"Son, you're a healthy, thirty-four-year-old man. You're supposed to desire a woman."

John nodded. "But it's not just about sex."

"Is it about not being alone?"

"No. I mean, it's been good having Shelby beside me, but what we have between us isn't the same as what I had with Rebecca, so I'm confused."

"What if there were no baby?"

"That's a moot point because there is."

"What if she lost the baby? What if there were no other reason for Shelby to stay in Magnolia Bend?"

John glanced out the window, turning over the thought of how he would feel if something happened to the baby. From the beginning, the thought of losing his child had hurt, but Shelby hadn't been as much a concern. But now the thought of losing Shelby…crippled him.

But how did he put a name to whatever it was that

held them together? Was it companionship? Sex? Friendship?

Or something more?

"I would want her in my life regardless of a child."

"But you didn't want her at first," his father said.

"I didn't know her."

"But now you do? So that means what?"

"I don't know. You're supposed to tell me. You're my dad. That's your job."

"My job, huh?" His father gave a dry laugh. "Okay, so how is what you feel for Shelby different than what you felt for Rebecca?"

For the first time since her death, thinking about Rebecca didn't hurt and didn't flood him with guilt. Strange.

He'd always felt safe with Rebecca. She'd been part of him, soul mates from the beginning, fitting together like a zipper. Was that the way he was with Shelby?

No.

But a zipper wasn't the only thing that held things together.

"Can a man truly love two women the same way, Dad?"

"Can a father truly love three sons the same way?" His father twisted his lips and lifted his dark eyes to the ceiling, carefully weighing his thoughts before he spoke. Finally, he nodded. "I don't love you the same, but I love you as much. Love comes in many forms, a gift from our Heavenly Father. God doesn't put Himself into a box, and so you shouldn't put his gifts into a box. There are no rules when it comes to life or love."

"I know I loved Rebecca, but I think I love Shelby, too. It's different, but not less. If something happened to Shelby..." He trailed off, the thought of losing her latching onto his heart, making his insides tremble.

"I understand, son. Loving a woman is always complicated, and no love is the same, just as no two people are the same. It's rather like a snowflake. You can't prove a snowflake is a snowflake because everyone's flake is different."

"So as long as the makeup is love, I don't have to worry about what it looks like?"

"Smart man. Just like your father."

"If you think talking snowflake analogies is smart." John finally smiled.

"Shelby suits you, son. She'll be a good partner, making you laugh, helping you heal and teaching you patience. But of these, the most important is love."

John laughed. "Always bringing the scripture."

"Hey, it's my thing."

Looking at the man who always seemed to know the answers, John's heart filled with gratitude. Family could be a pain in the ass...or a shot in the arm. Either way, he was happy to be a Beauchamp. "Thanks, Dad."

"Sure, and you will soon discover being a father doesn't end when your child grows up."

John walked around the desk, embracing his father as he rose to his feet. Feeling the strength of his old man, internalizing the wisdom, renewing the intent to create something beautiful and real from the mess he'd started that night in September.

JOHN SAT IN the living room reading the letter Shelby had left him on the kitchen table, along with a notice of eviction from the Stanton trust and the journal Rebecca had kept.

He'd returned home from his parents ready to share with Shelby the conversation he'd had with his father.

Ready to tell her exactly what she meant to him.

Ready to embrace a new love.

But Shelby's car had been gone and the house empty.

At first he'd wondered if she'd gone out to the store, but then remembered it was New Year's Day and outside of a couple of gas stations, the town was shut down for the holiday. So he'd gone up to her bedroom and found the bed made, everything tidy, which was totally unlike Shelby.

He came back down the steps, noting Bart's full food bowl, and found the letter.

He'd picked it up, shocked at what she'd written.

Dear John,

I know this will surprise you after the wonderful night we shared, but I have decided to go back home to Seattle. I know I should have had this conversation with you rather than being a coward like this, but I couldn't face you and not be swayed. You're my personal crack, remember? I've spent the afternoon thinking about our situation and contemplating your proposal of marriage. After reflection, I realized that as much as I want to I just don't belong at Breezy Hill. You, however, do. When I saw the eviction notice, I understood that in trying to do the right thing by me, you sacrificed your livelihood and all that you are, which is not fair.

I don't want you to worry about the baby. He or she is your child, and I think you know me well enough now to know I would never shut you out of our child's life. I will send you updates and we can later discuss the specifics. My attorney will be in touch with yours. Tell Carla I'm no longer in the picture. Tell her you belong there.

And I don't.

Shelby

Holy shit.

A real-life Dear John letter.

He crumpled it up and hurled it across the room, desolation consuming him…along with anger and fear.

God damn Carla Stanton.

And God damn Shelby, too.

The woman didn't even have the guts to tell him to his face that she didn't want him or this life. She didn't have the guts to stand and fight with him for happiness. John kicked the chair across the room and it clattered to the floor, making Bart yelp and run toward the living room. John slammed his fist on the table, knocking over the salt and pepper shakers, not caring he made a mess. His heart throbbed and tears clogged his throat.

Looking down, he caught hold of Carla's notice and ripped it into small pieces. He'd always loved the warmhearted woman who'd made fantastic lasagna and could beat him at dominos, but she'd lost her ever-lovin' mind in evicting him from his home... the place he belonged.

Carla wanted to erase his life here like it had never happened, like he hadn't poured his blood, sweat and every nickel he'd ever made into Breezy Hill.

"Goddamn it," he hollered at the top of his lungs, rattling the glass in the low-hanging light fixture centered over the breakfast table, and then he bowed, defeated, his head lowering to rest on the bound journal sitting on the table. He sucked in several deep breaths, inhaling the leather of the cover. Loss was an old friend—didn't take long for the pain to latch on.

A knock sounded on the front door and he lifted his head.

Maybe Shelby had changed her mind. Maybe she realized she did belong, not at Breezy Hill, not in Magnolia Bend, but with him.

Didn't she know she was his damn snowflake, different and wonderful?

More insistent knocking.

He rose and went to the door, throwing it open, half of him annoyed, half of him hopeful.

His sister, Abigail, stood there.

"Where's Shelby?" she said.

"Gone."

"Gone where?" Abigail made a face.

"Seattle. She left me a note so she's that kind of gone."

"I knew it," Abigail said, bulldozing her way inside like only she could do. She never asked. She just pushed and finagled her way into whatever she wished.

John closed the door, hoping like hell he didn't look like he'd been crying. He hadn't, of course. His eyes just felt raw and achy. "Knew what?"

"Shelby started acting weird. She came back from the kitchen all pale and quiet and wanting to leave. Then when we were in the car, she burst into tears, saying it had something to do with her mother, but then when we got here and Carla—"

"Wait, when she came back from what kitchen?"

"Mom's."

"Wait, what?"

"We were taking down the tree and Mom sent her in the kitchen for tape. I think you were in Dad's office."

In Dad's office.

Had Shelby overheard his conversation with his father? And if she did, why would she leave? Because she didn't want him to love her? Because she didn't like being compared to a snowflake? Or

maybe she heard the first part of the conversation...
the part where he doubted what he felt.

Abigail continued. "She got really quiet and sad
on the way home. I could feel a change in her. Usually she's so smart-mouthed and funny, but it was
as if someone had taken the wind from her sails.
Deflated."

John shook his head, trying to remember what
he'd said to his father at first. Crap. He'd said he
didn't want to bring shame on the family, that he
was sorry he embarrassed his father. He'd said he
wanted to do the right thing.

He'd never said anything about love until much,
much later.

"Then when we got here and she saw the notice,
she got even more subdued. I should have invited
myself inside, but she seemed to want me gone."
Abigail lifted an apologetic gaze to his. "So she just
left?"

"Yeah," he said, turning toward the mantel, to
where the painting she'd given him sat against the
pale cream walls Rebecca had repainted the summer before last. "She said things weren't working
and that she wanted to go back home."

"But she lied," Abigail said.

John snapped his head up. "Why do you think
she lied?"

"Because she loves you, idiot."

He ignored the insult because he was likely wor-
thy of it and concentrated on the important words.
"Loves me? Then why did she leave?"

"Men," Abigail said, crossing her arms. "You all are on some other plane of consciousness…the dumb-ass plane of consciousness."

He stared at her blankly.

Giving a beleaguered sigh, Abigail continued. "She left because she didn't want you to lose Breezy Hill. Because you're moving slowly in your relationship with her, and she's fallen head over heels for you. Obviously, you've given her the impression you're not in love with her or still grieving or—"

"I never said anything to make her think that."

Abigail looked momentarily guilty. "Yeah, but did you dispute it?"

No. He hadn't. Until earlier that day, he hadn't been sure what he felt was love. He'd had only one experience with it, and what he felt for Shelby was different than what he'd had with Rebecca. Not less. Just different. "I told her I couldn't promise love. I wasn't sure. But now I know."

His sister hooked a brow. "And you're sure? Because love is tricky. That flirty wonderfulness you feel at the outset won't sustain."

"Thanks, buzzkill," he drawled, his heart lifting, his anger draining at the thought of Shelby trying to fade out of the picture. At Shelby trying to "do the right thing." He left the room, heading for the kitchen.

"Hey, where're you going? And I'm not being a buzzkill. I think you're smart in being cautious with a new relationship."

John picked up his cell phone and turned to Abigail. "Of course, that's what you would think. You're jaded when it comes to love. Totally shut off. But I'm not. I love Shelby and want to build a life with her. If that's too fast, I don't care. I've already missed a whole year of life."

He'd dialed Shelby's number, but she didn't answer. He let it go to voice mail, deciding to hang up. What he had to say would be better done face-to-face. He clicked on the internet and began the search for airline tickets.

Abigail hadn't responded. Instead she crossed her arms and leaned against the cabinet.

"Damn it," he said, clicking off the phone.

"What are you doing?"

"Booking a flight to Seattle, but there aren't any out of Baton Rouge until morning."

"You're going to Seattle?"

"I'm going to bring her home. Where she belongs."

"What about the harvest? You've got cane—"

"I just got fired, remember?" He picked up the torn pieces of the eviction notice Carla had overdramatically nailed to his door. Probably wasn't even legal to serve it without the bank or law present, but Carla wanted effect. A twist of the knife for good measure. "Homer can take over for a few days. If anything goes wrong, what do I care?"

"But this is Breezy Hill," Abigail said, looking at him like his head had started spinning around.

"I know. But what is a house if it can't be a home?"

"My God, you do love her."

"Bingo. You're clueing in. Now, can Bart stay with you for a few days?"

Abigail looked down at the golden retriever at her feet, smiling up at her with a doggy grin. She sighed. "Sure. Birdie will be thrilled."

"Thanks."

"So you're going to give up Breezy Hill for a chance with that smart-ass blonde."

"You bet your own smart ass I am."

Abigail laughed. "Life sure surprises you sometimes."

John looked around the kitchen of the house he'd loved for over a decade and then looked back at his sister. "But thank God that it does."

CHAPTER TWENTY-TWO

SHELBY ARRIVED IN Seattle to overcast dark skies and her mother waiting in a Mercedes. That little fact shocked the hell out of her, because the Mackeys sent car service to the airport for pickup.

"Good God, Shelby," her mother said when she slipped into the front seat after having tipped the porter, "you look like hell."

"Thank you, Mother," Shelby drawled, pulling the door closed, grateful for the warmth of the heated leather seats. It was the little things that got a girl through the shittiness of life.

Marilyn pulled away, stopping to honk at someone who cut her off. "Idiots," she breathed.

Shelby's mother wore her dark blond hair in a controlled bob. Her touched-up eyes were dark blue, her long fingers elegant, her jewelry tasteful. She reeked of money, power and high expectations. Only the seats were warm in the car.

"How was your flight?"

"Long," Shelby said, passing a hand over her face, wondering for the sixth time in the past ten hours if she'd made a huge mistake in coming back to Seattle. She didn't feel like she belonged here, either.

Shelby didn't feel she belonged anywhere. "I'm surprised you came to pick me up. It's early."

"I have an early meeting and I couldn't sleep."

"Oh," Shelby said, knowing before Marilyn spoke it hadn't been about a mother concerned for her daughter.

"And I was worried about you."

Shelby sat up a bit. "Worried?"

"You know us mothers, we always worry when our children are unhappy."

Since when?

"Of course," Shelby said vaguely, staring out at the scant traffic on the road in the wee hours of the morning.

"Are you going to tell me about this man? About why you are back here?"

"Things didn't work out. It's best I come home and make a life here."

"You don't say it like you mean it," Marilyn said, shifting lanes and sliding a glance over at Shelby.

Shelby didn't know how to respond. Bone-deep weariness had settled over her and her mind was fuzzy. "I don't know what I mean. I'm confused."

"Yes, you've gone through much of your life the same way."

"I really don't need this right now, Mom. Really, really don't."

Marilyn closed her mouth and stared straight ahead into the darkness. Minutes ticked by. Uncomfortable minutes.

"Did I ever tell you about the time I ran away?" her mother said.

"Ran away?"

"I was twenty, home from Stanford for the summer. There was this guy. A surfer." Marilyn's eyes glazed over a little and a small smile tipped her lips. "He was something else."

Ah, that phrase again. "You ran away with a surfer?"

"For a month," her mother said. "It was the best month of my life. I planned to drop out of Stanford. We were going to open a surf shop in Laguna and live in an upstairs apartment of a friend."

"You're serious?"

Marilyn laughed. "I know it's hard to imagine, but I had hair down to my ass, smoked weed like a fiend, and my surfer taught me things that blew my mind. I would have done anything for him. It was the most wonderful summer of my life."

"What happened?" Shelby almost leaned over and pinched her mother to make sure she was real.

"Bobby robbed a liquor store and got sent to jail. I came back home heartbroken…and pregnant."

Shelby swallowed. "What?"

Marilyn shook her head. "Daddy almost stroked out, but my mother, who spent most of her life in an alcoholic haze, snapped to attention, whisked me away for an abortion and dumped me off on your father."

"What?"

"That's why I wish you would have told me before now that you were pregnant."

"Mom," Shelby said, taking deep breaths, fighting back the shock and the tears threatening to once again make an appearance.

"After all that, I swore I would take control of my life. I got my degree, set my mind to take over for Daddy and married your father. He's a good man and we've made a good life together, but I remember what it was like with Bobby on that beach, making love around the fire, getting high and being in love. You've always been like me."

"I—I…" Shelby couldn't even think of what to say. She'd never felt she was in any way like the tough woman sitting next to her. "I can't believe you just told me that."

Marilyn shrugged. "It was a secret I wasn't necessarily proud of, but it was mine. You know?"

Shelby nodded. "Yeah."

"So what do you want, Shelby?"

"A bed, some food and—"

"No, what do you want, sweetheart?"

Shelby looked at her mother. Marilyn set the car to cruise control and looked at her, eyes intent in the darkness.

"I wanted to live at Breezy Hill, have this baby and make a life in Louisiana."

"And?"

"Things got complicated."

"They always do. Do you love John?"

"You know his name," Shelby said, not believing she sat in her mother's car having this sort of conversation with the woman who'd disconnected herself from Shelby all her life.

"I make it my business to know everything about my children, which is why I'm really disappointed in Sela scheduling a nose job. She needs a lift. Her nose is perfectly fine."

"I love him."

"Then what are you doing here, baby?"

A tear escaped. Her mother had never called her *baby*. Ever.

"I don't know."

"Then I suggest you spend some time thinking about what you must do to get what you want."

And that was the last her mother said of it. She turned the radio to soft jazz, stuck in her Bluetooth and made a call to London.

Shelby looked out the window, wondering what parallel universe she'd just entered, wondering if her mother was right for once. Maybe she needed to think about what she wanted and then figure out how to get it. Maybe for once in her life, she shouldn't run from the things that were hard. If she wanted John, she should get him.

But maybe that was the kind of stuff that only existed in movies. The whole rush to the airport, feet pounding down the skyway, reaching the gate, yelling, "Wait!" She'd seen those movies, sighing at the implausible happily ever after.

She needed time to think. Shelby closed her eyes, her thoughts swishing round and round, and fell into exhausted slumber.

JOHN PRESSED THE button again, looking up at the huge ornate gates of Tangled Wood, the estate of the late George Montgomery Inabnet, founder of the largest furniture maker in the U.S., also Shelby's grandfather.

"Sir?"

"I'm here to see Shelby Mackey."

"May I say who is calling," the clipped voice asked.

The father of her child? The man who loved her? The idiot who let her slip through his fingers? He settled on "John Beauchamp."

"A moment, sir."

Several seconds later, the iron gates parted. John slipped back into his rental car, cursing the legroom of the only vehicle left at the airport car rental, and pulled into the long drive twisting through the evergreen forest. Thank God his uncle was the sheriff and had access to certain files or John would have never found the private residence. The stone mansion emerging through the clearing made John inhale.

Yeah, it was the most impressive house he'd ever seen.

He parked in the curving drive with the carved marble balustrade and walked up to the grand entrance and rang the bell.

The door opened and Shelby stood there.

"What are you doing here?" she asked, pulling the carved mahogany door closed behind her. He shivered in his light jacket, but didn't ask to be let in because he knew he was on thin ice.

"What do you think?"

"Did you call Carla?"

Shelby wore one of the outfits she'd purchased in New Orleans—a pair of jeans and a shirt that hung to midthigh. Her hair didn't look as bouncy as it usually did and her eyes were swollen. But she still looked like the most beautiful thing he'd ever seen.

"I'm not worried about Carla. I'm worried about you."

"I'm fine. The baby is fine."

She crossed her arms and looked at him with the same cute puzzled expression she'd given him time and again.

"I'm not here about the baby. I'm here about you." He sucked in a deep breath. "Why did you leave me, Shelby?"

"I left it all in the letter." She blinked away tears.

"You didn't even give me a chance to—"

"Change my mind?" Shelby asked, stepping toward him. "Look, I know you wanted me to stay and raise the baby there, and I get that when it comes to chemistry, we could burn up a science lab. But when I really thought about it, that's not enough for me. I don't want to be second best."

"Second best?"

"You still love Rebecca. Everyone knows it. Your sister loves to tell me."

"My sister's views on love are skewed."

"Yeah, but still you don't want me for me, you want me because I can fulfill some of your fantasies. And because I'm having your baby."

"Are you insane?"

"No," she snapped, her blue eyes igniting with anger.

"I love you."

"No, you don't."

He swallowed and looked around, like there might be something there on the marbled, fancy-schmancy entryway to help him. "Yes. I do."

"I heard you with your father."

"You overheard a conversation, likely a partial conversation, and jumped to all sorts of conclusions."

"You said I embarrassed your family. You said what you felt for me was not the same thing you felt for your wife. You have doubts. I heard that."

"Well, yeah. Don't you ever have doubts?"

She pressed her lips together, averting her gaze. She paused before mumbling, "You're twisting my words."

"No, I'm not. I'm trying to make you understand everyone has doubts. We've had them all along, but we also acted on something inside us. We listened to our hearts."

"What are you saying?"

"Can we go inside?"

"No. Say it here."

John sighed. "Okay. Yes, I've had doubts. I had doubts when I married Rebecca. I had doubts the entire time we were married, but that didn't change the fact that at the end of the day I thought she was worth the trouble."

"I read her journal. I know."

"You really like to snoop, don't you?"

"No, I tried to give the thing to you. I felt like Rebecca would want me to know about her…and you."

He made a face.

"What? It's true. And the only reason I heard you and your father is because of your mom's pie. And really you should shut the door when you have a conversation like that."

True. He should have made sure it was absolutely private. "I don't mind you read Rebecca's journal. I've read it, too, and it opened my eyes to a part of her I didn't get to see. But I want you to know I never forgot our anniversary. I just forgot where I put the present and wanted to wait until I found it."

Shelby gave him a little smile and hope blossomed. Rebecca had written some ugly stuff about him. Their marriage wasn't perfect. Far from it at times. That's the way marriage worked—some days you wanted to hug your spouse, the next kick them in the shin.

"I do feel differently about you, Shelby. I can't hide that. You're not like Rebecca, and the love I have for you is different. My dad called it a snowflake—the same, but different."

She swallowed and finally looked at him. "A snowflake?"

"You know. They say every snowflake is different."

"Oh."

"I don't love you any less than I loved Rebecca, and I may have gone a little crazy when I found your letter because I can't imagine you not in my life."

"This isn't about the baby?"

"It started with the baby, but it ends with you, Shelby. I love you and I want you to come home."

"But Breezy Hill is—"

"I love you more than I love Breezy Hill. My home is with you. If you want to live here, I'll get a job here. Don't know much about the agriculture in Washington State, but I'll learn."

"Seriously?"

"As serious as I know how to be."

Then Shelby smiled. "So you're saying you love me?"

"I love you, and not because you saved me from grief. Because you created new magic in me."

And then she was in his arms, her lips covering his, dotting hard, excited kisses. "You came for me."

He hauled her against him, lifting her from the ground, holding her tight. "Why in the hell would I let someone who made me laugh, hunger and feel again waltz out of my life? You taught me how to live."

"Oh, my God. I love you, too. I didn't know what to do. I didn't want to make your life worse."

He shook his head, setting her back down before kissing her again. She tasted so warm and good. She tasted the way love should. His heart swelled, filling all the leftover empty places, making him feel as if he might burst. "You could never make my life worse than what it was, Shelby. I'm a blessed man—I get you and a new life. What more do I need?"

She pushed against his chest, looking up at him

with eyes so full of joy it took his breath away. "We'll need a place to live."

"Where do you want to live?"

"Breezy Hill."

"That's going to be a problem, but we can find another house. Maybe a cute, country—" He glanced up at the magnificent arching stone mansion. "Your family is sort of well-off, huh?"

"We're freaking rich," she laughed, inching them back toward the door. "But when my mother picked me up this morning—which seems so long ago, by the way—she and I had a very interesting conversation. This morning, after sleeping like the dead, I had some thoughts about you and Breezy Hill."

She opened the front door to a breathtaking foyer with a double marble staircase. John doffed his old cowboy hat and swiveled his head around in wonder. "Jesus."

"Don't take the Lord's name in vain," Shelby said, assuming the same tone his mother had on that Christmas Eve long ago. "And come inside so we can talk about my plan."

"Your plan?"

She smiled. "This four-bit whore has tricks up her sleeves."

John laughed. Because that's what Shelby made him do.

CHAPTER TWENTY-THREE

Four months later

CARLA STANTON ACCEPTED the box from the FedEx guy with a heaviness she hadn't expected. Yesterday, she'd signed the papers selling Breezy Hill to IM Timber Industries. She had no clue what a Portland-based company wanted with a sugarcane farm, but the company had agreed to her price and the deal had required little negotiation. Even though the sale had been cut-and-dried, Carla had cried all the way home from the attorney's office.

Things weren't supposed to end this way. Breezy Hill was the legacy she and Hal would hand down to their child and her children. But that reality had shattered the September day when John had come home to find Rebecca.

Poof.

Gone.

Carla had entered the new year depressed. After spending nearly two weeks in bed and struggling to even dress, she'd forced herself into going to Baton Rouge to join a new grief therapy group. It had taken her several months and a lot of tissues, but now she felt better able to face what she'd done. Grief and anger had created a monster inside her. Even though she did feel a sense of loss at selling Breezy Hill and treating John so shabbily, she knew it was the first step in moving forward. One day she would have to tell him her regrets.

When she felt stronger.

Taking the box to the kitchen table, she turned on the light. She hadn't remembered ordering anything lately, but sometimes online purchases showed up later than expected. She glanced at the sender's name and swallowed.

Shelby M. Beauchamp.

Hot anger flooded her before she recalled she had vowed to let go of her hate and forgive the blonde who had insinuated herself into John's life. He'd married her. She was pregnant, proving Carla had been right all along. Giving a friend a place to stay, her ass.

She took several cleansing breaths and closed her eyes, stilling her anger, asking the Lord to fill her with the spirit of forgiveness.

There.

Grasping the edge, she pulled the tab and opened the box. Inside she found an envelope and the journal she'd given Rebecca the day before she married John.

Carla hadn't forgotten about the journal. She assumed Rebecca, who'd always hated any kind of writing, hadn't bothered with it. Unwrapping the leather cord looped tight around the button, Carla opened the book, a soft sound of gratitude escaping her when she saw the journal had been nearly completed, filled with the familiar boyish chicken scratch she'd teased her daughter about.

Turning the first page, she read the line in which Rebecca wondered if mothers were always right.

"We're not," Carla whispered, closing the journal and clutching it to her heart. "We're just human, baby."

Setting the journal down, Carla slid the flap of the envelope open, pulling out a handwritten letter. It was from Shelby, and the fanciful looping script was noticeably different from her daughter's.

Dear Carla—
I know you aren't expecting to hear from me. You've been quite clear on how you feel, but I felt moved to clarify a few things and to return the journal you gave your daughter long ago. It should rest with you.

By now you may know that IM Timber Industries is one of my family's corporations. At first I know this may infuriate you, but I hope with my words you will understand why I did this.

Carla set the letter down. "Why that little—" She snapped her mouth shut, gritted her teeth and prayed like tomorrow may never come she wouldn't march over to the rental house where a very preg-

nant Shelby lived with her new husband and snatch
her bald-headed.

After a full minute of asking for grace, Carla
picked up Shelby's letter.

I read Rebecca's journal. It was wrong of
me, and I admit my mistake. But I'm not sorry
I read it. When I first met John, I hated the face-
less wife he loved. But once I "met" Rebecca,
I grew to respect and admire her. Through her
eyes, I grew to love the man she loved and the
land she felt such a part of. At one point, she
mentioned how much John loved Breezy Hill
and how he fit the legacy her father had envisioned.

I know you're still angry at John, but knowing Rebecca somewhat intimately, I felt she
would have wanted John at Breezy Hill. I think
she would understand his need to be loved and,
I'm being presumptuous, but I think she would
have liked me. I think Rebecca and I would
have been friends.

I bought Breezy Hill, not out of spite, but
rather because I love it. Rebecca helped me love
the beauty of the sunrise over the Southeast
field, the hand-carved banister on the staircase
and the mantel salvaged from the fire. I do not,
however, like the curtains in the kitchen, but
beyond changing them, I want to preserve the
house the Stantons lived and loved in for over
a hundred years.

Lastly, through Rebecca I have seen the woman you truly are. She loved you so, and throughout the pages, I could see what an influence you were on her life. You were a good mother to her, Carla, the type of mother I hope to be to my own daughter.

In a month I will hopefully deliver a baby girl. She was conceived in grief, but will be born in love. I wanted you to know we plan to name her Lindsey Rebecca, after my grandfather and your daughter. You are always welcome at Breezy Hill. It is still your home and maybe one day you can forgive John and me, and be part of our lives. I hope you will find peace.

Sincerely,

Shelby

With trembling hands, Carla lowered the letter, dampness streaking her cheeks. She sat down so hard she scared Dim Sum, who flinched before rising up for a scratch.

"Down, Dim," she said, covering her face with her hands. Her body felt so heavy, so very, very heavy.

She uncovered her face and looked at the letter and the journal and shook her head.

I hope you will find peace.

At the hands of a woman she'd hated, Carla may just have found a remnant of faith and hope she'd tossed away in favor of grief.

Maybe the mother Rebecca had loved so well,

whom she had admired so much, had been so very wrong about so many things.

Outside the window a cloud scudded by causing a beam of sunshine to fall on Carla as she sat in her chair feeling like a failure.

The warmth of the light blanketed her, making her shiver despite the heat. She stared down at where her hands lay in her lap before looking up with a smile.

"I get it, honey. I get it," she said to the sunshine.

SHELBY LAY IN the hospital bed, still nauseous from the medication they'd given her during the delivery, but too giddy to pay much attention to the feeling.

John sat in the rocking chair across from her, counting the fingers and toes of their new daughter.

"She's so little," he kept saying, his dark head bent over the now-squirming baby with the full head of black hair.

"Wrap her in the blanket," Shelby said, her eyes lighting on her daughter as the baby opened her mouth and let out a squall.

"I can't wrap it like those nurses do," John said, rising and bringing the baby to her. Shelby took her daughter, nestling her to her chest, giving a little shush noise. Lindsey Rebecca calmed, but started immediately rooting to find Shelby's breast, which John had dubbed the jackpot for any infant in the nursery.

"You just ate, piglet," Shelby murmured, unhooking her gown, wanting to give the baby whatever she could to comfort her. Being born was not an easy task. For Lindsey or Shelby.

A knock sounded at the door, and Marilyn Mackey stuck her head inside.

"Mom," Shelby said, still in awe she called Marilyn "Mom" and not "Mother" the way she had all her life.

"Oh, are you feeding her?" Marilyn said, looking disappointed.

Shelby reached for the pacifier, refastening her gown. "Actually, she ate not long ago. Let's try this and maybe she'll settle down so you can—"

Marilyn scooped up the baby, expertly tucking the swaddling blanket around her granddaughter while popping the pacifier into her mouth. Cradling the crying infant, Marilyn strolled to the hospital window, humming a James Taylor song, looking like a pro. Lindsey stopped crying.

Shelby mouthed "oh, my God" at John, but he just smiled. The fool hadn't stopped smiling since his daughter had been born last night.

Another knock at the door.

"My family is going to drive us batty," John said.

But it wasn't a Beauchamp that walked in. It was the floor nurse, and she carried a gift.

"Something for the mama," the nurse said, thrusting the gift toward Shelby. John stood to take it and place it with all the flowers blooming on the large windowsill, but Shelby snatched it.

"She said for the mama," Shelby teased John, slid-

ing another glance at her mother talking sweetly to
her granddaughter.

Still so weird.

The nurse left with a wave and a promise to check
back later, and John sank back into his chair, still
smiling.

Shelby untied the bow and lifted the lid on the
gold box.

Inside the tissue paper, she found a beautifully
bound leather journal, with a leather strap to bind
around a large pewter button. Carefully, Shelby
lifted it from its home in the box.

Unwinding the leather strap, Shelby opened the
journal. On the first page written in tasteful pen-
manship were these words:

To Shelby:
May you find yourself in these pages and may
you chart the journey of a lifetime. May your
Rebecca bring you the joy my Rebecca brought
to me. Peace found.
Carla

Shelby set the journal back in the box, wrapping
the cord securely around the button.

"What did you get?" John asked.

"A new beginning," Shelby said.

John stood, glancing at the box, recognizing what
the journal represented. He lifted his pretty green
eyes, surprise reflected in them. "Carla?"

"I think she approves of the name."

John looked back at his daughter, still cradled in Shelby's mother's arms. "Thank you for turning your rental car into Boots Grocery and giving me a second chance at love."

Shelby took his hand and together they watched the CEO of a major corporation make a fool of herself with a baby.

It really was true.

A baby changed everything.

* * * * *

LARGER-PRINT BOOKS!
GET 2 FREE LARGER-PRINT NOVELS PLUS
2 FREE GIFTS!

HARLEQUIN®

Romance

From the Heart, For the Heart

YES! Please send me 2 FREE LARGER-PRINT Harlequin® Romance novels and my 2 FREE gifts (gifts are worth about $10). After receiving them, if I don't wish to receive any more books, I can return the shipping statement marked "cancel." If I don't cancel, I will receive 4 brand-new novels every month and be billed just $4.84 per book in the U.S. or $5.24 per book in Canada. That's a savings of at least 19% off the cover price! It's quite a bargain! Shipping and handling is just 50¢ per book in the U.S. and 75¢ per book in Canada.* I understand that accepting the 2 free books and gifts places me under no obligation to buy anything. I can always return a shipment and cancel at any time. Even if I never buy another book, the two free books and gifts are mine to keep forever.

119/319 HDN F43Y

Name _____ (PLEASE PRINT) _____

Address _____ Apt. # _____

City _____ State/Prov. _____ Zip/Postal Code _____

Signature (if under 18, a parent or guardian must sign)

Mail to the **Harlequin® Reader Service:**
IN U.S.A.: P.O. Box 1867, Buffalo, NY 14240-1867
IN CANADA: P.O. Box 609, Fort Erie, Ontario L2A 5X3
Want to try two free books from another line?
Call 1-800-873-8635 or visit www.ReaderService.com.

* Terms and prices subject to change without notice. Prices do not include applicable taxes. Sales tax applicable in N.Y. Canadian residents will be charged applicable taxes. Offer not valid in Quebec. This offer is limited to one order per household. Not valid for current subscribers to Harlequin Romance Larger-Print books. All orders subject to credit approval. Credit or debit balances in a customer's account(s) may be offset by any other outstanding balance owed by or to the customer. Please allow 4 to 6 weeks for delivery. Offer available while quantities last.

Your Privacy—The Harlequin® Reader Service is committed to protecting your privacy. Our Privacy Policy is available online at www.ReaderService.com or upon request from the Harlequin Reader Service.

We make a portion of our mailing list available to reputable third parties that offer products we believe may interest you. If you prefer that we not exchange your name with third parties, or if you wish to clarify or modify your communication preferences, please visit us at www.ReaderService.com/consumerschoice or write to us at Harlequin Reader Service Preference Service, P.O. Box 9062, Buffalo, NY 14269. Include your complete name and address.

HRLP13R

LARGER-PRINT BOOKS!

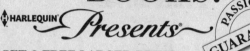 HARLEQUIN *Presents*

PASSION GUARANTEED SEDUCTION

GET 2 FREE LARGER-PRINT NOVELS PLUS 2 FREE GIFTS!

YES! Please send me 2 FREE LARGER-PRINT Harlequin Presents® novels and my 2 FREE gifts (gifts are worth about $10). After receiving them, if I don't wish to receive any more books, I can return the shipping statement marked "cancel." If I don't cancel, I will receive 6 brand-new novels every month and be billed just $5.05 per book in the U.S. or $5.49 per book in Canada. That's a saving of at least 16% off the cover price! It's quite a bargain! Shipping and handling is just 50¢ per book in the U.S. and 75¢ per book in Canada.* I understand that accepting the 2 free books and gifts places me under no obligation to buy anything. I can always return a shipment and cancel at any time. Even if I never buy another book, the two free books and gifts are mine to keep forever.

176/376 HDN F43N

Name		
	(PLEASE PRINT)	

Address		Apt. #

City	State/Prov.	Zip/Postal Code

Signature (if under 18, a parent or guardian must sign)

Mail to the Harlequin® Reader Service:
IN U.S.A.: P.O. Box 1867, Buffalo, NY 14240-1867
IN CANADA: P.O. Box 609, Fort Erie, Ontario L2A 5X3

**Are you a subscriber to Harlequin Presents books
and want to receive the larger-print edition?
Call 1-800-873-8635 today or visit us at www.ReaderService.com.**

* Terms and prices subject to change without notice. Prices do not include applicable taxes. Sales tax applicable in N.Y. Canadian residents will be charged applicable taxes. Offer not valid in Quebec. This offer is limited to one order per household. Not valid for current subscribers to Harlequin Presents Larger-Print books. All orders subject to credit approval. Credit or debit balances in a customer's account(s) may be offset by any other outstanding balance owed by or to the customer. Please allow 4 to 6 weeks for delivery. Offer available while quantities last.

Your Privacy—The Harlequin® Reader Service is committed to protecting your privacy. Our Privacy Policy is available online at www.ReaderService.com or upon request from the Harlequin Reader Service.

We make a portion of our mailing list available to reputable third parties that offer products we believe may interest you. If you prefer that we not exchange your name with third parties, or if you wish to clarify or modify your communication preferences, please visit us at www.ReaderService.com/consumerchoice or write to us at Harlequin Reader Service Preference Service, P.O. Box 9062, Buffalo, NY 14269. Include your complete name and address.

HPLP13R